ENTICING Me

TRUE PLATINUM SERIES

MORGANA BEVAN

Copyright © 2022 by Morgana Bevan

All rights reserved.

Enticing Mel is a work of fiction. Names, characters, places, and incidents are all products of the authors imagination and are used fictitiously. Any resemblance to actual events, locals or persons, living or dead, is entirely coincidental.

No part of this book may be reproduced in any form or by any electronic or mechanical means, including information storage and retrieval systems, without written permission from the author, except for the use of brief quotations in a book review.

Cover Design by: Pretty Little Design Co.

Editing by Dayna Hart

ISBN: 978-1-9196091-4-0

❦ Created with Vellum

To Janey. Thanks for going gaga over Dan.

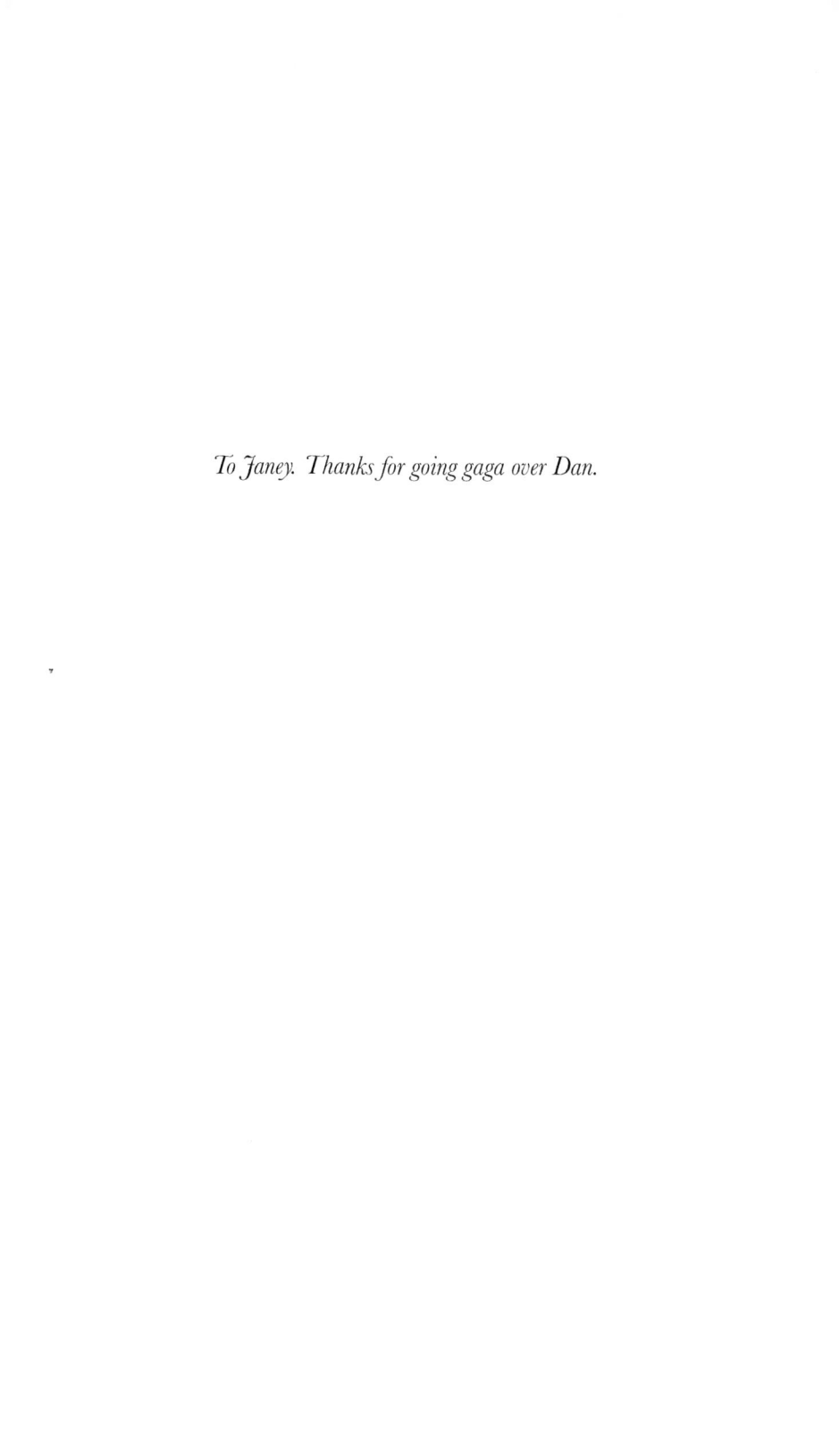

ENTICING Me

TRUE PLATINUM SERIES

MORGANA BEVAN

ENTICING MEL PLAYLIST

1. Until It Happens To You - Sasha Alex Sloan
2. Here I Go Again - Whitesnake
3. How Can We Be Lovers - Michael Bolton
4. When We Were Lovers - Jack Savoretti
5. Girl is a Gun - Halsey
6. Every Rose Has It's Thorn - Poison
7. Happy Place - SAINT PHNX
8. Willow – Taylor Swift?
9. Stabilisers (I Will Be) - The People The Poet
10. Memories - Maroon 5
11. Sweet Child O' Mine - Guns N' Roses
12. Don't Know What You Got (Til It's Gone) - Cinderella
13. Nails - Call Me Karizma
14. Darling - Roan Ash
15. Shivers - Ed Sheeran
16. Lady - Styx
17. If You Need Somebody - Bad Company
19. Used to Be - Matt Nathanson
20. The Fighter - Keith Urban
21. Mouth Tattoo - Murder Ballad
22. Little Lies - Fleetwood Mac

23. Start of Something Good - Daughtry
24. Feels Like That - The Reklaws
25. Sticky - The Maine
26. No Secrets - The Shires
27. River of Pain - Thunder
28. Stuttering - Fefe Dobson
29. Rooms on Fire - Stevie Nicks
30. Who Says You Can't Go Home - Bon Jovi & Jennifer Nettles
31. When You Love Someone - Bryan Adams
32. About This Boy - Collateral

PROLOGUE

Two lines.

The reality of what two lines meant crashed in hard.

"Shit. Shit. Shit," I hissed, picking up the tiny stick and shaking it.

It had to be wrong. I couldn't be pregnant. Yes, I couldn't stop throwing up, but I just had a bug. A very drawn out, only messes with you in the morning kind of bug. Yes, I hadn't had a period in two months but maybe that was...

"Shit." I sat down hard on the side of the bath.

I'm pregnant.

The test stick clattered to the floor. I pressed my face into my hands, and bent over.

Pregnant at twenty-three. Fuck.

Anger bit into me without warning. At myself. At Dan. At his stupid obsession with music.

The laugh that escaped me sounded far too bitter. *As if you didn't have front row seats to how this story was going to play out.*

I scrambled for the phone before I could really consider what I was about to do. Really, what was there to think about? I couldn't do this on my own. It was half his fault. No way was

I taking all the blame for forgetting a condom. It wasn't like I'd been expecting him to rock up at my door after a year of no contact.

Fucking musicians.

With the phone pressed to my ear, I found a reserve of strength. Where it came from, who knew. All I wanted to do was curl into a ball on the bathroom floor and will it all to go away.

I was on the cusp of getting an insanely important promotion that would set me on the perfect path to achieve all of my career goals.

Glaring at the ringing phone, I paced my tiny bathroom.

I couldn't stay here. My flatmates would definitely not be on board with sharing space with a screaming new-born, not when they were trying to get their PhDs. Shit.

What the hell was I going to do?

"Babe," Dan gasped, answering the phone at last. I stopped in my tracks. "I'm in the middle of something right now. Matt's going to take a message."

"Wait! I need to tell you something," I shouted, panic freezing me in my tracks.

"I'll call you later," he promised and handed the phone to Matt. *Who the fuck was Matt?*

"How can I help you?" the stranger said.

He pops into my life and expects me to drop everything. I call him once, and I'm relegated to human message services?

"Hello?"

Anger worked its way up my body. I stared at my reflection in the mirror. My face went red. Years of back and forth, of my trying to talk to him after he dropped in, yet again without warning, and decided for one night or week that nothing had changed… it all spiralled in my mind.

"I don't know who this is but you're going to have to speak if you want something from the band."

Dan never wanted more than a fling. Sure, he'd been my

loving boyfriend once, but that was before. Before he moved to Glasgow without warning five years ago. Before he formed Rhiannon. Before he became just like every other musician in my life… obsessed with the music, with the thrill of the road until they got so lost in it, no one else existed.

"The phone still says you're connected, but I'm not hearing anything," the guy, Matt, said. I rolled my eyes at him. "Hello?"

I hung up.

The phone stared at me, judging me.

Aren't you stupid? it said.

And the answer was yes. I knew better. If he'd ever loved me, he would have kept in contact between visits.

My grip tightened on the phone as anger flared. He wouldn't stop. I couldn't take any more unplanned, pointless visits. And really, why the hell would I subject my baby to the upbringing I'd had? With a father who loved an instrument and craved the thrill of a crowd more than he wanted me. Us.

My fingers flew across the screen as I blocked his number. It wasn't enough. I needed a new number. A new address.

I slid down the tile wall slowly. Moisture splashed down my cheek but I didn't try to stem it. All that angry energy had evaporated, leaving me a shell.

What am I going to do?

CHAPTER ONE

*F*our years and seven months later
CONFIRMED — ROCK BAND RHIANNON RETURNS TO WALES PERMANENTLY.

"What the fu — duck!" I muttered to myself. My gaze jumped to Phoebe splashing happily in the bath. My shoulders relaxed marginally when she didn't react to my almost slip.

She held out a rubber duck, her head tilting as she smiled at me. "Duckie?"

"Thank you, honey." I took it from her and placed it on the side, my phone still gripped tightly in my other hand.

Surely, it was wrong? Dan had always said he'd never come back to Wales.

My eyes were drawn to the screen. I couldn't stop scanning the article. My hands shook as I scrolled, searching for proof that it was nothing but a rumour. *Alt Rock Daily* had it wrong. They must have. Glasgow and Cardiff were two entirely different music scenes, and Rhiannon were taking off. I'd expected their next move to be LA. Not *home*.

"No Duckie?" Phoebe asked, dragging my focus back.

She frowned up at me, her copper locks plastered to her head, the foam almost turning her short hair white, and her smart green eyes narrowed as she studied me. *She looks more like him every day.* My breath caught painfully.

"Time to get out, Phoebs." I cleared my throat and forced myself to lock the phone and place it on the counter.

"No!" my toddler screamed. She backed herself into the furthest corner of the bath and pouted at me.

"It's bedtime, Phoebs."

"No," she growled.

If I wasn't exhausted and shaken, I'd laugh. If it wouldn't destroy all my serious parent leverage that is.

"Which would you rather, more bath time or a bedtime story?"

She pursed her lips, clutching her soaking wet doll to her chest.

Sometimes reasoning with my nearly four-year-old was harder than soothing the ruffled feathers of our biggest social influencers. One day, she'd make an excellent hostage negotiator.

But right now, I needed to beat her at her own game, and I wasn't above bribery.

"If you come out now, you can have potato waffles for breakfast."

Her green eyes widened. She flung herself at me with very little warning, trusting I'd catch her tiny body. My t-shirt soaked through instantly, and water dripped down my back.

My lips twitched and I bit my cheek. *Do not laugh, Mel.*

"How about standing back while I grab the towel?"

She stepped back. Her doll was still clutched in her hands. She took it everywhere, and no matter how many new toys I bought, she refused to get rid of it. The plastic was scratched, and her hair had been sheared off.

Phoebe stared at me, her face set in serious lines as she considered my see-through t-shirt.

"Sorry, Mammy."

I held out the forest green towel – the colour had absolutely not been influenced by how much I'd loved Dan's eyes – smiling, despite my reminders to be stern. I could never hold strong when she looked at me with that guilty look.

Getting her dry and into her pyjamas went by with the usual chatter, only tonight, concentrating was hard. There was a hand wrapped around my heart, squeezing until I could barely breathe. I needed a minute. I couldn't have a minute, so instead, I plastered a smile on my lips and pretended everything was fine.

Phoebe chattered obliviously as I dried her off and ushered her to bed. She'd had a full day at nursery but you'd swear she hadn't left the house or seen a soul. Her energy levels were off the charts, and if I let her, she'd make me read an entire book of fairy tales and still have the energy to run around the house. This kid did not like going to sleep.

Neither did I, but I'm pretty sure our reasons were very different.

She had a fear of missing out. I just feared dreaming. My subconscious liked to torture me with every what-if scenario.

What would happen if my ex knocked on my door tomorrow? Caught me at a cafe or park with Phoebe? Every time, I stood there, blinking, frozen with indecision and fear. The proverbial deer in headlights in the face of all my life choices and mistakes coming back to bite me in the ass.

It was like my subconscious was mocking me for the coward I was.

Maybe it was better than the first year of nightly reminders.

But then I'd traded dreams about our peaceful and heated past for guilt trips. I'm not sure it was a better development.

Despite all the dreams, I didn't know what I'd do if Dan Lloyd knocked on my door tomorrow. *Would I get the words out, explain it all, or would I hide behind the anger?* He was back in town, seemingly for good, so the chances of running into him had increased exponentially.

I'd made it my life's mission to avoid him for nearly five years but that luck wasn't going to hold up.

The time was coming, and I needed to prepare myself.

My dad had given me a front-row seat to the kind of relationship musicians wanted, and I wasn't capable of it. I didn't want to be someone's second choice, and Dan had made it abundantly clear that I was. In school, he'd left me with no warning. One day he was going to Cardiff uni, and the next, he was on a plane to Scotland. No explanation, no discussion.

I sighed as I sat on Phoebe's bed. She glanced up at me sharply. Her tiny brows pulled tight as she stared up at me.

"What wrong, mammy?" Her tiny, soft baby hands settled on my cheeks. "Don't be sad."

Despite the uncertainty turning me inside out, I smiled at the sweet girl before me. *At least he gave me her.*

"Do you want to do my work for me?" I asked, grinning conspiratorially. "It'll be fun."

She pursed her lips, unconvinced. *Smart kid.*

If that had been the end of it, ten years ago, I might have recovered, might have gotten over him. Instead, he kept dropping in, reappearing with no warning. One random text, and he was outside my flat, and I couldn't for the life of me push him away. I wanted that loveable asshole too much.

I smoothed a brush through Phoebe's rapidly drying hair. My hands followed in its wake.

Every time he'd disappear just as fast as he appeared, no warning, no texts, just poof. Each time I'd promise myself that would be the last time. Next time, I'd be stronger. I never was…

Until I got pregnant with her.

The week the band signed, he danced in again and just as quickly danced out. A flying visit. But it was enough. Two months later, I'd called him.

I have no idea what I wanted from that call. For him to tell me it would be alright. He'd always had a way of putting me at ease, even when it felt like life was spiralling out of control.

Instead, he picked up the phone, heard my voice, and handed me off.

I didn't tell him. I didn't tell *anyone* for so long.

And now it was all going to come back to bite me. Staring into Phoebe's softening features, fear gripped my heart too tightly.

What if he walked back into our lives and then vanished again?

He was a musician. A good deal of his job involved travelling. He would leave me again. Only this time, he wouldn't just be leaving me.

He'd be abandoning Phoebe.

How do you explain to a toddler that her dad cares more about his job than her?

The thought of her looking at Dan the way I'd looked at my dad – with distrust and resignation – it would break my heart.

No, I'd protect her, as long as I could.

"Story," she demanded, dropping a large, hard book in my lap and freeing me from my thoughts.

I chuckled. "Which one would you like tonight?"

She clambered into her little bed, tucking herself in while I settled back against the headboard.

"Gretel."

I glanced at her sharply. It was one of her favourites, so I shouldn't have been surprised. Did she understand that Hansel and Gretel's father abandoned them? I'd never been courageous enough to ask.

Instead, I cracked open the book and read.

She knew who her dad was. There were enough omissions in my life, I wasn't going to outright lie to my daughter. The day would come when she'd go searching for him, but at least by then she wouldn't be the trusting innocent she was now.

She'd go to him with an open mind, rather than with a defenceless heart.

The witch was just inviting the kids into her house when Phoebe's breathing evened out. I placed the book on her bedside table and edged away.

It was still early—the sun shone outside the wall of windows taking up one of the living room walls. The waters of Cardiff Bay glistened, and in the distance, I could just make out the people spilling onto the pavement, enjoying the bars. The rest of their night stretched out before them.

I'd given all of that up when I found out I was pregnant. Sometimes I missed it, being carefree with my entire future laid out before me. This mystical thing that could branch off in so many directions.

Regret wasn't a thing I allowed myself. I couldn't regret Phoebe, but sometimes on nights like this, when the flat was quiet and the world outside so vibrant, I wondered. Wondered what it would be like if I'd been stronger, if I'd said no to Dan the first time? Had I shut the door firmly on him when he left me for Glasgow with no warning, my life would have ended up so differently.

I shook myself, breaking the endless cycles of what ifs and turning my back on the window.

It was inevitable. Cardiff might be a city, but it had a way of drawing lost friends back to each other. If the article was right, my time was running out.

※

One Month later

I was dressed up for my first Friday night out in years. The nature reserve had been crucial to Nia's happiness over the years, and I wanted to support her. She was involved in a local community auction trying to raise funds for a visitor centre at a coastal nature reserve. She adored the place, and when she asked me and Sophie to go to the event, we couldn't say no.

Especially not when her dickhead of a boyfriend had up and disappeared on her with no warning. He'd spent a month trying to work his way back into her good graces after a ten-year absence, and then pulled something as stupid as getting on a plane to the other side of the world, without a word, on their anniversary, because a producer said jump.

Spoiler, she was going to forgive him, but I couldn't see why.

Once my mother left with Phoebe, I shimmied into my dress and heels. It was a little more flash than a local town auction called for, but Sophie and I had decided that we might as well enjoy the occasion and maybe hit up a bar afterwards. If I was going to feel guilty for having a night out, then I might as well make it a night to remember.

People were milling about when I arrived. The car park was packed, and the old social club filled with row upon row of chairs. The noise level was like a wall of sound, distant from the entry, but once you stepped through it, it embraced you, driving you to shout at your friends to be heard over the conversation happening next to you.

I needn't have worried about being overdressed. This was an event for the local town and everyone present had pulled out their good clothes. Teenagers loitered in the corner while their parents looked on with frowns and their grandparents smirked at their discomfort. It was a regular family affair.

Spotting Nia and Sophie off to the side, I weaved my way through the densely packed crowd. The sooner people took their seats, the better. Sophie hugged me when I stopped at her side.

As well as being my best friend since we were toddlers, Sophie also happened to be the sister of Nia's boyfriend, and oh how she hated that.

"Nia's gone a bit doolally," Sophie whispered close to my

ear so our best friend wouldn't hear. "She almost forgot her camera and nearly shut her fingers in the car. Watch her."

She pulled back and threw Nia a sunny smile. Nia glowered at her with suspicion clouding her icy blue eyes.

"What's with that face?" Nia asked, circling her finger in front of Sophie's face.

"Nothing." Sophie glanced around the room. "Is that frame on a slant?"

I bit my lip, trying not to laugh at Sophie's distraction attempts. Nia didn't even look; her eyes just narrowed on Sophie.

"Okay, so you're being a bit…" Sophie waved her hands. "Intense. Maybe you should just call James."

Nia's mouth dropped open.

"Is that what you want to do?" I asked before Nia could launch herself at Sophie, because I would, in her shoes.

"No. I had to wait ten years, he can wait until he's in the bloody country," Nia said, a hard bite in her tone. "I just don't understand what's taking them so long. Record the damn thing and come home."

"They're perfectionists." I shrugged, feigning a nonchalance that I would never feel when faced with Dan's return.

Nia hummed in agreement.

They always were.

Some days, I didn't begrudge Dan his success. He'd gotten what he wanted—his dreams were coming true.

The fire drained from Nia and her shoulders slumped. "What if I've got it wrong, Mel?" she whispered, uncertainty shaking her words. "What if he's changed his mind again, and he's decided there's no point in telling me?"

It was a very real concern. One we both shared.

We'd learnt early on that musicians were a fickle lot. Thanks to my dad, Dan, and James. My dad was hardly ever home growing up, always on the road, missing birthdays and milestone moments he always promised to stick around for. In the end, the music always called louder.

He loved it more than he loved me.

That's how things were with Dan.

And with James.

In the last month, James had come to his senses and fought for Nia. He'd messed up again, but this time, he wasn't giving up without a fight.

"I don't think that'll happen, Nia." There was a conviction in my voice that I envied. I wished I could be so certain about my own life. "This time is different. Hold onto that, and if you can't wait, you can always call him."

She huffed. "Not happening. I'm not the easy girl I was in uni. This time he'll come to me on his knees or not at all."

I laughed. It came out strained, muddled with the conflicting wants warring in my head. I wish I had her strength. Instead, I'd spent the last month hiding like a coward from Dan Lloyd. Technically, I'd gone on holiday, but it was directly influenced by his supposedly permanent reappearance in my city. I'd managed to avoid running into him thus far, but it was only by sheer force of will. And the girls giving me the heads up. My luck was going to run out.

What if I was going about this all wrong? What if sharing the secret wouldn't be as bad as I imagined?

"Everything alright, Mel?" Nia asked, reading me like a fortune cookie.

"What if I made a mistake, not telling Dan in the first place?" I whispered, the words barely a wisp of sound.

Sophie and Nia shared a look, each of them daring the other to ask the hard question.

"Do you think you made a mistake?" Sophie asked.

"I don't know, but I'm still scared."

"Scared that he'll find out, or scared that he'll leave?" Nia whispered, her gaze dancing around our quiet corner.

It was just the girls—I could say anything to them, and

they wouldn't repeat it or force me to follow through. Talking didn't mean I had to take action.

"Scared that he'll stay, out of some sense of obligation and either resent me for it or break Phoebe's heart when he realises we're not enough." They were just words. Just letters strung together. And yet, they had the power to make my eyes burn and stab a knife through my chest.

"I don't know the answer," Nia said, her words measured but thick with emotion. She understood better than anyone else. She'd nearly pushed James out of her life again through fear too. "Our situations are alike, but you have more to protect than me. But if you're thinking about this now, maybe you should consider whether you're willing to take the risk. If you are, do something, and if you're not…"

Then life was going to get extra painful.

The city hadn't been big enough for Nia to avoid James. If Dan was here to stay, we would run into each other eventually, and then I'd be faced with a choice.

Lie, or let him in.

The auction got underway and Nia circled the room, photographing the event, while Sophie and I hung out at the side with a plate of appetisers.

It wasn't all that exciting, but still, it was nice to be somewhere different. Usually, we spent our time together in one of our flats or at our favourite pub on a Saturday afternoon. This was a refreshing change of scenery, and I enjoyed watching the people around us. Some furiously threw their paddles in the air, glaring at their opponents like they'd personally insulted them by daring to get in their way. Others were more leisurely in their movements, too busy chatting to their neighbours to really pay attention to the fact they were about to bid £500 on a photograph of the lighthouse. The look of shock on their faces when Phil, the white-haired warden acting as auctioneer, declared them the winner was priceless.

Things were starting to wrap up when the doors opened.

A hush descended on the room; heads craned to catch a glimpse of the latecomers.

My heart stopped.

James stood in the doorway, grinning and surrounded by his stone-faced bandmates. His gaze fixed on Nia next to me, but I couldn't keep my eyes from Dan. His stoic features warmed as they roamed my face, causing my pulse to flutter in my throat.

Alys and Lily pushed past the guys, tutting as they waltzed into the room. They wrapped their arms around Nia, whispering in her ear.

I couldn't focus on their words. My ears were ringing. I was frozen, just like in my dreams.

Distantly, I noticed Alys returning to Ryan, and Lily approaching the stage, but it might as well have been happening in another room.

"You alright?" I asked Nia, hooking my arm through hers, trying with all my might to be normal.

She side-eyed me, noting what was probably panic in my eyes.

He couldn't be here. I wasn't ready for this.

Why couldn't they have waited for a less public event to make their return? Or better yet, no event at all? A random day when I'd be tucked away in my flat with Phoebe.

"Finally," Dan seemed to say.

Rats.

She patted my hand. "You can leave if you want."

I studied her, trying to assess whether she meant it. She couldn't possibly. If I were in her shoes, I'd be a bag of nerves and want my friends around me.

"It was going to happen one day," I whispered.

"You're not going to tell him now?"

"No, but I will." Determination broke through some of the panic, infiltrating my voice and helping me put up a much-needed front. My grip still tightened on her arm.

"Ladies and gentlemen." Phil's excited voice boomed around the room and I jumped. "We have some new entries to the auction."

More lots were announced and a bidding war ensued but I couldn't focus on any of it. James approached slowly, Dan edging along behind him. The closer he got, the tighter my grip on Nia's arm grew.

"Sold for ten thousand pounds." Phil slammed his gavel down, the noise ricochet through the huge open room and I flinched.

On the lots went, and still I couldn't tear my gaze from his. Thankfully, he hung back, clearly trying not to overshadow James's moment. I'm not sure if that was worse or better. The longer they took, the stiffer I grew. I couldn't feel my toes from lack of movement, and my shoulders positively ached.

"Hey," James said, finally stopping in front of Nia. I could barely take in his nerves, my gaze fixed on the red-haired giant at his back.

As James's speech wound on and the tension drained from Nia, my tolerance hit the bottom of the barrel. Staring into his gorgeous green eyes was too much. I shouldn't have come. I should have stayed home, just in case. I didn't need to be here, Nia would have understood. No one would have missed me.

And I definitely wouldn't be staring at the man who broke my heart… over and over and over again.

The man I thought I'd grow old with.

The only one to light me up and uncover truths I didn't know existed.

The one who gave me my hyperactive little munchkin.

God, one look at her and no one would argue that she was his. She had his eyes, his hair colour. Her nose and poker straight hair were all me, but that was where our resemblance ended. In appearances, one could argue that she's more his kid than mine.

No, if I'd just kept playing it safe this wouldn't be happening. He definitely wouldn't be stood there, his eyes eating me up. I steeled my shoulders against the shiver trying to overtake me.

Gah, why did he have to get hotter with age? How was that even fair? Couldn't he have gained some weight or have one of those irritatingly long beards?

It was too soon. I wasn't ready.

James was apologising to Nia and I couldn't focus on a word of it. Whether I'd have heard him over the pounding of my heart was questionable but still, Dan was making me be a shit friend and miss a very important moment.

There was a security door right next to me. One quick shove, and I'd be in the car park. I'd be free.

I wasn't a coward.

I could do this.

I needed to get it over with.

Dan stopped before me, wearing the biggest grin. My stomach flipped as it lit up his eyes.

"You haven't been avoiding me, have you?" he asked, his tone light and teasing. He didn't believe it. Probably couldn't fathom why I wouldn't want him, despite his piecemeal offerings.

He reached for a hug, his arms wide but his movements slow, like he thought I'd disappear in a puff of smoke.

Screw being brave.

I turned tail and ran.

CHAPTER TWO

Thankfully, the security door wasn't alarmed. The slamming of the metal door behind me would have drawn enough attention.

I sprinted across the carpark, cursing my choice of footwear. I'd lived in trainers since Phoebe learnt to walk, and I chose tonight to wear heels? Stupid hindsight.

The door slammed again and my heart sank.

Dan shouted my name. I didn't turn, I didn't slow. My gaze was fixed on my perfectly safe car, parked in the back corner of the small, tree-lined car park.

"Slow down." His arm snagged around my waist. The momentum swept me off my feet and he spun us, like he used to before it all started going to shit. "Where's the fire?" he asked, chuckling as he set me on my feet.

Him holding me like this was odd. Different, yet familiar.

My eyes fell shut for a moment, my head lolling back against his strong chest.

"I've been trying to reach you for weeks." His breath puffed against my neck in the chilled air, tickling me while also lighting a fire inside me.

It felt… nice.

How long had it been since someone had held me? Since *he* held me?

My entire body stiffened at the thought. It was his fault, not mine. And just because the press of his hand against my stomach felt familiar, it didn't mean I should let it stay there.

I pushed his hands away, quickly putting distance between us. I held up a hand, my eyes begging him to stop — could he even read me that well anymore?

"What's wrong?" His face hardened, and that gorgeous 'sweep me off my feet' smile vanished.

Do not feel guilty. It shouldn't have been there in the first place.

"We're not doing this." I gestured between us.

"Do you have a boyfriend or something?" He frowned, confusion blanketing his features. "I thought Sophie or Nia would have told me if you did."

I could say yes. That would give me at least a little reprieve.

Haven't you kept enough from him?

Guilt slithered through me. The denial tripped off my tongue and my heart sank as his entire body relaxed at the news that I was unattached.

"So why not? I'm back now."

"Because it's been *five years*. I've been there, done that, and moved on."

I crossed my arms and glared at him, not trusting his crestfallen look for a second.

"Babe, I'm home now. It's okay."

"As if that changes anything." I glared at him.

"But it does." He took a step closer. "The distance isn't an issue any more. We can make this work now."

My brows shot up at the conviction in his voice. *How could he honestly think the distance had been the only problem between us?* He'd barely talked to me. If he wasn't in town for one reason or another, I didn't hear from him. We went months without contact. That was not a relationship.

I frowned at him. "I don't want to make it work."

His jaw dropped and I had to glance away to avoid the sharp stab of pain in *my* chest at his sharp intake of breath.

"I don't believe you," he whispered, forcing himself to straighten.

"I can't help you see reality, Dan." I gritted my teeth, trying to bite back the anger and the longing swirling through me. "If you can't understand the actual reasons we never worked, that's not on me."

"Why am I getting animosity here?" Dan asked, his voice raising as he pointed at himself. "I'm not the one that changed their number, moved, blocked you on social media and forbade her friends from answering questions about you. What the hell did I do to you to deserve all that?"

I shook my head. "I'm not going into it in a freezing cold car park."

He studied me with far too much clarity in his gaze. There was very little this man didn't know about me and I had been clinging to the biggest of those secrets with two hands. It was all going to come crashing down on top of me, but it didn't have to be tonight. It didn't have to be here, in a dark car park, miles from home with no one to back me up when he freaked out. Yes, *when*. I knew him, remember?

"Of all the people in my life, I was not prepared for you to ghost me,' he muttered, hurt and indignation dripping from his tone.

I laughed, but the sound was not pleasant. "Like you didn't do that to me on a regular basis?"

"I was working."

"And I was trying to move on with my life." My face hardened along with my voice as I took a step forward. "You expected me to wait around until you remembered I existed. It *never* mattered what I wanted. Nothing was stopping Dan Lloyd the trucking rock star getting his way."

"Trucking?" he asked, smirking. I glared at him. No way was I explaining my child-friendly swearing. "It wasn't like that. I love you," he whispered, taking a step closer. "I never stopped."

I snorted. "If that was love, I don't want any part of it."

Resolve settled on his face. He tucked his hands into his pockets and fixed me with his wounded puppy dog eyes.

"Can you stop looking at me like that?" I growled.

"Like what?" he whispered, feigning ignorance.

I rolled my eyes. "This isn't happening. We've been done for five years, and we aren't starting anew."

Something was happening in his head. He seemed to relax for the first time since we got out here. His face smoothed out, his frown replaced with a gentle smile that had once lulled me into agreeing to anything he said. *What the hell was he thinking?*

"Then can't we just go back to being friends and see how that goes first?" Dan asked, imploring me with his words and his eyes.

My laugh was not kind, but I couldn't help it. Friends! Us?

"We tried that. It didn't work."

He scrubbed a hand across his short beard, hiding the smirk I could clearly read in the creases of his eyes.

"And that says you know full well it was a ploy you had no intention of abiding by." I circled my finger at the evidence.

He dropped his hand and outright grinned at me. My breath caught somewhere in my throat, and I focused on not melting into a puddle at his feet.

"Alright, so you know me too well for that to work."

I scowled. "So why try it?"

He shrugged, the playful expression disintegrating in a cloud of confusion. "I don't understand where we went wrong."

My jaw dropped. "You don't..." I blinked, unable to comprehend the way this man's mind worked.

"Alright so my leaving for Glasgow didn't help much." He took another step towards me and I was too shocked to react. "But things were good, weren't they?"

"Define good."

"My moving didn't really change anything."

I snorted. "You mean other than our relationship?"

Another step. "But did it really?"

My nod was swift. "I'd say it put a pretty big fudging hole in our lives, yes."

Dan blinked. "Fudging?"

I crossed my arms. "Yes, fudging. It perfectly describes the mess you made of our plans."

His lips twitched. "How so?"

"Chocolate fudge cake is messy, impossible to clean up, and it makes everything sticky."

His eyes twinkled. "You just described our sex life, babe."

I blanched. "I did not. I—" —was describing the chaos of Phoebe running around the flat after her first bite of one. What the truck.

He'd gotten too close. I had to tip my head back to meet his gaze. I needed more space. I couldn't be this close to him and trust myself. I'd learn one day. Tonight wasn't it.

"Yes, I didn't touch base as often as I should have. Things were pretty crazy those couple of years with the band." Dan caressed my jaw as he stared into my eyes. I shivered at the feel of his calloused fingers scraping against my skin. *Back away now!* "We were working to get signed, and then when it happened, we had to deliver every bloody time. There was no room to think half the time. So yes, I was a shit boyfriend, and I'm sorry I neglected you. But babe, things are different now, let me prove it. Please?"

"Why?" I asked, biting the word out between my clenched

jaw. "So you can decide to move to another country without me again?"

He shook his head, and my brows rose.

"Isn't that exactly what you all just did to Nia?"

"It wasn't permanent."

"Yet," I spat. I forced myself to take a step back and break his hold on me. His hand dropped to his side but he didn't notice, his hopeful, determined gaze fixed on me.

"How many times do I have to say I'm sorry?"

My scowl went up a notch. "Until I say you're done." I jabbed my finger into his far too solid chest. *When had he gotten serious in the gym? Why did I touch him?* The thought of all that muscle was going to keep me up all night. "I made no promises to go along with your selfish plans. I didn't say I'd wait for you. I definitely didn't say I'd give up my goals and leave my home for you. You got to follow your dreams, now please respect mine and —" I punctuated each point with my finger. "Leave. Me. Alone."

He scoffed. "That's rich. Cardiff had nothing to do with your dreams. Yet you're still here." He glanced around the deserted car park. "Tonight's probably the most excitement you've seen in a long time and —"

"Hey! Don't insult my life. You know jack sip about it."

His eyes darkened. "And who's fault is that?"

Yours, and your inability to put me first when I needed you most. I dropped my gaze. "Don't."

The fire door opened again, and the band strolled towards us, carefully. The only happy expression to be found was on James's face.

My gaze bounced back to Dan, drawn by some invisible string.

"I didn't cut you out, Mel. I didn't change everything so that you couldn't find me." His voice grew louder and angrier the more he spoke. "You shut the door on me with no warning." He swallowed. His eyes glittered with unshed tears and mine burned just as badly. "You robbed me of my best friend just as things were starting to take off, and I needed her."

His voice gutted me. It shouldn't have.

You robbed me of a lot more.

His expression softened slightly, tracing the sad lines of my face with too much love, too much reverence. "I needed you, babe, and you fucking abandoned me," he whispered, his hand reaching out to caress my cheek again.

The press of his strong fingers against my skin was the jolt I needed to free me from his spell. I backed away again and this time I didn't stop.

"Pretty words, Dan. Maybe talk to Ryan about writing for the band." My lips flatlined. "Your fans will appreciate them far more than I do."

"Mel, please."

"No," I almost shouted, my own anger overtaking me. "You don't get to waltz into my life, yet again, with your pretty words and empty promises. Don't paint yourself as the victim, the light's not pointing at you." Surprise flickered across his feature at the venom in my voice. "You didn't honestly think I'd wait forever, did you? You had to know I wouldn't be happy taking your morsels of attention whenever you remembered I existed."

He blinked at me, seemingly stunned. I didn't buy it.

"You and I are past tense," I shouted, holding out my hands, gesturing towards the grim-faced band. "You must have realised that by now."

"I've been busy with the band, and I should have tried harder to get in touch." He took a deep breath, his expression gentling in a way that was not allowed to sway me. He started to follow me, but I just kept moving towards my car. "I love you. I just want a chance. I'll be your friend if I have to. Start slow."

"You can repeat that as much as you like, but I still won't believe you." I held my arms out in an exaggerated shrug.

"This is it, Dan. It might look boring to you, it might not match my dreams from five years ago, but it's mine. You got what you wanted. Rhiannon is going places, and I'm happy for you, but that doesn't give you the right to mess with my life."

"I'm not trying to mess with you."

My laugh sounded bitter. "Maybe not intentionally. Then the next big thing will come along and you'll be on a plane without a word of warning, leaving me behind yet again." My gaze drifted pointedly to James.

"I would never do that to you," Dan said, his voice cutting in the watchful silence. James winced behind him and Nia rubbed at his chest. Kind of her, considering he'd put her through hell.

With a dreary smile, I shook my head. "I don't believe you."

"Mel." He held his hand to his chest, pain shadowing his eyes.

"What did you expect? You can't just waltz into the city and tell me you're here to stay." My voice shook with emotion. I needed to get it under control but my throat felt too tight. "Dan, I don't trust you. Please just leave me be," I whispered.

My face burned as tears welled in my eyes. If I didn't leave immediately, I'd turn into a sobbing mess in front of him.

Ryan approached Dan and lay a hand on his shoulder. He leant in close, whispering in his ear. Dan's face hardened, but he nodded all the same.

I walked away, and this time, he let me go.

CHAPTER THREE

Sleep eluded me. My night was spent tossing and turning, struggling to shut down thoughts of Dan and what might have been, what might be. He was delusional. I was not. The teenager who trusted him when he made promises had seen the light and grown up.

Even if my body had other ideas.

There would be no romantic what ifs. The only relationship in our future was that of co-parent.

If I decided to tell him. When. If.

It felt odd to not have Phoebe running around my feet and I missed her. She would have pushed my confusing thoughts from my mind with just her presence. But I'd sent her home with my mother so I could enjoy the auction last night, and she usually spent every Saturday with her favourite grandmother. She hadn't met the other, and I'd honestly like to keep it that way for as long as humanly possible.

On to happier thoughts. I had a standing date with the girls at our favourite pub. Once upon a time, it had been our local. Now, we all lived in different parts of the city. Sophie was the only local left.

I walked into the bar just after midday with at least three

layers of concealer fighting to eliminate the circles. The girls took one look at me and saw straight through it.

"You look like shit," Sophie said, her brows soaring. She glanced at Nia, a scowl pulling at her features. "I told you we should have gone with her."

I slid into the booth next to Nia, a small smile pulling at my lips. "I'm pretty sure Nia had more important things to deal with last night."

Nia blushed but continued to stare at us, satisfaction written plain across her face.

Sophie's face scrunched up. "Ew, don't say shit like that in front of me. I can live without the visuals, thank you very much."

Nia and I chuckled. Sophie still hadn't forgiven her brother for breaking her best friend the first time. He'd have a way to go to win her back now, but she wasn't a hard nut to crack, he'd figure it out eventually. If Nia didn't scar her with too many details.

"Tell me all the details later," I whispered to Nia.

Her gaze roamed my face, uncertainty in the icy blue depths. "Are you sure? You really don't look so good."

I shrugged. "I'll be fine. Just need to actually sleep."

I glanced around the bar, searching for James's familiar dark blond head. We were surrounded by strangers, which was a surprise. I didn't think James would let Nia out of his sight.

The back room where we always sat was made up of large six-seater booths and a couple of smaller tables. There was no TV back here, so the area was always quieter than the front, where all the football and rugby fans congregated. Music played softly overhead, just loud enough to cut out the chatter from the tables nearby but not so loud to stop a conversation.

"He decided to stay back at the house," Nia said, reading my mind. She bit her lip, studying me. "We kind of agreed you might need some girl time."

I wasn't surprised. I'd have done the same thing to her.

"How are you really doing?" Nia asked. She pushed an empty wine glass towards me and Sophie filled it up.

Picking up the glass, I sipped, stalling. My thoughts were a jumbled mess. It felt like factions of me were at war, part of me wanting to throw caution to the wind and let him break me, another part wanting to just introduce him to Phoebe and deal with the fall out, and another desperately screamed at me to run away and hide. That part was speaking a lot louder than the rest.

Moisture filled my eyes as I glanced between my two amazing best friends. They'd go along with anything I decided. They wouldn't necessarily like it, but they'd do whatever I said.

"It's all such a mess," I said, my voice choked with unshed tears.

"Do you still want to keep the secret?" Nia whispered, scanning our surroundings just in case the wrong person walked in and overheard.

My head fell back against the booth and I groaned. "I don't know. I want to tell him, and then I don't. I want to throw myself at him, but I know how that ends. I want to trust him, but how can I, when he'll drop me the moment something new, shiny, and musical comes along?"

The tears overflowed and they both reached for my hands, squeezing. Their faces were open, their care and understanding plain to see. They'd never judged me for keeping it from him—neither had my mother—but that didn't mean it was right.

"I will tell him. I don't think there's any world in which we could both live here and keep it secret." The conviction in my voice shocked me.

The fact was, we'd only managed to keep Phoebe a secret this long because the guys had been insanely focused on building the band, and Sophie point-blank refused to speak to her brother for nearly ten years after he broke Nia's heart. If any of us had been on good terms with them, the cat would have been out of the bag so fast. I wasn't exactly inconspicuous in the beginning with my huge belly, and then the pram and screaming new-born. The only reason his mother didn't know was down to the fact she hated me well before Dan and I had broken up.

"No, I'll tell him. I just need time to figure out how."

They both nodded.

"Of course. It's not every day someone drops a child on a man." An amused glint entered Sophie's eyes. "Can I be there when you tell him? Preferably with a camera?"

I chuckled, amused despite the dread coiling in my stomach.

"Who are you planning to torture with the footage?" Nia asked, failing to hide her grin behind her wine glass.

"I'm sure it'll come in handy someday." Sophie shrugged. "Maybe when he freaks out at Phoebe going on her first date."

"Be honest, you just have a sick sense of humour," I muttered, my tears all but forgotten.

She nodded. "That too." Her tone was so serious that neither Nia nor I could hold in our laughter.

Sophie had her touchy moments but she could lighten even the darkest atmosphere. I released the fear, if only for now. She squeezed my hand again, relief shining in her eyes.

"Now, please tell me you gave James hell when you got home," Sophie demanded, turning her attention to Nia and moving the conversation away from me.

"I thought you didn't want to hear all the details?" Nia reminded Sophie, a teasing note in her voice.

Sophie groaned. "Please, just keep it PG rated."

I sniggered and Nia shook her head.

"They don't do PG, Soph. What on earth are you thinking?"

"That it sucks I can't live vicariously through either of you," she muttered, her brow quirking.

Nia snorted. "Why don't I believe you?"

I chuckled. "You're welcome to do the party planning for me, if you're that desperate."

She shook her head at me, grinning "That is not what I meant, and you know it, but I'll happily take some of it off your hands for my favourite niece."

"Hold on, let's rewind a minute," Nia said, turning fully to Sophie until she sat with her back to the room. "You didn't want to hear the details before James came back."

"Maybe I had a change of heart."

She couldn't have been more obvious had she waved a red flag. Nia leaned forward, her gaze avid as she assessed Sophie.

"Spill."

Sophie laughed nervously. "Spill what? There's nothing to spill." Her voice climbed, giving her away.

I settled back against the booth and sipped my wine, content to watch Nia dissect Sophie. *This should be fun.*

"Then why are you looking at us like that?" Nia asked.

Sophie's eyes widened. "Like what? I'm just looking at you."

Nia humphed her disbelief and continued to eye Sophie like she could crack her if she found the right pressure point. She probably could.

"I'm not the one about to let my ex sweep me off my feet," Sophie muttered, her panicked eyes catching mine.

I frowned, barely registering the regret that flitted across her face.

"What the hell, Soph?" Stunned was too weak a word. I was floored. "What happened to understanding and letting me be?"

She mouthed "sorry" but didn't retract the declaration.

"I am not going to *let* him do anything," I growled, the very idea digging into my mind with sharp claws.

Doubt darkened her eyes.

"You don't actually think that?"

Sophie lifted her shoulder in a half shrug, and I turned to Nia. She wore an equally sceptical expression.

"You too?"

Nia bit her lip and nodded slowly. "I'm sorry. It's just you and Dan are like me and James, and I didn't have a hope in hell of resisting him." She gulped down her wine, placing the empty glass back on the table. "I just don't see him laying down this time, Mel."

Laying down? Try walking away.

"There's one salient difference between us, Nia."

"Oh?"

"You didn't have a small child relying on you," I said. That conviction flowed through me again, bolstering my weakening defences. "Yes, I'm drawn to him but that'll only end in fireworks, and not the good kind. For Phoebe, I need to stay detached, and letting him sweep me off my feet,"—I glanced at Sophie pointedly—"would only hurt her in the end."

Nia's shoulders slumped. I hadn't spotted it before but there was a grain of hope in her eyes. My words snuffed it out.

"What if it didn't end in fireworks?" she murmured, her voice subdued but still challenging me. "What if he's grown up and opened his eyes?"

"Like James?" I asked, barely containing my disbelief. She nodded and I snorted. "Nia, I love you, but James growing up and opening his eyes didn't change who he is. He's still music-obsessed, he'll still follow the band anywhere at a moment's notice. The only difference now is you're letting photography consume you, and when he picks up and goes, you can go with him."

Her eyes dropped to her empty wine glass. She frowned at it as she twisted the stem, drawing a circle on the scarred table top.

Silence fell. Neither of them could argue with me. I was right, and I wasn't like Nia. I didn't have a passion to consume me and help me understand. I had a toddler who would eventually share in my hurt every time he skipped town.

"There's no romantic end to this story," I said, steel filling my tone. "Phoebe might get her father, and I —" I swallowed hard. I was painting such a dreary picture but it was for the best. "I'll lock my heart in a box and keep him at a distance."

Tears glistened in both Sophie's and Nia's eyes.

"You deserve so much better," Sophie whispered, her voice low and pained.

Nia nodded. She glared at her empty glass. "We need another bottle."

"You're driving," Sophie said.

She growled. "So I'll get a taxi."

"To work?" I asked, my nose scrunching up at the idea of her wielding a camera in a crowd of music lovers while drunk.

Her glare went up a notch. "Fine, you two need another bottle. And food." She pushed at my shoulder. "Let me out, I'll go put in our usual order."

I freed her and slid into her seat. Sophie and I stared at each other. We sipped our wine in silence, well and truly lost in the dour atmosphere my words had created.

"I didn't mean to kill the day."

"Pretty sure that was my fault," Sophie said, trying for a smile. It didn't reach her eyes and she gave up. "I'm sorry, I shouldn't have pushed like that."

I couldn't blame her. I'd gladly use someone else as a human shield right now. I just hadn't expected Sophie to use me.

"Guess I'm not the only one suffering," I muttered, eying her for a reaction.

She tilted her head, considering me. She'd always been easy for me to read, and right now, she was working hard through her options.

"I'm just bored."

I frowned. "Bored with what, exactly?" She loved her job.

Or I thought she loved her job. She was happily single by choice, and fiercely independent.

"I'm not sure." She shook her head, a thoughtful light in her eyes. "I just need something to change."

Before I could comment, a red-haired giant caught my attention and my stomach flipped. Rats.

"We're about to have company," I whispered to Sophie, not even bothering to hide. He'd already spotted me and was striding purposefully towards me.

Couldn't a girl have a day to catch her breath?

CHAPTER FOUR

"Fancy seeing you here." Dan slid into the booth next to me, his face set in happy lines, but his eyes watched cautiously. Good, he'd learnt something last night.

"Try that line with someone who doesn't know you."

I turned in my seat until my back pressed against the wall and an entire seat sat open between us. The more distance from this man, the better. Even so, my eyes were drawn to the rigid line of his body. My fingers itched to touch him, to discover if his biceps were as toned as his chest.

He chuckled, the low sound playing havoc with my self-control. It licked at my skin and heated my blood.

"Alright, so I'm crashing on purpose." His green eyes were dark, mirroring the lust burning through me.

I dragged my eyes away from him, focusing instead on Sophie. She'd slid into the corner of the booth, her head back against the leather, her eyes shut.

"Where's my brother?" she asked without opening her eyes. Resignation filled her voice.

"At the bar with Nia."

So much for him giving us the afternoon for girl time.

Sophie nodded. I poured her another glass of wine, using

up the last of the bottle of red. Her smile was grateful when I slid it towards her. We both sipped from our glasses, trying to ignore the demanding presence that had invaded our booth.

"Radio silence, huh?" Dan said, amusement dripping from his words. "You don't remember how that always backfired on you?"

I quirked a brow. "For it to backfire, I'd have to want something from you."

He smirked, leaning towards me, resting his forearm on the table. With my back against the wall, I had nowhere to go, and he ate up the space between us quickly, caging me in and barely shifting from his seat.

"You're not indifferent to me," he whispered, his eyes dropping to my lips. "I just have to be patient."

"Yet another quality you don't possess." I stared into his eyes, refusing to join his dance, refusing to let my gaze drop to his lips.

But it was so hard, and he was so close. His eyes dared me to lean forward, to catch his mouth with mine, to take what was mine.

"What's the other?" he asked, his voice low, so low I doubted Sophie would have heard him over the hum of the music. It played through my body, as if he'd plucked me like a guitar string.

"What?"

"The other quality." His voice was soft, enticing me just as much as the close heat of his body. "You said another quality I don't possess."

"Oh." I shook my head, trying to clear some of the fog. "Reliability. You're not reliable."

His head snapped back as if I'd slapped him. He settled back into his seat just as Nia returned with another bottle of wine. James trailed behind her, two pints of golden liquid in his hands and a careful expression painted on his face. Nia slid into the booth next to Sophie, her eyes fixed on mine, an apology in their depths that she had no reason to own.

I emptied my wine glass and pushed it towards her, grateful that I always got a taxi to our lunches. Just because Nia had to limit herself didn't mean Soph and I did. Neither of us had anything else to do with our Saturday, and as long as I was sober by dinner when my mother would return Phoebe, everything would be fine.

"I hope you don't mind us joining you," James said, his tone making it perfectly clear that he knew they weren't welcome.

"You're always welcome, *James*," I said because what else were we meant to say?

We couldn't ask him to leave. Nia had gone through enough, and where James went, so did the band. We wouldn't push him away, even if Sophie wished she could shove her brother off a cliff and get away with it.

Sophie snorted but otherwise remained silent, twirling her wine glass and watching the liquid coat the edges.

Dan studied me from the corner of his eye. It made me defensive but I also itched to close the distance, to lean into him like I used to. Before he'd left for Glasgow, we had been good together. Evidently not good enough to stop him going, but we never argued. The radio silence had been a game half the time and the other half was nothing but small disagreements.

We'd been comfortable. Even when he was walking in and out of my life in the seven years that followed. When I was sad, he was the one I wanted to hold me. When I had a bad day at work, I itched to call him, to have him sit in my kitchen, absorbing every word no matter how arbitrary my issues.

In the moments before sleep, I missed him. And that was a very bad thing. Because no matter how safe he made me feel, he wasn't permanent. Back then, he'd stick around for a week and then be gone without warning. No note. No texts. Nothing until the next time he turned up at my front door.

Instead of sliding closer to him, I crossed my arms and stared right back. I filled my gaze with the remembered pain, with years of betrayal.

How was I going to be friends with him? Because I'd have to be friendly at least. Phoebe loved him, and she didn't even know him. Poor child. The moment she laid eyes on him, I'd never get him out of my life. Friendship would make his constant presence easier.

Maybe.

A tiny voice laughed at me.

Friends with Dan. The concept of either of us keeping our hands to ourselves was less than believable.

"What's that scowl for now?" Dan asked, turning fully towards me again.

My gaze flicked to our friends. Nia was trying to engage Sophie in conversation but her eyes kept straying to me. Worried furrows marred both their faces. James was outright staring at Dan, his body rigid as he waited for Dan to mess up.

All of our friends were on edge, and I had done it. Why couldn't we just have a peaceful afternoon with no drama? I missed it.

"How's your sister?" I asked, changing the subject entirely. Or trying to. He frowned at me, his lips sealed. "Is she still in London?"

He glanced at James.

"Can we grab another booth and talk?"

I was shaking my head before the words had finished forming. Bad idea.

"We need to talk, babe," he whispered, his voice and eyes imploring me to just follow him.

"Don't call me that."

It was just an endearment. In the grand scheme of things, who cared? But he'd given up the right to talk to me with that loving hitch when he kept leaving me… when he'd pawned me off onto his manager on the one day I'd needed him to tell me everything would be alright.

Dan sighed. His shoulders slumped and he let his head fall back against the booth.

"How do I fix this?" he asked, rolling his head towards me, pinning me with the desperation in his green eyes.

The urge to just let him in was strong, but one glance at Nia and Sophie's watchful faces froze the words before they could leave my tongue.

"I don't know that you can."

"But I can try?" His voice sharpened with hope.

Attempting any sort of relationship with this man could go horribly wrong, but the alternative was bleak. Maybe if I promised to give friendship a go, it would ease the shock of Phoebe.

Gah, who was I kidding? Nothing was going to ease that bubble bursting.

I studied his face. He'd been clean-shaven most of his life, but now a short-trimmed beard covered his jaw, ageing him in enticing ways. It made him more rugged.

"Let's start with friends." The words were out before I could overthink it.

Surprise widened his eyes, a hesitant smile toyed with the edges of his lips. "You said it wouldn't work."

And I still believed that, but what else was I meant to do? Avoiding him wasn't going to work. He and James were practically attached at the hip, and James had just become a permanent feature of my inner circle.

"I don't really see any other options, do you?"

His gaze dipped, roaming my body with a devilish light in his eyes. My stomach flipped.

"Any other platonic options," I bit out, my voice annoyingly hoarse.

He shook his head, smirking at the blush creeping into my cheeks.

"Okay, so friends." I held out my hand to shake. It was a stupid move, letting him touch me. Not on the level of forgetting the condom, but it was up there. I'd had two glasses of wine—I'd blame the alcohol.

His hand engulfed mine, callouses grazing my sensitive skin. It set off a chain reaction, one I equally loved and loathed. The sensation was so soft but it sent sparks through my nerve endings. I shivered, and his grip tightened. His green eyes darkened as he watched me. The knowledge that this, our friendship, was a very bad idea sat between us while my body urged me to close the gap.

His head started to dip and the spell broke. I turned sharply in my seat, my gaze latching onto Sophie like a lifeline. She tried to hide a smirk behind her hands but her eyes creased as she silently laughed at me. Nia and James stared back at me with a mixture of hope and concern.

Thankfully, our food was delivered before I had to figure out how to put a pin in the tension permeating our booth.

We all dug into our burgers and fries. James and Dan eyed our food with envy. James leaned into Nia, whispering in her ear. She shook her head and continued to eat.

Without even trying to distract me, Dan nicked a fry.

"Hey!" I dragged my plate further into the corner. "Get your own fries."

"But yours are right there." He reached for another, and I swatted his hand away. He chuckled, the tension draining from him. I liked the sight of him relaxed far too much. "And friends share."

"You know well enough that I don't share food." I covered my plate and turned my body until I was guarding the food. I glared at him over my shoulder. "Go order your own."

Eyes dancing with mirth, he held up his hands. "Good idea." He slid from the booth and stretched. His black band shirt rode up, revealing a teasing glimpse of what might have been a six pack. My mouth went dry.

Friends. Just friends. I could do it.

Shit.

"James, do you want anything?" Dan nodded towards the bar.

James followed him out. Their low murmurs faded fast and the girls turned to me as one. It was startling but also expected.

"Friends?" Sophie muttered, her eyes spitting fire. "What the hell are you thinking?"

"That we need boundaries, and keeping him completely out of my life isn't possible anymore?"

She covered her mouth and stared at me like I'd toppled her dominos again. It happened once when we were kids. She never set them up in front of a closed door again, but she also gave me grief about it for months.

Nia cleared her throat. "It was brave."

"Masochistic more like," Sophie muttered. She picked up her glass and downed the contents. I'd be carrying her out if she kept that up.

Nia snorted.

"What? It is," Sophie squeaked. She peered over Nia, trying to see the door. Lowering her voice, she continued, "He doesn't know the meaning of friendship. It's nothing more than a challenge for him."

I glanced at Nia to see if she agreed. Given the way she worried at her lip, the answer was obvious.

"She's got a point. James did the same thing to me." Her eyes trailed over the dark space, realisation settling across her features. "Right here, actually." She reached across the table and grasped my hand, fixing me in her stare. "Just be careful."

CHAPTER FIVE

*S*unday
Dan: I'm bored. What are you up to?

I stared at it, indecision warring inside me. If I answered, he'd keep pushing. If I didn't answer, I'd feel bad, and he'd continue blowing up my phone.

Phoebe happily munched on an apple slice in her highchair. Totally oblivious to my dilemma.

Dan: Remember that bar we used to go to in town? Is it still there?

It wasn't, but I could see right through him, trying to goad me into responding. It seemed perfectly innocent, just reminiscing about the past, nothing to see here.

Until I answered with a yes or a no, and then suddenly I've agreed to meet him, and I'm on my way into the centre to make some more bad decisions.

Dan: Nope. How could they shut down? That place was amazing.

It really wasn't. It was a dive bar, overflowing with drunk students sucking down cheap drinks. But our priorities had been so different then. It wasn't about the quality of the alcohol but the buzz and saving money. If I drank the sugary crap I used to, now, I'd end up with a three-day hangover.

I watched as those three little dots appeared, threatening me with another text.

Dan: Mel. I'm bored. Be a good friend and talk to me.

My brows climbed.

He was still predictable. Next he'd be outright calling me out…

Dan: Stop ignoring me. I promise you'll have a good time.

And there it was.

I chuckled beneath my breath, and Phoebe's head shot up, her apple slice all but forgotten.

"What's funny, mammy?"

Looking at her quizzical face, guilt flickered in the back of my mind. I should have been focusing on her. Not him.

Dan: Did I hear you're in the Bay too? We could get a drink on the waterfront. That place with the deck and the fruity cocktails you like still there?

My heart almost stopped. He knew where I lived? Or at least the right area. My time was running out. I glanced at Phoebe, gnawing innocently on her apple slices. Guilt slithered through me for keeping them apart, but life was simple right now. Tiring but straightforward. I wasn't ready to expose her to the drama. I needed to find the courage to get this over with fast. Who knew, maybe he'd stop chasing *me* once he knew.

Why didn't that fill me with joy?

I couldn't figure out how to tell him. Yes, it was as simple as opening my mouth and letting the words come out, but what exactly was I meant to say?

'Oh hey, remember the last time we hooked up? Yeah, well it seems we weren't as safe as we thought. Here's your toddler. Please don't break her heart like you broke mine.'

I guess I could just let him come over, and Phoebe would spill the beans for me. But I wasn't enough of a chicken to expose her to his shock. I had no idea how Dan would react to kids. His sister Freya was only four years younger than him. What if he didn't know what to do with her exuberant welcome? Because it would definitely be exuberant.

There was the age-old text option, but again, cowards' way out. And talk about tactless.

Fact: there was no good way to tell someone they were a father.

I silenced my phone and put it down, pushing the whole thing behind a wall for now.

"Do you want to go see auntie Sophie?" I asked Phoebe, my smile too wide.

"Yes!" she screeched before immediately trying to clamber out of her high chair. "Can we go now?"

"Sure." I caught her before she could leap from the chair and hurt herself.

"Can I take my dolls?" Her eyes shone with the barely contained joy of a toddler. Just looking at her eased some of the tension inside of me.

"I'm sure she'd love to see them."

She wriggled in my arms, eager to get down and start selecting. I squeezed her tighter, not ready to let her go. The thought of someone hurting her put a lump in my throat. Especially not her dad. Tears pricked my eyes, and I blinked furiously.

Fathers should be heroes in their daughters' eyes. I didn't have that, but I wanted it for her.

Though would it be fair of me to expect Dan to step in like that?

I'd loved him once, and he was a decent guy then. What if his growing fame had gotten to him and that had changed?

"Mam!" Phoebe growled, desperate to be put down.

Guilt hit me again but for an entirely different reason. I

was too distracted to pay attention to her. I couldn't control the outcome, but the how and the when were mine to manoeuvre. I was going to have to let it happen, on my terms. The suspense wasn't good for either of us.

I set her on her feet and she shot off, chatting to herself as she gathered toys.

I forced a deep breath, willing the worry away. It would fall as it fell. I'd take the week, get work out of the way, and face the music next weekend.

※

6 AM came around far too quickly. No matter how much sleep I got, getting up was always painful. Groaning, I forced myself out of bed and into the shower. If I didn't get moving before Phoebe woke up, I'd be leaving the house with my unwashed hair in a ponytail again.

No, there was too much riding on the day for me to walk into the office a bedraggled wreck. So, out came my blow dryer. My side parting and lack of fringe meant that I didn't really have to worry about how it felt, either. I'd worn it that way for years.

Despite all those pros, it was starting to drive me insane. I resisted the urge to cut it all off every time I set foot in the hairdressers — which was… once in a blue moon. I might hate it now, but if I cut it short like Nia's, I'd have to do more to it. Right now, I could throw it in a ponytail and rush out the door, no styling product required.

"Mammy," Phoebe called just as I put the makeup brushes away.

She wandered into my ensuite bathroom, her green eyes shining bright. All her energy from the night before was back in full force and she could barely stand still. Her short copper hair was dishevelled and stuck to her head, the ends curling slightly.

"Waffles now?" she asked, her small voice hopeful. My heart squeezed at the sight of her.

I picked her up and sat her on the bathroom counter. "How about we brush your hair first?"

She pouted. "Fine."

The kid hated the hairbrush. I could never figure out why, but she'd learnt not to argue with me after she convinced my father to let her go to nursery with her hair a matted mess. Safe to say, he was never allowed to get her dressed in the morning.

Phoebe pulled a face as I ran the brush through her baby-fine hair.

"It's not that bad." I chuckled. She didn't agree.

With her hair straightened out, she raced into the living room and turned on the TV. Cartoons blared through my flat as I popped potato waffles in the toaster.

"Turn the volume down, Phoebe."

The sound dropped as I poured her juice.

A quick glance at the clock put me on superspeed. I was running out of time. I needed to get Phoebe fed, dressed, and in the car by 8AM if I was going to get to the office on time. I'd eat breakfast at my desk, so that was one less thing to worry about at least.

The toaster popped and I dished the squares onto a plate.

"Food, Phoebs." I placed the plate and her juice cup on the breakfast bar and pulled out her high chair.

"Can I eat in front of the TV?" she asked, her voice telling me she already knew the answer because she asked it every single day, and my answer never changed.

"No, turn it off."

Grumbling, she did as told, and I lifted her into her chair.

The clock on the oven was taunting me. Time was slipping away, and Phoebe was picking at her waffles like she wasn't really sure she wanted them.

"I thought you wanted waffles?" I held another piece out to her.

"I do."

"Then stop playing and eat them."

She wouldn't stop kicking the back of the island, too focused on tapping out a beat to pay attention to me or her food. I ignored the niggling comparison between her and Dan.

"Can I listen to music in the car?" She asked around a piece of potato.

"Sure, but don't talk with your mouth full."

It didn't speed her up, unfortunately. It was ten minutes to eight and I was frantically brushing her teeth. I sent her into her room to put on the clothes I'd laid out for her while I cleaned up.

I walked into her bedroom to find her still in her pyjamas, playing with ponies in the corner of her room. Her clothes sat untouched on her bed.

"Phoebe!"

She jumped, glancing over her shoulder at me with her lips pressed together and her eyes wide, too wide.

"Stop playing and get dressed. We have to leave right now."

I picked up her dress and she scrambled off the floor.

Yeah, I wouldn't change a thing.

❄

When I turned my laptop off on Friday, everything was under control. The graphics were on the verge of being approved. I'd confirmed all the influencers involved with the launch and sent a list to the person handling the shipping of their swag for their own content to launch next Friday.

It should have been an easy Monday.

Why then, did I drop Phoebe at the nursery downstairs and find my team in chaos?

"What happened?" I asked the moment I dropped my purse on my clean desk. I hated clutter, I'd had to get used to it at home with Phoebe, but I wouldn't accept it in my workspace. It was too distracting.

We worked for a marketing firm, but there were four of us managing the entire social media marketing branch. That number was gradually growing, thankfully. Lisha, Charlotte, and I handled different accounts with Dylan assistant to us all, but this one was so big that we'd decided it was best to pool efforts.

"Another brand just dropped a similar strategy," Lisha said, her blue gaze catching mine briefly before returning to her screen. There was a slump in her shoulders that wasn't typical.

"How similar?" I asked, collapsing into my chair and bracing myself for the worst.

"Word for word identical." Charlotte sat in her chair, spinning aimlessly. Another not bizarre sight.

"How is that possible?"

Charlotte and Lisha shrugged.

Dylan, our assistant, was on the phone. She held it clasped between her shoulder and ear. When she noticed me assessing her, she grimaced. It morphed her young face. Usually she was all bubbles and fun, the picture-perfect blonde who could be a social influencer herself if she wasn't so uncomfortable about strangers staring at her.

We'd worked together for almost two years, since before she graduated from university in Cardiff, the same one I went to. She'd started here as an intern and quickly ingratiated herself to the company. It was a start-up, and they needed all the eager bodies they could get.

Which explained how I kept my job and returned to a

promotion despite dropping to part time during maternity leave.

"That would be a question above our heads," Charlotte muttered, continuing to spin. Her long, raven hair lay across the back of the chair, spilling down the back.

"Okay, we can fix this." I powered up my computer.

Charlotte stopped spinning, Dylan put the phone down and Lisha's furrowed brow deepened.

"How the hell are we going to do that?" Lisha asked.

"By assessing the damage to our plans and finding an alternative."

Charlotte sat up, she leaned towards me with the look of someone who'd been slapped. "But the foundations are gone."

"Then we'll get new foundations."

"In a week?" Dylan squeaked.

"By the end of the day."

Everyone's eyes widened. Yeah it was a crazy ask, but we had to get the job done.

"Now somebody show me the problem."

"The memo's waiting in your inbox," Lisha said, continuing to stare at me like I was in denial and a breakdown was imminent when I realised the full scope of the problem. If I could handle a toddler on my own, I could handle a snag in our plan.

❄

Dan: I haven't been on the ice in years. Wanna go tonight?

Neither had I, and my heart leapt at the thought.

Mel: Sorry, I'm busy.

Better to be safe. Was it fear or joy that tricked the brain into thinking it was in love with someone? I couldn't remember, but either way, spending time with him, alone, was not a good idea. Even if the thought of ice skating was extremely tempting.

I'd talk to the girls about redirecting our weekend date to an ice rink. Still get a fix in a way that's safe.

Dan: What about tomorrow?
Mel: Busy.
Dan: -.- Why don't I believe you?
Mel: Not my fault you turned into a suspicious person.

I stared at the screen, hoping he'd stop but hoping he wouldn't. I shouldn't be hoping for anything with him.

Dan: Uhuh. How about a film and takeout then?

Persistence had always been his best quality.

'Be careful' Nia had said. Like that was easy to do when the man wouldn't take a step back.

Mel: Busy means busy, Dan.
Dan: Still not believing you, babe. Maybe if you call me...

Ha. Not happening.

He'd hear the lie in my voice with very little trouble. Plus, hearing his voice just wasn't good for me. It would turn smooth, tempting me in all the best and worst ways. No, silence was best, so I silenced my phone and went back to work.

❈

As snags go, this one was pretty frustrating. Another cosmetics company had used the same slogan we had printed on an obscene amount of merchandise for swag boxes and party favours. To right the ship, we needed a new slogan, and a kind ear at the printers.

It had taken six months to get Efa Michaels to sign off the first slogan for her zero-waste green cosmetics company, but miracles could happen. So out with the old and back to the drawing board.

While Owen, our owner, locked himself in the conference room with the copywriters and Efa's assistant, we started sweet-talking the printers, drafting updates for all the influencers and partners, and taking stock of the copy we'd need to update across the company and through a month-long digital campaign — the bare bones of which we'd already scheduled.

"Ladies," Owen said, approaching our corral of desks in the back corner of the office just after lunch.

We all glanced up at him with eager eyes and said nothing. He was smiling. Why was he smiling? He'd walked into the conference room with tension riding his broad shoulders. Now his handsome face was the picture of relaxed.

"It's done."

"Define done." Lisha leaned back in her chair, her blue eyes narrowing. She'd lost control of her short blonde hair as the day progressed. Her fingers had run through it so often that it was now conducting static, and she'd had to wrangle it into a bobble.

"Make them swoon, not the planet." He rubbed his hands together, his calm blue gaze travelling between us all. It settled for longer than necessary on Charlotte.

She focused on the window instead of him.

"It's signed off. Make the changes, and get out of here as early as you can," Owen said, settling on me with a slight furrow to his brow.

We nodded but no one spoke. How had he managed to get that out of them in a couple of hours, when the copywriting team had to go over their ad copy a hundred times before they'd settled on the first?

Owen sauntered away.

"The fuck just happened?" Lisha muttered, shellshocked and catching my eye over the tops of our computer screens.

I shook my head. Hell if I knew.

"I don't really want to ask questions, do you?" I asked, raising my brows at her.

She winced. "Yeah, let's not turn away a gift today."

"Right, I'll update the influencers." I glanced at Dylan and Charlotte who stared back at me, poised to jump into action. "Dylan, start tweaking copy. Charlotte, call the printers back and take them off standby. Lisha…" Our eyes connected again—amusement twinkled in hers.

"Will browbeat any fucker who steals this one," she muttered, typing furiously at her keys.

We all sniggered but it was subdued, fear filled.

"Let's not tempt fate," I said, rubbing at my eyes. "Can you coordinate with the events team?"

"On it." She pushed her chair back and smoothed her pencil dress down. A wicked grin stretched her lips. She sashayed away, leaving us all laughing off the nerves that had gripped us all day.

We could do this. Six days to turn it all around.

Welcome to my life.

❄

Tuesday

Dan lasted the entire day without texting me. I was able to get a decent chunk of my to-do list done, and the week was starting to look like it might go off without a hitch. Friday was the launch of one of my biggest brand campaigns and nerves were starting to get the better of me. Each time I crossed an item off the list, it quelled them, allowed me to breathe for a couple of moments.

I was collecting Phoebe from the nursery at the office when my phone blew up. I couldn't help but sigh. Standing outside the centre, I pulled it out of my back and glanced at the lock screen notifications.

Five messages from Dan Lloyd.

What surprised me was the three messages from Nia.

Nia: Red alert.

Nia: Dan is grilling James for your address.

Nia: He's holding strong but he won't last.

My heart jumped into my throat. I didn't want Dan at my door, surprising me. No, I needed to be prepared for him.

Mel: Did he tell him?

Mel: Wait! How does James know where I live?

My face hurt from the mammoth frown gripping it, but I couldn't stop, couldn't tear my eyes from the screen.

Nia: I might have told him.

"Why would you do that, Nia?" I growled. Thankfully, there was no one around to see me losing my shit over a text message, but what kind of idiotic move was that? I rubbed at my temples, the pressure doing nothing to ease the incoming headache.

Nia: He's picking me up on Friday night. Figured we'd be breaking out the wine, and I'd need a lift. I'm sorry.

The pressure unravelled slightly. Okay, that was fair. It was a perfectly normal thing to ask your boyfriend. Too bad perfectly normal was going to drop me in a pressure cooker.

Mel: Not your fault. It's fine.

Nia: Really?

Mel: Yes.

Nia: -.^ Really?

Mel: YES! Why should you get a taxi when you've got a bf at your beck and call? I get it.

Nia: Oookay. What are you going to do?

Mel: Not a bloody clue.

Mel: Wait, did he tell him?

Nia: Not yet, but I can't watch him at all times.

Nia: Does it help if I tell you my cake-maker friend agreed to do Phoebe's birthday cake?

Mel: The one with the awesome salted caramel?

Nia: Is there another?

Mel: Yes, that definitely helped. Thank you. You're the best.

Nia: Repeat that for Sophie on Friday night. :p

I was chuckling as I opened Dan's messages, but the amusement quickly faded. I shut my eyes, unable to look. *Please tell me he's not at my door.*

Peeking through my lashes, I scanned the messages, chewing my lip as I scrolled.

Dan: Which building are you in? James won't tell me.

Dan: Friends hang out. Stop avoiding me.

Dan: Okay, that was a bit harsh. Sorry. I'm antsy to catch up. Aren't you?

Dan: If you weren't avoiding me, would you meet me for dinner?

Dan: Hypothetically of course.

My shoulders sagged. *I'm safe.* For now.

Mel: Sorry, I have plans.

Dan: No one is that busy.

I was that busy. The only reason I made it home on time every night was because of Phoebe. Some nights, my job didn't stop when I put her to bed. It was the only way I could keep up. My boss was understanding, allowing me to work flexibly, picking up hours at home where needed.

Mel: Then I guess I'm no one.

I reread the text and groaned.

Way to sound defensive.

Now he'd assume he'd upset me, and the messages would never stop.

I silenced my phone and dropped it in my handbag. With all thoughts of Dan and his persistence pushed to the back of my mind, I opened the door to the nursery.

Phoebe ran at me, chattering too fast for me to keep up.

I crouched down by her side and tried to hold her still. "Try it again at a human speed, munchkin."

She bounced on the spot, her face split with a huge grin. "We made slime. It was gross and slimy, and I want more." Her tiny hands landed on my shoulder and her eyes widened comically. "Can we make more at home?"

A vision of my sofa plastered in green slime flashed through my mind. I pulled a face. She had tiny streaks of the stuff in her hair. There was a bath in her very near future.

"How about we make cookies, instead?" I touched the gunk, it was rock solid. There were going to be some tears while I got that out.

She hissed her agreement and broke from my hold, running for the door before I could stop her. I chuckled as I raced after her. She kept up the chatter as we drove home. By the time we arrived, cookies had evolved to three kinds — chocolate, skittles, and peanut butter. Probably a good idea to stock up with the stress Dan was inspiring.

I glanced at my phone while Phoebe danced around the room, unable to resist the itch any longer.

Four messages from Dan Lloyd.

Yup. He'd freaked out.

Dan: Shit, I didn't mean it like that. I just meant that it's an excuse.

Dan: That was worse, wasn't it?

Dan: Okay, I'm a bad friend. Help me get better at it?

Dan: Dinner at Harrys?

I shook my head, my lips twitching at the edges.

He wasn't going to stop, and I didn't think I was capable of ignoring him.

Sighing, I leaned against the counter. Phoebe bounced at my feet, her eager face shining and dragging my reluctant smile to the surface.

Avoiding him wasn't going to work. I'd have to agree to at

least one of his requests if I didn't want him to just turn up at my flat.

I typed out a quick reply, hoping it would put a pin in Dan for the night.

Mel: Rain check? I really am busy.

Dan: Okay. As long as there is a rain check -.-

❄

Wednesday

It was nearly lunchtime, the day was slipping away from me, and my newest social media influencer was having a meltdown. When my phone pinged, I braced myself for the worst.

Dan: Are you still a Marable fan?

I frowned at the message. Why would he want to know that? I'd been obsessed when we were kids — I bought every album the day of release and learnt the new lyrics within hours kind of obsessed.

Mel: That kind of love doesn't die.

Dan: We're supporting them on Saturday in Cardiff. Come to the gig.

Seeing Marable would be incredible. I hadn't been to a gig in years. I didn't even go to Axel's or Jackson's when Nia was working now. At some point, I'd decided to reserve my night off for quiet time with the girls, favouring spaces where we could actually talk and catch up. But the thought of going to a gig, feeling the music vibrating through me, was alluring.

My mother normally had Phoebe on Saturdays. It wasn't out of the realms of possibility.

But I'd have to see Dan.

The more distance I put between us the better for my resistance.

Dan: Stop overthinking it. You'll get to meet Marable.

I groaned. Oh, he knew me too well.

Dan: *groans* Mel!

I shut my eyes and fired off a reply before I could give it anymore thought.

Mel: Sounds great.

Dan: YES! Let me know if you want to come for soundcheck. We could hang out before the show.

I swallowed. That would be a lot of hanging out. My mind conjured memories of Dan pre-show when we were kids. His entire face had always lit up. You couldn't help but grin with him before and after. And when he was on the stage… I could never tear my eyes away from him, his enjoyment somehow communicated in his movements.

Was I actually ready for all that, or strong enough to hold firm?

I didn't want to know the answer.

CHAPTER SIX

Friday night was finally here. The campaign went off without a hitch, and the influencer realised that a temper tantrum wasn't the best way to ensure she got future work. I was more than ready to shut off work and put its problems in a box and enjoy my weekend.

Starting with film night with the girls.

The wine was out. The pizzas had been ordered. Sophie lay on the floor, winding Phoebe up like she did best, and Nia… well, Nia was staring at me across a glass of wine with worried eyes. It started almost the moment she arrived, and I'd been ignoring it ever since.

Phoebe shrieked as she rolled around the carpet. Sophie had her caught in a tickle attack and the toddler wasn't making much of an effort to escape. Tears streamed down her face while she laughed.

"She's going to look at you with suspicion when she grows up," I said, chuckling as I watched them.

"Nah, I'll be the fun aunt." Sophie sat up, breathing hard. She started to stand and Phoebe launched herself off the ground, into Sophie's arms. She clung to her, arms wrapped tightly around her neck. "What have you been feeding this kid?" Sophie muttered, straightening up with Phoebe's legs wrapped around her.

I snorted. "She might have had a couple of cookies before you got here."

"You did that on purpose."

"Maybe."

She was a pro at tiring Phoebe out. Of course, I was going to use that to my advantage tonight.

Sophie spun around the room to a chorus of excited screams, and I relaxed into the sofa. I had wine, I had my friends, Phoebe was entertained, there were no work fires coming for me.

Tonight I'd enjoy myself, and tomorrow…

Tomorrow I'd have the hardest conversation of my life with Dan.

Nia's gaze burned my skin from the other end of the sofa and I couldn't shake it.

"Everything okay there, Nia?"

She sank lower in her seat, her eyes bouncing between me and Phoebe. "How can you be so relaxed right now?" she whispered, confusion furrowing her brow. "So far, I've been there every time James almost cracked. I thought you'd be more stressed about Dan. Right now, I feel like I'm the only one panicking about this."

"I'm not stressed," I said, vaguely amused by her wide-eyed expression. I pushed my hair back, dragging my hand through the strands. "I'm scared."

"I can understand that," Nia said.

"Can I have a cookie?" Phoebe whispered in Sophie's ear, sneaking glances at me in what was meant to be a covert way.

Sophie glanced at me, her brows rising. "You'll have to ask your mother."

I pursed my lips, pretending to consider it. Sophie placed Phoebe on the ground and she rushed towards me. She flattened herself against my lap, her tiny arms trying to wrap around my waist.

"Please, mammy," she said, her voice sweet and innocent, like she hadn't already snuck one while I'd been pouring the wine.

It was hard to say no to that face. Her green eyes begged me to concede.

"If you have one now, you don't get one after pizza."

"Yes!" She scrambled off my lap and rushed into the kitchen.

"Don't run." I handed my wine glass to Nia and got up, following her into the kitchen.

Phoebe slowed to a spacewalk. Her little face shone with mischief. With that expression on her face, she was the spitting image of her dad.

I pulled the plate from the microwave and offered her a choice between the leftovers. She went straight for the skittles, no surprise. She'd turn into a skittle if I didn't keep an eye on her sweets addiction.

She skipped back into the living room and sat herself in her little armchair. My father had thought it would soften me towards him — one look at her in it and I'd had to concede that he knew me better than I thought.

"Do you two want one?" I asked, turning back to the girls.

"Wouldn't say no to one of your peanut butter ones." Sophie wandered towards me, practically salivating at the sight. She plucked it off the plate.

"Grab me a chocolate, will you?" Nia peered at me over the back of the sofa.

I picked up two chocolate and returned the plate to the microwave.

"Phoebe, do you want a drink to go with that?"

She was already halfway through the cookie before I had a juice box placed in front of her.

I returned to my seat, handing a cookie to Nia.

"But I'm also resigned to it." I shrugged a shoulder, picking up the strains of our conversation. "He's not willing to drop out of my life, right now, and the longer I wait, the worse it'll be."

And the harder it would get to spill the beans.

"I'm going to tell him, tomorrow at the Marable gig."

Nia smirked. "He invited you to that, did he?"

"I'm not sure any of us should be surprised," Sophie said, her voice oddly strangled as Phoebe chased her around the kitchen island. "The man's got serious game."

I snorted.

"She's right. And this way, I don't have to be on edge every time I leave the house with a toddler in tow."

Nia tilted her head in agreement. "Are you going to do it before or after their set?"

"Why does it matter?" Sophie asked as she plucked Phoebe off her feet to fits of giggles.

"Because if she does it before, it'll mess with my photos, and I'd like to be prepared."

Relief fluttered in my chest. "You're going to be there?"

"I'm Rhiannon's photographer. Of course I'm going to be there."

Sophie and I froze, our eyes going wide.

"You accepted the job offer?" A grin overtook my face as I spoke. Yes, it reduced my chances of escaping Dan, but we'd already ascertained that escape was very, very unlikely. "Nia, that's amazing."

Her smile was huge. "Yeah, it is."

"Want to see my ponies?" Phoebe asked Sophie, her little voice oblivious to the way her life was going to change in twenty-four hours — why had I told her who her father was?

But it wasn't really a question I needed to answer. I knew why. I didn't want her to ever think I'd hidden anything from her.

She tugged at Sophie's hand with more strength than Sophie was prepared for, pulling her towards her bedroom.

Sophie grabbed Nia's wine glass as she passed her and downed it. Nia's brows shot up. "Sorry, yours was closer, and I need fortification," she muttered, glancing at us over her shoulder.

We both snorted. She was definitely Phoebe's favourite aunt. She didn't need to wait for her to grow up to claim that title. The kid wouldn't stop talking at her and Sophie went along with it at every step.

Nia and I stared at each other in shared amusement, worries momentarily forgotten.

But the sharp edge was always there.

"I'll tell him after their set."

The amusement on her face faded. She nodded.

"He'll nag you to go for a drink. Maybe go along with it."

"Yeah, I figure it'll be best to do it without the band around." I twirled my glass, my gaze following the swirl of the liquid. "I can see his shocked face already."

She pulled a face. "What if he doesn't take it well?"

"The secrecy or the addition of a toddler to his life?"

"Both?"

I met her concerned gaze with one of steel. "If he flips at the secrecy, I'll take it. But if he flips about Phoebe…" I bit my lip, searching her face for reassurance. There wasn't enough reassurance in the world to make this easier. "If he does anything to upset Phoebe, I'll bury him."

She shook her head and reached for mine. "It's your job." She squeezed. "Who else is going to make sure she grows up sensible? It definitely won't be Sophie," Nia said, her voice louder than necessary.

"Oy!" Sophie shouted from the bedroom. "I'll have you know I'm the most sensible one in this flat."

Nia's brows rose, daring me to argue with her. I smirked

and kept my mouth shut. If she wanted to wind Soph up, she could do all the work.

Nia pouted. "You're no fun."

"Or I just appreciate the free babysitting," I whispered, a devious note to my voice.

"Okay, that's pretty genius."

Nia's phone started vibrating across the coffee table, shaking the glass loud enough that we both jumped. Text after text lit up her phone. Nia and I chuckled at ourselves as she picked it up. She frowned as the phone rang in her hand before she could unlock the screen.

"Who is it?"

"Hey, babe, I'm with the girls, remember?" Nia's brows climbed. "Slow down, I can barely understand you. What's up?"

The doorbell chimed before she'd finished speaking. Phoebe stomped out of her bedroom chanting for pizza.

"I'll get it," Sophie called, following the giddy toddler down the hall.

"Phoebe, calm down." I knew better than to try and reason with her, but I couldn't stop. I turned back to Nia. Her face had turned ashen. "Nia, what is it?"

Her horrified gaze clashed with mine. "He tried to distract him," she whispered, speaking slowly as if she couldn't believe what she'd heard.

Phoebe screeched in the hallway. "Pizza, pizza, pizza."

I placed my wine glass on the table. "I live in a bloody circus," I muttered, rushing towards the door to calm Phoebe down before she scared the pizza guy away.

I stubbed my toe on a plastic pony. Water leaked from my eyes as I hissed, kicking the thing towards Phoebe's bedroom.

I turned the corner and froze when I laid eyes on my open front door.

Sophie stood rigid in the doorway, her back to me, but I knew she'd be mirroring my shock.

If the building felt like collapsing, now would be a good moment.

CHAPTER SEVEN

Sophie stood frozen in front of the open door staring up at the perplexed look on Dan's face. Perplexed because my lovable daughter had wrapped herself around his leg. James stood behind Dan, rubbing his face. He was cursing beneath his breath.

"Did you have to make me run?" James grumbled, glaring at Dan as he pushed past him and into the flat. James approached me with hesitation in his face. He placed his hands on my shoulders and squeezed. "I'm sorry, I tried," he whispered low enough so that no one else would hear.

I caught his arm as he tried to pass me. "It's fine," I said and his serious expression cracked a little. "But watch your language around my daughter."

His eyes widened, glancing over Phoebe poking at Dan's tense leg. "Sorry about that."

I nodded. "You got lucky. Just don't do it again."

He walked away, and my eyes settled on Dan again.

I don't know what I expected, but it wasn't what I got.

His eyes were fixed on Phoebe with a softness I hadn't seen since we were kids.

Maybe it would be alright.

My eyes burned and I pinched myself. Hard. There were going to be no tears. I'd deal with this... somehow.

I forced my shoulders back and a smile to my lips that itched with how wrong it felt. Getting my feet to move was a heck of a lot harder. Like my floorboards had morphed into sticky mud. My heart beat in my throat.

Dan's gaze finally rose to mine. It both terrified and floored me.

"Daddy, can I have ice cream?" Phoebe asked. She snuck a glance at me from the corner of her eye, a mischievous grin on her lips.

Dan stared down at her with wide eyes, the look of a man who had no idea what to do with himself or the small child staring at him with stars in her eyes. Damn it.

She knew she wasn't allowed sweets this late.

"It's nearly bedtime, Phoebe," I said, my voice betraying none of the unease squirrelling inside of me.

Sophie snapped into gear. "Phoebs, want to go to the park?"

Phoebe glanced up at her, her face screwed up as she thought, her eyes bouncing between us. "Can't. Not allowed."

I almost smiled at that sweet voice. Normally, she'd be right, and on her way into the bath. Tonight, however...

"It's fine. Sophie needs you to teach her how to use a slide."

Her eyes widened in a mix of excitement and disbelief as they returned to Sophie.

"Sure." Sophie chuckled. She picked Phoebe up and rushed back into the flat.

"Can Daddy come?" Phoebe asked as Sophie reached the living room, the sound drifting down the hall and squeezing my heart.

This is what I didn't want. I didn't want her to be so trusting, so vulnerable. If he disappeared now, she wouldn't understand.

Dan hadn't moved an inch. His shell-shocked green gaze rested on me, but he said nothing.

"Do you want to come in?" I tilted my head towards the flat and caught the door.

He nodded and sauntered in. I shut the door and forced air into my lungs. It'll be fine. Just be honest. Can't control how he reacts, but I can control everything else.

Sophie rushed around the corner with Nia and James in tow. Flustered was the word of the day. All three of them looked extremely uncomfortable. I needed to do this alone anyway.

"Nia and James are coming, too." Sophie skirted past us with a giddy Phoebe bouncing in her arms. "Text when you're good."

I nodded and they all took off. The door shut behind them, and silence descended, wrapped in tension and expectation. It was stifling.

I led Dan into the kitchen, my mind whirling, searching for the words. How was I meant to start?

He leaned back against the island, studying the toaster behind me with a very white face.

"She said…" his voice was low but emotionless.

I thought he was in shock, but what if he just didn't care?

"I heard."

He glanced at me sharply. "Is it true?"

I nodded.

The emotionless mask slipped away. His jaw shifted, and his face hardened. "Why didn't you tell me?"

"I tried." I bit my lip and willed the pressure behind my eyes to stop. "You fobbed me off…."

"I think I would remember you telling me you were pregnant." His words cut as deep as the disbelief painting his face.

"I'd just gotten the results, and I was freaking out." I forced myself to keep staring into his green gaze, searching for proof that my words were ringing a bell for him. "I called you, and you passed me off to Matt. You were too busy to talk to me."

His brows furrowed. I'm not sure why I'd hoped he'd remember, but he didn't. I could see the cogs ticking over the past and coming up short. My heart sank. *Don't be ridiculous. Of course, the rock star doesn't remember a phone call.*

"When was this?"

"May that year."

He crossed his arms, leaning back against the counter, his hard focus never leaving me. "We'd just signed, and the label had us locked in the studio until we came up with a hit." He nodded, piercing me with his own hurt. "That was the last time you called me. Why didn't you try again?"

"Because I needed you and you fobbed me off? After the initial panic, I didn't think it would change anything for you. Why would I try again?"

He was bristling. "I would have done anything for you."

I stared at him, my thoughts of that statement blatantly obvious. "I'm not naive enough to believe that," I whispered.

"You should have told me." He dragged his hand through his hair, tugging hard at the thick copper strands. "Why did you wait until…" he paused, his mouth working as he did the math. "I've missed four years of her life, Mel. Why did you wait?"

I was going to wait a heck of a lot longer. That would just add a spark to an already tender situation.

He had always been happy, doling out pieces of himself and leaving me. He'd never given me a reason to believe he would put my life and my problems first. How to say that kindly? I took a deep breath and let instinct take charge.

"It was a lot to deal with at the start, still is. I didn't…" My hands were starting to shake and I shoved them behind my back, gripping the counter like it might anchor me. "I was scared of what you'd do."

He opened his mouth to argue, his gaze incredulous. "Not

like that." I held up my hand, warding off his argument. He pressed his lips together and waited. "You were always leaving, Dan. You didn't think we would last a long-distance relationship, you didn't want me with you in Glasgow. All I got were stolen moments, whenever you came home."

"It wasn't fucking like that, Mel." His cheeks reddened as he glared at me. "I always came home. I always answered the phone. If you needed me, I would have been here."

I snapped. "Don't try to rewrite our history now. I was good enough for a roll between the sheets but pitted against your musical aspirations, I lost. Every time."

He ground his teeth together. "So you kept a daughter from me as punishment?"

"Yes, Dan, I made my life a complicated hell for nearly five years just to spite you. I'm raising a terrifyingly smart toddler, working an extremely busy full-time job, I have barely any social life, and a heck of a lot less sleep, just to get back at you." I snorted, shaking my head in disgust. "Get real."

"Hard to do that when you kept something as big as this from me." He pinned me with a hard look and I squashed the urge to step back. I had nowhere to go anyway. "How long has James known?"

"I'm not sure." My brow furrows, how did he know? "I didn't tell him."

"Who else knows?"

"My parents, Sophie, Nia, my boss, and co-workers." It was a relatively small list. I didn't really have time for socialising.

"But not my sister or any of the guys?"

I shook my head. *I had no reason to speak to any of them.*

"Okay, now tell me what the fuck you were thinking?" he asked, his voice almost booming. I flinched. "I should have been the first to know. Yes, I didn't take that one call, but you could have kept trying." He fixed me with another of those piercing, 'I know you better than you know yourself' looks.

"You can be a hardass when you want to be. If you really wanted me to know you would have hunted me down and slapped me with the test stick. I wasn't exactly hard to find." Sadness filtered into his expression. "I could have helped you."

A bitter chuckle escaped me and I hated the sound of it. "What would you have done, Dan?" I crossed my arms and glanced away from him, letting my eyes rest unfocused on the pink sky outside. "If I'd told you, and you'd still left or stayed away… It would have broken me," I whispered, my voice hoarse and my eyes flooding with tears.

"You don't know that I would have left." Something about his tone drew me back. I studied his face. "You should've given me the benefit of the doubt."

"You would have tried, but you wouldn't have stayed," I said, the words soft, careful. I didn't want to hurt him, but he needed to see reality if we were going to have any chance.

Wait.

That sounded like…

I mentally shook myself.

No.

He needed to see reality for his own sake.

It had nothing to do with us. There was no us.

"This is fucking different and you know it." His face darkened and his voice hardened. "We're talking about my daughter here, Mel."

It took seconds for his meaning to settle over me. It felt like all the blood drained from my face.

At least I knew now. I didn't have to wonder.

"What just happened?" he asked, his voice more subdued, eying me like I might fall over. Funny, I actually might.

"Nothing," I murmured, shaking my head.

He didn't believe me, but tough. He'd lost the right to the contents of my mind years ago.

"Were you ever going to tell me?" Dan whispered, the words catching in his throat.

"Of course."

"When?" A line appeared between his brows as realisation flashed in his eyes. He tilted his head, lost in thought. I could practically see the pieces crashing together inside his mind. Confused awe filled his expression. "She knew who I was." He straightened from leaning against the counter. "How did she know who I was, Mel?"

"I told her," I said, my voice weak. "Showed her pictures, videos."

He nodded, slightly appeased. "When were you going to tell me?"

I hesitated, bracing myself for his anger to relight. "When she was old enough to protect herself."

He repeated my words to himself, puzzled. "What does that mean?"

The way he said it made my blood boil. Like he hadn't realised how painful his past choices had been for me, like he just expected me to be waiting for him every time he remembered I existed and felt a sudden whim to see me.

"Not to sound like a broken record, but you're clearly not understanding how much damage you did," I bit out through a clenched jaw, unearthing some of the fighting energy he'd robbed me of moments ago. "Given my experience growing up with a musician for a father, who was never home, why the hell do you think I'd expect any differently from you?"

"Because I'm not your father!" Dan roared.

"No, you're not," I shouted back. "But you do a damn good impression of him."

He shook his head. "That's not fair," he growled, tension still riding his voice.

My brows rose. "Seriously? He chose the road and music over his family, repeatedly, and you chose it over me, repeatedly." Tears burned my eyes again. I had to keep it together to get through this. I could curl up in a ball and cry later. "I'm not a guitar you can put down and come back to when it suits you."

"It *would* have been different, had I known about her," he said, conviction riding his tone and animating his features. "I would have been here. You couldn't have kept me away."

I wished he'd stop. Yes, it eased some of my concerns about introducing him to Phoebe's life. But did he have to keep slapping me in the face with the fact that I wasn't a good enough reason on my own?

I turned away from him, busying myself making tea that he probably didn't want. I needed to hold something, it would stop the barely restrained shaking in my hands. I hoped.

"Anyway, that's where we're at. I'm sorry I kept it from you but…"

Dan caught my hand as I reached for a mug in the cupboard. I turned to him with wide eyes, all the better to stop the tears from falling.

"But what?" he asked when he had my full attention.

Staring into his eyes, my pulse slowed. He'd always had this effect on me. Something about him had always calmed me, forced the truth I really didn't want to speak out of me.

Moisture splashed down my cheeks as I swallowed hard against the lump in my throat. "I didn't want you to break my heart again." The words came out hoarse.

Too late to worry about that. He'd already done it.

Regret flickered across his handsome face. Without warning, he tugged me against his chest. The feel of his rock-solid pecs pressed against my cheek was a shock but it couldn't stem the tears. He wrapped his arms around me, and I was helpless to fight him.

For minutes, I sobbed into his chest while he comforted me. I couldn't understand why he did it. I couldn't understand why I cried now, after promising myself I wouldn't.

If someone had dropped this big a bombshell on me, I'd

have been raving mad. I'd have reacted just like he did, except I would have been out the door, a fuming, swearing mess.

Having his arms wrapped around me, knowing how upset and angry I'd made him... It made everything worse.

He was everything I'd ever wanted, and he was here now. So what if he'd clearly said he'd have forced himself to stay out of duty? At least he'd be here. I could sacrifice my pride and just enjoy that.

But for how long?

I'd never been able to anchor him. After seeing it with James and Nia, I didn't have it in me to believe he'd never vanish on me again. Music would always come first and I didn't have something else to drive me to distraction like Nia. Even if I told myself it was going to happen, that he was only staying with me for Phoebe, he would break me again.

I also had a small child relying on me to raise her right and keep her safe. That included protecting her from a repeat of my upbringing.

I shut my eyes hard, willing myself to stay strong. Giving in right now would be easy. It wasn't the now that scared me, it was a week from now, six months even. I had to remember that, even while my body tingled at the press of his against mine.

His fingers pressed into my back, drawing comforting circles, tracing invisible patterns that only he had ever followed. He rubbed his lips back and forth over my hair, whispering reassurances in the quiet space. Sinking into him like this, it was too easy, too comfortable. Yet knowing it was a bad idea was one thing, stopping it took a heck of a lot more strength.

Dan leaned back, forcing my head up until I was staring into his excited eyes. One look, and my heart started galloping again. "But it was always you, Mel. You must have known that?"

"How was I meant to know that?" I whispered, my voice thick with tears.

"I have never wanted anyone else." He stroked my cheek, his calloused fingers scraping against my sensitive skin while his eyes bore into mine, trying to communicate something that I really didn't understand. "I thought you knew that. It's why I kept coming home."

My eyes narrowed. "That's not even slightly true. I was nothing but a booty call to you."

Dan laughed and I turned my face away.

"Babe, I was always coming back to you." His smile was easy, confident, and it grated on me just as much as it weakened my knees. "We agreed I had to get this done first."

I spluttered and pointed at myself. "I didn't agree to any such thing. You said you were going to Glasgow for the music, and that was the end of the conversation."

He scrubbed a hand across his beard. "Yeah, but I didn't say we were done."

My eyes widened and I broke from his grip, backing away. "Was I meant to read your flipping mind?"

"I thought it was pretty clear," he muttered, perplexed. "Why else would I keep coming back?"

"For sex?"

He smirked. "That was part of it."

"Well it's the only part I believed."

The amusement drained from his face. "What do I have to do to convince you that I was always coming back for you?"

I crossed my arms. "You don't need to. It's not important anymore."

"Bullshit."

"The only thing that matters is Phoebe, so get on the same page, or leave. I meant it when I agreed to try and be friends but that's all I can give you." My gaze hardened as I met his hopeful one. "I can't take the roller coaster anymore, and if you pull any of that shit with Phoebe, if you break promises and skip out on her... There can be no half measures. You have to commit to her."

"And you honestly expect me to believe that you want nothing else from me?" He stepped towards me, a smirk tugging at his lips as he closed the small distance I'd created.

"Yes. I don't want you like that."

"Sure," he drawled, his green gaze daring me to keep arguing. "That's why you went soft the moment I touched you."

Dan stepped so close his shoes nearly touched my toes and I had to crane my neck to meet his eyes. He leaned down, his forehead almost resting against mine. A hair's width separated us. My breath stilled, and I braced myself for the feel of his hands on my skin again. I could hold in my reaction, I had too.

"You're so full of shit," he muttered.

His hand settled on the nape of my neck and his head descended. It happened so fast I'd have missed it if I'd blinked. His lips brushed against mine, delicate, soft, patient. Just a feather light caress and I was his.

I really needed to work on my resistance.

His hand tightened and he pulled me towards him, until I leaned against his chest again and my arms wrapped around his waist. For balance. I swear I wasn't clinging to him.

With light touches, he coaxed me into responding. Against my better judgement, I sighed against his lips, sinking into his hold. For a minute, I allowed myself to forget that this was a bad idea. I fed all of the anger, heartache, and stress he'd caused me into that kiss. The pressure amped up until we were gasping for breath, and for a moment, I could believe it would all work, that he would love me enough to put me and Phoebe first.

This is fucking different and you know it.

His words echoed in my mind, souring his kiss. No matter

what sweet words he breathed, duty was all it was. He needed a reason to be with me. I wasn't enough.

Panting, we broke apart. I let my forehead rest against his chest while I recovered, while I wrestled with the thoughts threatening to drive me into a hole.

He tilted my head back, chewing his lip while his fingers tapped out a nervous beat on my back. If my pain was visible, he missed it.

"Can I meet her?" he asked, his voice shaky.

"You just did," I said, somehow injecting enough emotion into the words for my voice to not sound robotic.

Dan chuckled. He stepped back, releasing me, and I ignored my body's plea to put his hands back on me. He rubbed at his beard, sheepish after all that.

"Not properly. Can you call them back?"

I didn't have it in me to deny him, so I picked up the phone and did just that.

CHAPTER EIGHT

When the door opened five minutes later, I sprang from the sofa and rushed down the hall. Dan's chuckles followed me. He was still nervous, but apparently *my* nerves made for a great distraction. Nice to know.

I found Sophie and Nia divesting Phoebe of her shoes and jacket.

"If you stood still, it would come off faster," Sophie muttered, tugging at her jacket which had somehow gotten tangled around her arms. Nia placed her shoes on the shoe rack and stepped in to free her.

For a second, watching them eased the ache in my chest.

"How hard is it to take off a jacket?" Phoebe scowled at the wall while they tugged at the material.

Smiling for the first time since Dan had set foot in the flat, I jumped into the fray. I caught Phoebe and held her still. She grinned at me as I freed her arms.

"How was the park?" I asked just as the material released her.

"Great. Sophie sucks at slides." She spun around, poking her tongue out at Sophie.

"Hey! That was meant to be our secret," Sophie growled.

"Where's Daddy?" Phoebe asked, dodging me and racing down the hallway.

"Slow down," I shouted over my shoulder. It did no good. A shriek was my only response. It sounded vaguely like a battle cry, and I itched to get in there.

Instead, I stood and forced myself to stay with my friends. "Thank you for taking her."

Nia and Sophie wore identical worried expressions. They tore a small hole in my hastily patched defences.

"It's no problem. Are you okay?" Sophie asked, reaching out for my arm. She squeezed, her concerned gaze fixed on my face.

I nodded. "I'll be okay."

Going by the way their faces fell, I wasn't convincing. There may have even been a sniffle.

"I'll talk to you guys later."

We said our goodbyes, and I shut the door. Happy chatter from Phoebe drifted down the hallway. It should have relieved some of the nerves, but it only seemed to make it worse. I braced myself and returned to the living room.

Phoebe sat in Dan's lap on the sofa, talking his ear off. Thankfully he had abandoned his cup of tea on the coffee table. He stared at her with a blend of fear and awe that amused me, while also squeezing my heart.

"I don't like 'Run'," Phoebe said, referring to their latest hit songs.

Surprise rippled across Dan's face. He glanced at me sharply as I returned to the sofa. I picked up my discarded cup and settled into the corner to watch them.

"Why's that?" he asked, his voice low and measured, the jitters firmly under control.

Phoebe's nose scrunched up. "It's stupid."

My daughter, the music critic.

"What's stupid about it?"

Dan's hand rested against her back. It was probably an

unconscious gesture, fear that she'd fall over, but the fact he'd done it, that he was holding on to her—my eyes started to fill up again.

"Not real. Grownups don't chase each other," Phoebe answered, the steely conviction of a child running through her voice.

Dan's focus shifted to me. It was brief, but I was so attuned to him that I'd have had to be blind to miss the flicker of pain in his eyes. I hadn't told her about our past, how he'd essentially played cat and mouse with my feelings. All she knew was that he was making music somewhere else and he couldn't be with us. So her interpretation of Rhiannon's latest hit had a remarkable insight into our situation? It was nothing but a coincidence.

"What is a stage like?" Phoebe bounced in his lap, falling slightly against his braced hand. Fear widened his eyes but he righted her immediately. "Are you deaf now?"

He stared at her for a moment, trying to work out where she was going with her questions. Good luck to him. I'd learned to never question her tangents. There were far too many of them to make sense of.

"No, we have earbuds to protect us."

"But then, how do you hear the music?"

"It's still really loud."

"Then why wear them?"

"Because they protect our ears."

Phoebe frowned. "But how?"

Dan wore a pained expression. His smile was in place, but I could tell from the tightness around his eyes that he had no idea what to do with her. I hid my face behind my mug and chuckled. He shot me a dirty look.

Conceding that I should probably help him, I lowered the mug.

"Phoebs, give Daddy a minute."

Saying the word in front of him felt weird.

"But I don't understand." She pushed her lip out, pouting as her eyes travelled between us.

"I know, but he's not used to your high-speed questions like I am."

She considered it for a second before nodding. Dan's jaw tightened and his eyes narrowed on me, seeming to scream 'whose fault is that.' I couldn't focus on him now, not with Phoebe studying me with a sly glint in her eyes.

"Does Daddy live with us now?"

It was such a simple question.

Spluttering, I sat forward and placed the mug on the table before I threw it all over myself. Dan rubbed my back. It was nice, but it didn't help.

"Annie's daddy lives with her," Phoebe said, continuing as if nothing had happened.

I sat back, leaning into the sofa again. "Yes, munchkin, but Annie's parents are together," I said, wheezing slightly but powering through.

She furrowed her brow at that. Displeasure pinched her features and I tried not to laugh. I knew what her next question would be, but how else was I meant to answer something like this?

"Why aren't you together?"

Dan froze, showing me just how ill-prepared he was to outsmart a toddler. Mind you, I'm not sure I could, and I'd raised her.

"Annie's parents are married."

She squinted at me. "Why aren't you married?"

My lips twitched. Dan stared on with wide eyes. Poor man had no idea what he'd gotten himself into.

"Not everyone gets married, Phoebs."

She tilted her head, her eyes narrowing. I bit the inside of my cheek as she turned to Dan with an order flashing in her eyes. "Get married, so we can have sleepovers."

It was Dan's turn to splutter. I couldn't hold the amusement in for much longer. I needed to shut it down. Dan clearly had no clue how to do it.

"Can't, munchkin. Daddy's too busy with his music."

Okay, so it was an incendiary thing to say, but it silenced her.

"Thanks for that, babe," Dan growled. He turned back to Phoebe and whispered, "I'd happily marry her, but she won't let me."

I glared at him. I'd hit him with a pillow if it wouldn't make this a memorable moment for Phoebe. But I didn't need her fixating on this.

Phoebe was less than impressed. She turned in Dan's lap and climbed onto her knees. Her tiny hands rested on his cheeks, forcing him to look at her. For a second, he looked like a wild animal, freaked out by the tiny human trying to manhandle him. Then it cleared, leaving only curiosity in its place.

"Well, duh, because you like music more," she said, her face deadly serious. "People are better than music."

Surprise curled through me. I had not expected that. Of course I'd told her why he wasn't here but I'd never put it quite like that.

With that done, she glanced at me and yawned. "I'm tired. Can I go sleep now?"

I nodded, resolutely keeping my eyes off Dan. She scrambled down from his lap and stomped towards her bedroom.

I peeked at him from beneath my lashes as I shifted off the sofa. He was staring out the big windows with a bemused smile tugging at his lips. What did that mean?

"I'm just going to get her ready for bed," I said, shuffling through the gap between his legs and the coffee table. "Just give me a sec."

He glanced up at me, the smile fading away. "Do you need help?"

"It'll be faster if I deal with it."

Despite my words, he followed me down the hall.

Phoebe stepped out of her bedroom wearing pyjamas. This might have been the first time she'd actually taken the initiative on her bedtime routine.

"Well done, Phoebs," I said. She grinned, her teeth on full display. "Teeth and face, then story."

She nodded before skipping into the bathroom, her red hair bouncing. I flicked the light on as I followed her in. Lifting her, I settled her on the bathroom counter. Dan leaned against the doorframe, a shadow in my periphery. It felt weird, having someone watch me go through the daily motions. This was just my normal life. There was nothing interesting about it. But Dan absorbed every movement as I brushed her teeth and washed her face.

"Which story will it be tonight?" I asked as I lowered her wriggling body to the floor.

"Gretel," she said, swiping her doll from the sofa and wandering into the hall without so much as a glance at Dan.

I frowned. "But we've already read that one this week."

Phoebe shrugged before disappearing into her room. I followed her, Dan not far behind. She pulled back her duvet and climbed into bed, scooting down until her head rested on the pillow. She blinked up at me, all innocence. I wasn't believing it. The devious child was trying to make a point with her choice. She was mine, after all.

I picked up the book, resigned to letting her plan play out. She shuffled in until her back pressed against the wall, making room for me.

When I was seated, she glanced at Dan and pointed to the end of her bed. "You sit there."

He complied instantly.

Oh, this was going to be fun.

She was going to walk all over him, and I wasn't sure if I should warn him. It might actually be fun to watch him squirm.

This time, she fell asleep before the witch could even capture the children. All the excitement must have gotten to her. I carefully stood, placing the book of fairy tales on her nightstand.

Dan watched her, a soft expression on his face that just about ripped out my heart. He'd only just met her, and he was smitten. Good. Maybe he'd think twice before he broke her trust.

I cleared my throat softly. His eyes shot to mine, and I nodded towards the door. If the way he watched her tore out my heart, that smile stole my breath. He was potent on a normal day, but right now, with those hard edges softened….

Dan followed me out, closing her door gently. I went straight to making tea. I really wanted wine, and I'd had enough caffeine, but I needed something to do with myself. Eyeing him was just too damn dangerous and painful.

He scrubbed a hand down his face, and a smile overtook his face. "She's incredible."

A lightness filled me at his words, like we were cocooned in a bubble and bad emotions weren't allowed in. My lips quirked. "Yeah, she is."

He crossed his arms. "Although I think it would really help my case if you stopped telling her I chose music over you."

I scowled. "It's the truth."

He took a step towards me. "Am I ever going to be able to convince you that I never gave up?"

"Probably not." I didn't have to think about it.

"Can you at least give me a chance to try?"

"Why?"

He blinked at me. "What do you mean why? I love you. What else do I need?"

I snorted.

"Why is that funny?" he asked, his voice rising. "I never stopped."

I shook my head and turned my back on him. I abandoned the tea and went straight for the fridge. Sod it, I needed a drink to deal with this man.

"Time and distance didn't change anything for me, Mel."

I closed the fridge and turned to find him right in front of me. He watched me with a predatory look in his eyes. Like I *was* his and always would be. If only I could be that delusional.

I stepped around him. "Well, it changed things for me."

"I don't believe that."

Shrugging, I pulled a wine glass from the cupboard. "Tough. You don't get to cherry pick our memories," I said, my voice low, mindful of the sleeping toddler less than twenty feet away.

I poured a glass of wine and took a deep, fortifying sip before I turned to face him again. I'm not sure what I was expecting, but the defiance on his face was definitely not it.

I had to steer this away from us. It wasn't about us anymore.

"But while we're discussing things not to say. Please refrain from telling our daughter that you'd marry me if I let you. I don't lie to her."

He crossed his arms. "It wasn't a lie. I would."

"That isn't true." I averted my eyes — his stare was intense and I couldn't take it. Swallowing more of the wine, I tried to project calm.

I'm not sure it worked.

"That's bullshit, and you know it," he said far too loudly.

"Mammy, what's bullshit?"

I jumped at the sound of her little voice. Dan's smirk fell, and he muttered beneath his breath, clearly not learning his lesson from the situation unfolding before us.

Ignoring him, I turned to my errant child. Her short red

hair stood on end, and she rubbed at her eyes, still very much in the grips of sleep.

"What are you doing up, love?"

She shrugged and continued to stare at us, awaiting her answer. She was shaking off the sleepiness far too quickly. I had to get her back into bed fast.

"It's poo that comes out of a bull."

Her brow quirked, screaming her scepticism at me. I put the glass down and walked towards her.

"Want me to tuck you in again?" I asked, ignoring the doubt in her expression.

She shook her head hard, dodging my reaching hands. Her green eyes went straight past me, resting on Dan. "I want Daddy."

My breath caught, and a funny feeling settled in my chest. Was this… surely not. I couldn't be jealous. I got her every single night, why should it matter if she wanted him for once?

I turned to the man in question, trying to gauge his response. He didn't so much as pause, didn't look fazed at all. He sprang into action, slipping past me with a sneaky swipe of his hand across my lower back as he skirted between the kitchen island and me. My skin tingled, tightened unbearably and I scowled as I watched them go.

"What does bullshit really mean?" Phoebe asked him as he trailed after her.

"What your Mam said." His voice was muffled thanks to the room between us but even I could hear the desperation in his voice. He'd put his foot in it yet again.

There was a brief pause and I could imagine her staring him down. I edged towards the door. Was he squirming?

"I'm nearly four, I can know things."

Dan chuckled. "Sure, you can, baby. Why don't you tell me what I'm meant to do?"

She gave him instructions on how to tuck her in, and all the while, I watched from the doorway with my heart in my throat. When she'd finally settled, he smoothed his hand over her hair and kissed her forehead. There might have been a tear in my eye after that.

When he returned to me, he looked mesmerised. We stood in the doorway together and studied her. The light from the kitchen framed her, setting her red hair on fire. She looked so tiny and innocent — an act, but one I was willing to believe in these quiet moments.

Dan cleared his throat, and I glanced up. He was staring at me with something like awe in his eyes. "She looks like me."

My smile was small as I turned away from him. "That's how genetics work, Dan."

He followed me back to the kitchen. He wisely didn't comment when I went straight for my wine glass.

"I know, but it's different… knowing and seeing it, you know?" He leaned across the island, his elbows holding him up as he focused on me.

The first time I'd seen it, I'd cried. He'd given me a daily reminder of him. So I got it, it was magical and painful, all at once.

He pressed his lips together, amusement flickering across his features. "But remind me never to swear when she's in the same space again."

"Yeah, you definitely don't want to do that again. She's relentless."

Straightening up, the amusement faded, leaving behind nothing but that quiet determination. My throat dried at the sight of it and dread uncurled in my stomach. *What now?*

"Are you still coming to the gig tomorrow?" he asked, hope shining back at me.

I bit my lip. Seeing him was a bad idea, but how could I say no? For Phoebe, we needed to have at least a friendly relationship. I nodded.

"And bring Phoebe? There'll be a headset to protect her ears, but I'd just —" The smile fell from his lips and drained from his eyes until the unsure boy I used to love stared back at me. "It would mean a lot if you could be there."

That look…I couldn't say no.

His shoulders relaxed. He rounded the island and caught my hand, pulling me into another hug. I didn't fight him. I'm not sure I had the energy left.

"We'll figure it all out, okay?" he whispered against my hair.

I was in way over my head.

CHAPTER NINE

"Are you sure you're ready for this?" Sophie asked as we stopped outside the venue.

Outside, it didn't look like much. It was one of those old concrete monstrosities from the seventies. Despite the ugly exterior, it was still one of the best places to watch a gig. The hall was big, and yet, no matter where you stood, you'd always have a good view. Bands both big and small had graced its stage, and once upon a time, I'd spent most nights lost in the crowd with Sophie and Nia.

But that had been uni, and things had been simpler.

The show was due to start in half an hour, and I'd stalled long enough. Phoebe was out cold. I wasn't surprised. It was well after her bedtime.

Was I ready?

No, but at this point, it didn't matter.

Instead, I took a deep breath, then nodded. The doorman checked our passes and tugged the door open. We clattered up the steps before we flashed our passes at another checkpoint. A stony-faced woman escorted us through the merchandise area to a set of double doors.

"Follow the signs on the wall to the green room." She pointed at the green line on the white painted breeze block wall, like something out of a hospital. "If that fails, follow the voices."

She stepped back through the doors, carefully shutting them behind us.

"Last chance to turn back," Sophie said, dragging my attention back to her.

"The ship sailed already, Soph." I strode on, my boots clicking on the varnished concrete floor.

Was there a single part of this building that wasn't concrete?

In the end, the security woman had been right. We didn't need the signs. Ten paces down the corridor and the sound of raucous laughter reached us. Phoebe stirred in my arms just as we turned a corner and confronted the full force of it.

The room wasn't, in fact, green. I had no idea where that name came from. The walls were dark grey that contrasted with the white of the shiny concrete floor. Sofas and armchairs were arranged in groupings along two walls while a banquet style table stretched across the back wall, filled with drinks and every snack imaginable.

"Looking good as always, Mel," Tommy said, pecking my cheek in his usual welcoming manner. "Are we in for a show tonight?"

His eyes were fixed on Phoebe's face. Her grip on my blouse tightened, telling me that she was, in fact, awake.

I chuckled. "Most likely."

Waking Phoebe was always a bad idea. If it wasn't on her own terms, I rarely avoided a meltdown. Bringing her to something so late was a risk.

Across the room, the Rhiannon guys laughed at Dan and his scowling face. I nearly rolled my eyes at the jealous routine. Try it on someone else.

Tommy moved on to Sophie, tugging her into a hug. He

whispered something in her ear but I tuned it out as Dan approached me.

His smile was hesitant, a stark contrast to his easy confidence last night.

"You made it."

My brow furrowed. "Said I would."

He bit his lip, indecision warring on his face.

A nervous Dan was an odd sight to behold. No matter how uncertain he was, he used to be forthright with his opinions, never hesitating to call bull on something he didn't like or didn't believe. Bravado was his best friend. I wasn't sure I liked this development.

"Phoebs, do you want to say hi to Daddy?" The word stuck in my throat.

I jolted my shoulder, trying to get some reaction out of her. She pressed her face into my neck and shook her head.

"But he asked to see you, munchkin," I said, turning on the mam guilt. "You don't want to upset him, do you?"

Again she shook her head. Dan studied us both, drawing closer until his hand rested on her back and I could feel his breath skittering across my face.

"It's alright. We can catch up tomorrow." He met my gaze. A question waited in the depths of his eyes, and I braced myself. "The weather's meant to be good. We could have a picnic."

Predictably, Phoebe's head shot up. She glanced at him with slightly narrowed eyes. "Will there be ice cream?"

"Sure," Dan drawled, his shoulders sagging. I eyed him, looking for other signs that he was on edge. I hadn't realised he'd tensed up in the first place.

"Chocolate ice cream?" Phoebe asked again.

This time Sophie and Nia heard. Both groaned in spectacular fashion.

"Please tell me Dan gets clean up duties?" Nia asked, her eyes wild as she glanced between us.

"Well I'm not doing it, so yeah," I muttered, enjoying Dan's confused expression.

He leaned towards me, his voice dropping. "What did I just get into?"

I grinned at him. "You'll find out tomorrow."

"And then can I feed the ducks?" Phoebe asked, holding her arms out to Dan.

Again, he gave her a quick agreement.

"Oh no," Sophie whispered, horror dripping from her tone.

I barely heard her. I was too focused on watching Dan as he took Phoebe from me with so much care that my defences cracked a little. She rested against his chest, staring up at him without an ounce of concern. I never wanted her to lose that trust.

"What now?" Dan asked, turning towards Sophie with a sceptical scowl.

"Just keep her away from the geese," Sophie muttered, her eyes wide.

"What happens with the geese?" he glanced between Nia and Sophie like they might just fess up and put him out of his misery. Unfortunately for him, they were both too traumatised by past experiences.

"They get a little overzealous," I said, trying to ignore the heat of his body, still so close to mine. It felt intimate. I didn't want intimate.

Nia snorted.

"Sophie ended up with stitches after saving Phoebe from one that got impatient and tried to nip her leg."

I glanced at my sacrificial friend. She'd sat herself down on a sofa with Nia, they each had a drink in hand, and each were in the process of draining those drinks, their knees bouncing with nervous energy.

"And if you would like to avoid the same fate, don't let her near a body of water with birds," Sophie muttered, her voice dry.

"I'll just refill those, shall I?" James asked, amusement colouring his tone.

"Thanks, gorgeous," Nia said, handing him her glass. He shook his head and stood, taking Sophie's too.

"Yeah, thanks, gorgeous." Sophie batted her lashes at her brother.

Everyone sniggered. Watching my friends interact with the band like they were family eased some of the pressure riding my shoulders.

"Ten minutes to show," someone called from the open door. "Lovers Knot, if your asses aren't at the side of the stage in five minutes, I'll personally make sure the label hear about it."

Tommy groaned. "Alright, Matty, we're coming."

The Lovers Knot guys filed out of the room, trailing after a blond guy in a suit. Only Rhiannon and Marable were left.

"Would you like a drink?" Dan asked me, tilting his head towards a table overflowing with bottles of booze and soft drinks.

"Can I have pop?" Phoebe piped up before I could answer.

"Which kind?" Dan asked without so much as a glance at me.

"No, it's too late," I said, using my 'don't argue with me' mam voice.

Phoebe pouted. "But Daddy said yes."

"Daddy doesn't know the rules yet."

"Not fair," she muttered, burying her face in Dan's neck.

Dan's smile turned sheepish and he mouthed sorry.

"I'll catch you guys after the show," Nia said, tugging me into a hug. "You going to be alright?" she whispered in my ear, low enough for no one else to hear.

It was the question of the night, it seemed.

I nodded. I wasn't sure if it was true, but what else could I do?

She picked up her camera bag and wandered into the hall. Almost everyone else followed her out.

I grabbed a water and filled Phoebe's travel cup with blackcurrant squash before following Dan to the sofa tucked into the back corner. He set Phoebe down on the cushion between us and I handed over her cup. She scowled at it but accepted it without an argument.

By the time we settled either side of her with our drinks, guitar reverb echoed in the hallway, the muted sound filtering into the almost deserted green room. Only Alys and Ryan remained. Nia'd tried to talk me into going dancing with Alys once, but I'd felt guilty about asking my mother to babysit for another night. Plus there was always a risk that Dan would appear.

I glanced back at him, leaning over Phoebe, ready to catch her if she decided to slide off the sofa and make a run for it. She might. She could be a nuisance when she wanted to be. They stared at each other, their green eyes clashing with equal amounts of curiosity, their red hair making them look like the picture-perfect family, despite Dan's sleeves of tattoos.

I couldn't have predicted this outcome back then. Worse, I couldn't have prepared myself for the hole it opened in my heart. I wanted it—the family, the partner, someone to step in when things got too much and I was about to crumble. I'd been so close too many times now, and relying on the girls wasn't fair to them.

Letting my eyes trail over him, I gave myself a moment to imagine what it could be like between us if I ignored my worries and my pride and accepted anything he wanted to give me. I'd get to watch him adjust to our new lives, to experience his strong hugs whenever I needed it, and the sex… I hadn't had sex since we made Phoebe. It would be phenomenal. It had been before.

But would I be happy?

Or would knowing that he wasn't all in for me get the better of me and overshadow all that joy?

"We're going to head up," Ryan said, making me jolt. "I'll see you before the show?"

I'd completely sunk into my head and missed him and Alys standing. They eyed us with sweet smiles, neither of them missing Dan's gentle manner with Phoebe.

"We might catch a bit of the show in a little while." He glanced at me, his easy expression telling me he'd do whatever I wanted. "I'll catch you in a bit."

Ryan nodded and led a muttering Alys out the door. She kept shooting me glances.

"What was that about?" I asked Dan, my eyes still stuck on the doorway.

Dan chuckled. "She wants to befriend you, but Ryan's trying to give me space."

My brows climbed. "Why would you need to stop her from talking to me?"

He bit his lip, eying me from beneath his lashes, smouldering. That look had gotten me into trouble a time or two.

"I might have told them I want you to myself for a little while."

There was a promise in his voice I couldn't handle. Despite my wishing and my dreaming, I knew better, and I knew myself. I needed to be strong, but if he threw himself at me... I wasn't sure I could resist him.

And I had to. If not for my peace of mind, then for Phoebe. We didn't need this to get complicated, and she didn't need to witness me hating her father when he inevitably chose the band over us.

"I can talk to lots of people and still help you get to know Phoebe." I settled into the corner of the sofa and pressed the glass to my face, trying to hide.

His eyes darkened. "That's not all I want."

I was well aware. Didn't mean he was getting it.

"So, picnic?" I asked, steering us to safer topics.

Disappointment chased away the lust on his face. "I could pick you up at one? I haven't been to Roath Park in years. We could check it out?"

He braced himself, as if I'd deny him now that he'd dangled it before Phoebe.

"That sounds good," Phoebe said, her gleeful little voice breaking the tension growing between us.

"It does?" Dan smoothed his big hand over her head of red locks. His eyes creased as he smiled down at her. My chest hurt watching it.

Phoebe nodded vigorously. "Lots of ducks there."

Some of the colour drained from Dan's face.

"We'll keep her away from the ducks," I said.

The 'we' hung in the air between us.

❅

Dan found Phoebe a pair of industrial ear muffs and we braved the stage. I wasn't convinced she'd like it and honestly, who takes a toddler to a rock concert? The answer was, of course, rock stars, but equating Dan to that word was still new.

I'd worried for nothing. Had I not put her on a harness, she would have run onto the stage at multiple points. It got worse when Rhiannon's time came.

The lights dipped and the crowd started chanting their name. It was insane. A wall of deafening sound that seemed to feed adrenaline into the guys.

"Will you stay to the end?" Dan asked, leaning close until his lips brushed my hair. His bass was flung over his back and his eyes were wild, excited for the show to come.

I turned my face towards him and shouted, "If she doesn't have a meltdown, sure."

He pulled back slightly to catch my eye. "Does that normally happen?"

"When she's tired, yeah."

He nodded, his gaze dropped to my lips. Before I could react to that hint, his head descended. His hand pressed against my lower back, forcing me into the circle of his arms. His mouth nibbled at mine, coaxing me into responding.

I knew better, but stopping him when my lips were tingling and my body instinctively sagged against him? Get real. I kissed him back, everything else faded away, and I let myself enjoy the press of him against me.

Was it stupid? Of course.

Apparently, neither my heart nor my brain cared in that moment.

"Now, can you get married?" Phoebe shouted, her voice raising above the backstage chatter. People laughed around us.

I tensed and tried to pull away. Dan's arms tightened around me. He raised his head slowly, reluctantly. His lips were swollen, his green eyes filled with heat.

"I'm up for it," Dan said, grinning at me.

"Don't even joke," I muttered, glancing down at Phoebe. She stood at our feet staring up at us with a grin of her own.

Dan followed the direction of my stare and finally released me. He knelt in front of her, leaning in until he could speak directly to her and be heard over the commotion.

Whatever he said, I missed it. Phoebe's face lit up as he spoke, filling me with dread. If he'd made her a promise he couldn't keep I'd flip.

He straightened with a mischievous expression that did not help his cause. He pressed one final kiss to my forehead, that I didn't lean into in the least (lie).

The band took to the stage, and the volume in the hall skyrocketed. Drum beats sounded, and Rhiannon swung into their first hit song. Phoebe danced around my feet like a little lunatic. For the first couple of songs, she'd tugged me hard towards the stage, but I was stronger.

By the twenty-minute mark, she started to droop. Five minutes more, and she sat herself down on the dirty backstage floor. That was enough for me. I scooped her up and carried her out.

Was it cowardly to leave without talking to Dan? Maybe, but I had a tired toddler to get to bed.

CHAPTER TEN

The doorbell rang, and Phoebe shrieked from the living room. I glanced at the clock on my bedside table. Twelve thirty. He was early.

Phoebe danced around my feet as I walked to the door, dragging a reluctant smile from the responsible mask I was trying to force in place.

"Stop it, Phoebs. I don't want to step on you."

She ignored me, racing ahead to the front door. Bouncing on the balls of her bare feet, she shot me an impatient look over her shoulder.

So, maybe I was taking my sweet time to open the door. He was early. I'd expected another thirty minutes to psych myself up.

"Maaaam," Phoebe growled.

Bracing myself, I opened the door. Phoebe shot at Dan before I could so much as blink. She launched herself at him, a feat considering she was pint sized and he was over six foot. He chuckled, lifting her.

"I could get used to this sort of welcome." He stepped into the flat, pausing as he passed me. "Want me to carry you too?"

My stomach flipped at the heated promise in his eyes. I'd never been one to back down from a challenge, but this one wasn't happening. I averted my gaze and shut the door, avoiding touching him entirely.

"Are you ready for the park, munchkin?" Dan asked Phoebe as he walked into my kitchen. "What's that look for?"

"Mammy calls me that too."

I caught up with them just in time to catch his satisfied smirk. He'd placed Phoebe on the worktop and leant down until he was eye to eye with her.

"Is that so?" He glanced towards me, his eyes twinkling before his attention returned to Phoebe. "Is it okay if I use it, too?"

Her agreement was instant. She had that sly look on her face again.

"Sorry. I wasn't expecting you so early, we're not ready." I crossed my arms, my brows climbing, demanding an explanation.

"I might have been a little eager." He tickled Phoebe lightly until her shrieking giggles filled my flat and tugged at my heart strings. "Phoebe doesn't mind. Do you?"

"No," she cried, collapsing onto the island with tears of joy shining in her eyes.

I sighed. How could I be annoyed at him when he did that? From the smirk, I was sure he did it on purpose to get to me. He had me pegged.

My shoulders sagged. "Fine. Get your shoes, Phoebe. We're leaving."

I left them to collect my own shoes from my bedroom. When I returned, it was to find Dan kneeling in the hallway, holding a pair of green sparkly shoes while she ran circles around him.

"Phoebe, sit down or no park."

She didn't always obey, but today, she must have been

feeling helpful. She collapsed onto the floor and presented Dan with her feet.

He got her shoes on without another incident. I grabbed my purse off the side table and we were out the door.

Walking into the park with Phoebe on her harness and Dan at my side, we almost looked like every other family enjoying the rare October sunshine.

I shut the box hard on that thought. The yearning had to stop. I'd lose my damn mind if it didn't.

We found an open spot, and Dan pulled a blanket from the top of the mysterious basket he'd prepared. He lay down the blanket and gestured for me to sit. Eying him with suspicion, I did just that.

"I promise I have no surprises," he said, laughing at me.

"You wouldn't let me see in there, so why should I believe you?"

"Because I'm a trustworthy guy?"

I snorted.

He flicked the lid off the basket and tilted it towards me. "See? No silly string in sight."

"Don't remind me," I muttered, studying the contents.

We were the odd kids who didn't just agree to be boyfriend and girlfriend on a whim. I made Dan work for it, and each date got more and more inventive. We went on a picnic for our fifth or sixth date. He'd rigged the basket with silly string. I'd taken the lid off, and the thing popped, scaring the life out of me and plastering me in sticky string. It set his progress back two weeks and I never accepted boxes from him again.

Despite the trauma at the time, the memory brought an easy smile to my lips. We'd been good together once.

I spotted a bottle of fizzy pop. "If you give her that, you're chasing her."

He followed my gaze to the offending item. "Does she get hyper with it or something?"

Phoebe sat up like a meerkat, excitement blooming on her

baby face. "Is it pop? Can I have pop?" She grinned at me, her eyes already wide and manic as she silently begged me.

"Why don't you ask your father?"

She spun around to face him, turning the full force of that desperation on him. "Please, Daddy."

His gaze flicked between us. Indecision skittered across his face and my lips twitched.

"Maybe just one," he said, but the way he drawled the words made him sound unsure, like he was asking for permission.

For once, I didn't need to take the responsibility for the way our day would end. I gave him a sugar sweet smile and slipped my sunglasses on. Leaning back on my forearms, I spread out and left him to fumble his way through. It took real life experience to outwit a toddler. How else was he going to learn?

With a pained expression, he poured some pop into her travel cup. He hesitated as he held it out to her but Phoebe didn't notice. She snatched it from him and started chugging it.

"Slow down before you make yourself sick," I muttered, my voice brooking no argument.

She slowed down, just. Dan stared at her with shock colouring his face.

"Why do I have this sinking feeling that I made the wrong choice?" he asked, shellshocked.

I just smirked.

He pulled a circular tube from the basket and waved it in front of Phoebe's face. "If you give me the cup, I'll give you bubbles."

Phoebe lowered the cup but didn't release it. Her eyes narrowed as she considered it, and him. I could see the calculations taking place in her head. How could she get them both?

Dan unscrewed the cap and blew on the stick. Soapy

bubbles scattered around us and Phoebe avidly tracked their progress.

"Gimme bubbles," she ordered, holding out her hand for the stick.

Dan stayed strong. "Give me the cup."

She pursed her lips. Her gaze fell to the almost empty cup and she shrugged, dropping it on the blanket without fighting further.

"Good girl," Dan muttered, handing over the stick and the tub of liquid.

She sat herself down on the edge of the blanket with her gains. The satisfied smirk on her face matched Dan's, only she had a reason to revel in her success.

Dan sprawled out next to me, leaving just a couple of inches between us. He grinned up at me like he'd won the lottery. It was too much for me and I had no qualms about wiping it away. I edged away from him to make sure I wouldn't resort to anything more than words.

"You realise she just played you, right?"

His amusement faded slightly.

"What do you mean?"

I nodded towards the cup. "There's drops left in there. She got the pop and the bubbles." I chuckled as the realisation settled across his features. "Face it, Dan, your daughter's smarter than you."

He scowled. "She got lucky." His elbow held his head and torso at the perfect height for a kiss. "I just need practice."

Phoebe sat in front of us like a lifeline.

"You'll get plenty of it with her," I muttered, the words coming out slightly hoarse. "I mean, the longer you're around, you'll be able to read her."

His fingers pressed into my chin, turning my head until I couldn't escape the promise in his eyes. "I'd be around twenty-four seven, if you'd let me," he whispered, so that Phoebe couldn't hear.

I swallowed. I guess I should be thankful that he was being tactful about it today. Unlike last night.

"You shouldn't act like this in front of her."

Dan frowned. "Like what?"

"Like you're in love with me." I shook off his grip and sat up. "It'll give her the wrong idea." I turned my back on him and focused on Phoebe. We were only together for her.

※

We got home just in time for dinner. Dan talked his way into staying for food and the hours slipped away until he was helping me put Phoebe to bed. Then he was still here, and it was just us with the sun setting across the bay.

Nervous energy overtook me and I started cleaning. Me, cleaning! I didn't clean unless forced or Phoebe got out of control. I had better things to do with my evening hours… like work.

I started emptying the dishwasher with singular focus. So singular that when Dan stopped next to me, it scared me. My heart racing, I straightened and caught the amused twinkle in his eyes. He knew I was avoiding him. Of course he did, because he knew all my tells.

"Want some help?" he asked, his voice deep and sliding over my nerve endings like melted chocolate.

This was a very bad idea.

"Sure."

He took over the dishwasher, handing me items while I returned them to their homes. For moments, we worked in companionable silence. It didn't last.

"So other than having Phoebe, what have you been up to?"

I shrugged. "Just work."

"Are you still with that start-up?"

"Yup, six years and going strong." I rounded the island to get to the glasses' cupboard on the other side of him. He smirked at me, but I didn't care.

"And you still like it?" he asked, curiosity dripping from his words in contrast with the amusement on his face.

"Yeah, I'm good at it." I filled the glasses into the cupboard, avoiding looking at him wherever I could. "And they must agree, 'cause they promoted me, despite my flaky moments with Phoebe."

"That's great, babe." He handed me the last glass, but when I reached for it, his grip tightened. I stared into his gaze with my pulse fluttering wildly in my throat. "But if you ever need help, you know you just have to ask, right?"

"What does that mean?" I asked. A frown tightened my face as I tried to puzzle out his meaning.

Was he offering me money?

And if so, why did the thought of that turn me kind of sick? It would be the right thing for him to do, but it just felt… if him choosing to be with me now was only because of Phoebe, him offering up money would be like wiping his hands of us. They were complete opposites but both made every inch of me break out in a cold sweat.

"I'm just recording at the moment. The album's nearly done, and we're probably going to do a one-month UK tour in November." His eyes danced across my face, trying to read me. Whether he was succeeding was up for debate. I'm not sure he would have anticipated the sudden plummet my stomach took at the mention of him touring again.

"What I'm trying to say is I have time. If you need to work late, I can be here for her," he said. His expression gentled and he continued, "If you need to spend a night with the girls to unwind, I can babysit. Any night." He took a step closer to me, placing the glass on the worktop. "And if you ever decide you want me here with you both permanently, all you have to do is ask."

My mouth opened and closed as I processed that last one. He'd been back ten days. It had only been three days since he'd learnt about Phoebe. And he thought this was the perfect time to say something like that to me?

He cleared his throat. "I'm not saying right now, babe. You need time, I get that," he whispered, lowering his head towards me. He closed the space between us. "But I meant what I said the other day, I was always coming home to you. I just had to figure out how."

Tears burned my eyes and I blinked furiously. What the hell was it with the crying?

"We had a nice day," I said, stopping when my voice came out hoarse. I swallowed and tried again. "It was a nice day, please don't ruin it with talk of the past." I stared up at him, imploring him to listen to me.

He shook his head. "How can I not? When we're with Phoebe, you don't want to give her ideas, but when we're alone…" His fingers trailed up my arm, leaving goose bumps in their wake. "This feeling doesn't go away. It's been twelve years and the desire to be near you has never faded. So tell me how to shut it off, Mel, because every time I tried, I came home to you."

I shut my eyes against the longing on his face. Seeing it didn't help me stay strong. It just dragged all my hopes to the surface, ready for him to smash them to pieces when his next whim took him.

His fingers smoothed along my skin, cupping my jaw and tilting my head back until I couldn't escape him. He pressed his forehead to mine.

"Tell me you haven't thought about us. Tell me you haven't dreamt about what life could be like with us together." His other hand slid over my hip and around to my lower back, pulling me towards him. "Tell me that, and I'll stop, I'll leave. I'll be Phoebe's father and nothing more."

His heart hammered against my chest and his feverish

gaze burned into mine. I should say it. Two simple words — *I don't* — and he would back off. It would get easier.

But it would be a lie.

His lips claimed mine so fast it caught me off guard. I gasped and his tongue swept into my mouth, taking every advantage he could get. For once, I didn't resist. What would have been the point? He knew I wanted him, against my better judgment or not. Depriving myself of this kiss would be a waste.

So I sank into him. My arms wrapped around him and my hands smoothed up his back, glorying in the feel of him pressed against me. He recognised the change in me instantly. He turned us until my back pressed against the cupboard. His hands grasped my butt and lifted me onto the worktop. He wedged himself between my legs, dragging me forward until I could wrap my legs around him. There wasn't an inch of free space between us, and my body went into freefall. So many sensations, I didn't know what to do with them all.

One of his hands glided up my thigh, dragging my light jersey dress up. They coasted up my side, his calloused fingers grazing against my sensitive skin. I shivered, moaning into his mouth. If it was possible, he pressed himself harder against me, the bulge in his jeans hitting all the right points to start a light buzz in my core. He rolled my nipple through the thin material of my bra, and electricity shot through me.

Dan pulled back, a smirk on his lips and fire in his eyes as he took in my dazed expression. His head dipped just as the cool air kissed my exposed breast. His tongue swirled around my nipple, and my fingers slid into his hair, tugging at him, urging him on. He chuckled against my sensitive skin, the vibrations just as effective as his mouth at driving me crazy. I lost the ability to stay upright when he increased the pressure. Sinking back against the counter, my shoulder held me up so I could watch him through my lashes.

A small voice of conscience tried to penetrate the sexual

fog. His calloused fingers grazed against my hip bone before I could grasp the words and it faded away.

A finger hooked into the waistband of my woollen tights, dragging them down. All the while, he watched me, refusing to let me escape him for even a moment.

You should stop him.

I bit my lip and dragged his face back to mine. Our mouths crashed together as his fingers delved into my tights and underwear. The shock of him was too much, and reality set in. I leaned back, breaking the kiss.

"Wait," I said, my hand pressed against his chest, holding him off.

"Mel," he groaned.

I shook my head. "This can't... we can't..."

The lust faded fast in his eyes. Annoyance replaced it and I ignored the pang of loss. His hands fell to my thighs, holding me on the counter as he stared at me.

"It will and we can."

"No, I'm sorry. I should have stopped you sooner." I pushed him back and slid off the counter, marching away from him and around the island. Putting all the space between us I could. "I'm not sure about you, and... and Phoebe's in the next room."

"Okay, if that's an issue for you, we can wait until she's at your parents," he said, trying to be understanding, but tension still rode him. A pang of guilt hit me in the chest but I shook it off.

"No, it'll get messy if we get together. She — we don't need that."

Anger darkened his face and he rounded the counter towards me. I backed away, but I had nowhere to go. My legs hit the back of the sofa and I was trapped.

"Stop lying to yourself and me. We deserve more than that," he snapped, stopping so close I could feel his body heat against my skin. "We are giving this relationship a chance.

Even if I have to wait a week, a month, a bloody year. I'm not going to let you self-destruct us before we've at least tried."

What could I say to that? His determination washed over me. It didn't take my resistance with it, but staring into his face, reading the lingering signs of our kiss in his eyes and the puffiness of his lips, the inevitability of it all settled over me. I knew he would break my heart again, but he wouldn't stop trying.

CHAPTER ELEVEN

Three days passed before I answered his calls. Just because our relationship was inevitable did not mean I had to fall headfirst into it. I'd spent nearly four years learning to be the most cautious version of myself. That didn't go away overnight.

So, when Wednesday rolled around, and a crisis presented itself at work, I caved and called him. True, I could have asked my mother. Or Nia. Or Sophie. But this was my olive branch. It put me on edge to hand Phoebe off to him, but he was her father.

He met me at the day-care centre at 3PM without a moment's hesitation. My body was still hung up on the events of Sunday night. The fact my mind reminded me of it every time I shut my eyes wasn't helping. So when I saw him, with his trimmed beard and his unruly red hair sweeping over his head in mild waves, the permanent example of beautifully windswept, my stomach flipped and started my heart racing.

Priorities.

"Hey," he said, his voice subdued. His hands were shoved into his pockets and his eyes devoured me in much the same way as I had him. "Thanks for calling."

I nodded. "Thank you for agreeing to watch her at the last minute."

An intense light entered his eyes. "I told you I'd be here for anything you needed and I meant it."

"I know." I glanced to the right, catching sight of people side eying us. "Can we talk about this when I get home?"

Whether they were trying to eavesdrop on our conversation or checking him out, I wasn't sure. I couldn't blame them. He'd always been gorgeous.

Dan smiled. It was ropey around the edges but it still made something inside me sit up and take notice.

"Of course. We'll be waiting for you at home."

My heart fluttered. He did that on purpose. There was a devious glint in his eyes.

I handed him the keys to the flat. "I'll be back around 8PM I expect." I bit my lip, glancing at the door to the daycare. "Are you okay to put her to bed?"

His rough hand caught mine, drawing my gaze back to his. He'd closed the distance between us while I'd been distracted and now he wove our fingers together. He squeezed them, silently reminding me that this was where he thought he belonged.

"We'll be fine. Let's get her out of there, and then you can get back to your desk."

I nodded, but my feet wouldn't move. I wasn't sure why.

Using our twinned hands, he tugged me until I fell into him. His other arm wrapped around me and he leaned down. "I promise I'll take good care of her," he whispered, his voice low, so no one else would hear.

I took a deep breath and let the building anxiety go. I let my body relax against him, absorbing the heat and smell of him while I could.

"Ready?" he asked. His hand rubbed up and down my back in reassuring sweeps.

I nodded, and we went in.

❄

I'd gotten a good chunk of work done when the phone rang at 7PM. Dan's number flashed across the screen and I scrambled for it.

"What happened?" I asked, anxiety making my voice breathy.

"I don't know," Dan said, his worry audible. "One minute she was fine, and the next she was throwing up. Mel, I don't know what to do."

"I'm on my way." I shut the lid on my laptop and stood, my brain running a mile a minute while I tried to figure out what to tell Dan and what to pack in case I had to work from home tomorrow. "Does she have a fever?"

"I think so."

"There's a bottle of Calpol in the fridge. See if you can get her to take a spoonful of it."

"Calpol," he repeated. The fridge door squeaked on the other end. "Is it purple?"

"Yes."

"Okay, got it. How long will you be?"

There wouldn't be much traffic out of the city centre, so... "Fifteen minutes maybe."

Heart in my throat, I hung up, shoved my notebook into my handbag, and picked up the laptop. Then I rushed to the lifts, hit the button a dozen times in an agitated hope it would make the damn thing climb the fifteen floors faster.

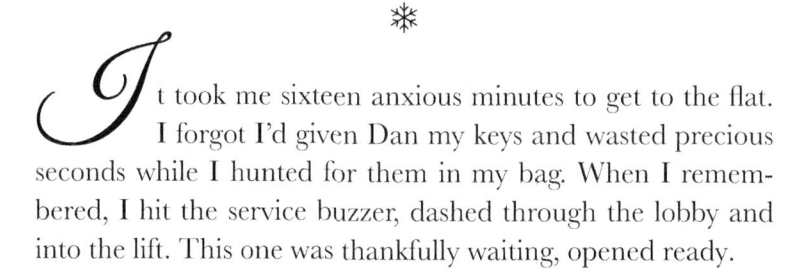

❄

*I*t took me sixteen anxious minutes to get to the flat. I forgot I'd given Dan my keys and wasted precious seconds while I hunted for them in my bag. When I remembered, I hit the service buzzer, dashed through the lobby and into the lift. This one was thankfully waiting, opened ready.

Ringing my own doorbell felt weird. The door flew open before even one chime had passed. Dan's eyes were wide, disturbed. His hair stood on end and his t-shirt and jeans were covered in dried vomit. It was an alarming sight but not unexpected.

"Did she take it?" I asked, breathless as I brushed past him.

"Yeah, but she fought me. She said her throat hurts," he called after me.

I found her on the sofa, wrapped in a blanket, her tiny face white against the dark green cushion beneath her head. Her eyes opened as I approached. There wasn't an accusatory edge on her face, but still, I felt guilty. I should have been here. I shouldn't have been working late.

"Mammy," she croaked, trying to sit up.

I knelt in front of her and helped her up.

"Where were you?" she whined, moisture filling her eyes.

"Sorry, munchkin, I had to work." I pulled my phone from my handbag and flicked on the torch. My hand shook as I held it up. "Open up."

I angled the light into her mouth, already knowing what I was going to find. Her tonsils were enflamed again. For the third time this year. I shut the light off and put the device down on her blanket.

"How do you feel now?" I asked, smoothing her hair back.

"Hot."

I nodded. "Do you want some ice cream?"

Even sick, she could give me stink eye. "I'm not allowed."

"Tonight you are."

Slowly, she nodded her head.

"Which flavour? Daddy'll put some in a bowl for you."

"Chocolate." Barely any sound escaped her mouth and I had to read her lips.

I glanced at Dan. "There's some in the freezer."

He sprang into action while I held her upright. I pressed my forehead to her feverish one and sighed.

"I think you might have scared him," I whispered to Phoebe. She didn't grin or chuckle or give me any of her usual mischief. "You'll be okay." She just stared at me, saying nothing but trusting me implicitly.

Dan handed me the bowl and sat down on the edge of the seat. His leg pressed against my side. Whether intentional or not, his strong presence told me he was staying.

Bit by bit I fed Phoebe the ice cream. She only managed a couple of mouthfuls, but hopefully it would help calm the inflammation in her throat. She fell asleep before the ice cream could melt.

❄

*P*hoebe lay tucked up in her bed. All I wanted to do was hover over her like I usually would, but for the moment, I couldn't. Dan was waiting. I reluctantly shut her door and returned to Dan.

"Do you want me to wash your clothes?" I asked as I opened the fridge door and retrieved the open bottle of wine.

Dan cleared his throat. "I've got nothing to change into."

Pausing mid pour, I glanced up at him, tracking slowly up his body. It was almost second nature, being this attuned to him. But tiredness pulsed through me, and I really didn't care if he was dressed or semi-naked right now. Between the worry and the anxiety of the evening, I was exhausted.

"Nothing I haven't seen before." I shrugged and continued pouring the wine. "I'm assuming you aren't leaving yet?"

"No, I'd rather make sure you're both okay." He approached me at the island, his steps slow with hesitation as he eyed me.

"Her bouts of tonsillitis are getting more frequent," I said, a hitch in my voice. I put the bottle down, my eyes fixed on it.

"She's too young to have them removed yet, but the doctor's counting down the days at this point."

"Why can't they do anything now?" he asked, his voice gruff.

"No tonsillectomy for children under four." I shrugged, I'd been through it enough times now, I was resigned to the wait. "Too much risk of bleeding."

His lips flatlined at the information.

"It won't put her completely out of the woods anyway." I put the bottle back in the fridge. With my back turned, I whispered, "It's my fault. She got it from me, and even with an operation, it doesn't completely go away."

"Blaming yourself won't help, babe," he said, his voice strong with his belief. I tensed at it. Why did he have more faith in me than I did? It hadn't always been that way. "Yes, you got the occasional bad cough when we were in school, but you're still perfect and healthy. Phoebe will be too."

I tensed at the quiver in his voice. Turning back to him, I wasn't sure what to expect. Dan stood closer, on the same side of the island, but he didn't try to touch me. The mixed expression on his face confused me. He seemed equal parts shaken and determined.

He also smelled really bad.

My nose wrinkled as I considered the shades of yellow on his t-shirt.

"You didn't let her eat cheese puffs, did you?"

He bit his lip and glanced away. "Maybe."

For a second, the worry lessened and I smirked. "Was she running you ragged before she got sick?"

He scratched at his jaw, still not meeting my gaze. "There might have been some bribery."

I nodded, the glass pressed to my face. "I blame you for that part."

"What?" He spluttered. "I was not that bad."

My brows rose and I waited.

"My sister was worse."

I pressed my lips together and leaned back against the counter. His eyes finally settled on me, amusement in those beautiful green depths and I could happily spend every waking moment with that look.

"Alright, so I was a bit of a nuisance, and I couldn't be trusted with a fizzy drink either."

I chuckled at his petulant expression and pushed a glass of wine towards him. "Glad you could admit to your part in making that little monster."

A soft smile over took his features before he picked up the glass and eyed the clear liquid with suspicion.

"Sorry, I don't keep cider."

He nodded, tentatively taking a sip.

"Now, give me the clothes." I held my hand out to him.

His brow shot up, playfulness in his eyes.

"You stink. If you're staying, you need to not make me feel ill."

"Fair enough." He sighed and placed the glass back on the counter.

Before I could say another word, he tore the t-shirt off, and my tiredness evaporated. I devoured the defined ridges of his muscles as he bundled his t-shirt up and placed it on the counter. Too entranced by all that skin, I missed him shucking his jeans. Talk about sensory overload!

Dan placed his folded jeans on the counter and crossed his arms. I didn't stop staring. I'm not sure I could.

Sick child in the next room.

That thought broke through.

Clearing my throat, I averted my eyes, heat burning my cheeks. "Why don't you throw a blanket over yourself for now?"

Grabbing the clothes, I turned away from him. There was no need for me to see the interest in his eyes to know it would be there. We were predictable, like moths to flames.

What a morbid thought.

"Sure," he said, his voice soft. "There's food in the microwave for you."

Surprise rippled through me. He cooked for me with a manic toddler?

I loaded his clothes into the washing machine and set it off. He sat on the sofa, his body turned, so he could watch me over the back of it. Something about it stilled me. I usually hated people seeing me crumble.

With him, the anxiety no longer plagued me.

I turned my back on him and focused on reheating the pasta he'd left me. Plate in hand, I picked up my glass and joined him on the sofa. The moment I sat down, my shoulders sagged and I sank into the cushions.

"Well tonight did not go the way I expected," Dan said. He side eyed me with concern. I ignored him and ate my food. "I thought I'd get to be the fun dad and spoil her for the evening." He shook his head, a mildly traumatised chuckle escaping him.

"Instead, you got a baptism by fire," I muttered, my voice devoid of all lightness. "Sorry about that."

"It needed to happen sometime, right?" He sipped his wine, watching me over the rim.

At some point, I'd forgotten how intense he could be. I used to love it and if I wasn't so exhausted and worried about Phoebe, I probably still would. I sighed. It would make my life so much less complicated if I could resist him. There would be no messy feelings, no fear that he only wanted me now because he had to…

"You know you don't have to make an effort with me for Phoebe, don't you?" I asked, placing the empty plate on the coffee table and picking up my wine glass. "We don't have to be a perfect family. Yours wasn't and you turned out fine."

Maybe it was the exhaustion, but the words just spilled out. Inside, my common sense was screaming at me to stop but the message wasn't getting through to my mouth. I could see his face closing up and still I didn't stop.

"Your mother was always a little on edge." I shrugged and let my head rest back against the cushion. My eyelids grew heavy and I fought to keep my eyes open. "But then she had you and Freya driving her up the wall, breaking curfews, so what did we expect really?"

"Stop talking, Mel," Dan growled, his voice low and annoyed.

I rolled my head to the side. His jaw worked, and his lips flatlined. My stomach dropped as my mouth and brain finally got on the same page.

"I'm sorry, I didn't mean —"

"Yes, you did," he bit out. He leaned towards me, anger flashing in his gaze. "Did it not occur to you that I don't want Phoebe to grow up like I did? Wondering why her dad wasn't there for her?"

I frowned. "You always told me that you didn't care."

"I was a kid, Mel! Of course I said that," he snapped. "I wasn't going to admit, to the one person I wanted to love me, that a part of me was missing."

"It wouldn't have changed anything if I'd known, Dan."

"It would have for me. He was an arrogant asshole that got bored of his family." Determination flashed across his face as he leaned closer. "I won't be him. Phoebe deserves better."

"Yes, she does." I nodded, my brows still drawn. "But that doesn't mean we have to be together."

"Why are you so bloody resistant to this?" he asked. That guilt-inducing uncertainty flitted across his face and my chest tightened. "On Sunday, things were fine. We made progress, and then silence." The anger fizzled out as he considered me. "What am I doing wrong?"

I rubbed a hand across my face. I'd already spilled some of it. Why stop now?

"I don't trust you," I said, working hard to keep my voice

soft, vacant of accusation. Forcing myself to keep eye contact, I continued, "If you were here for only Phoebe, it would make life easier. I'd know where I stand."

"I came back to you before I knew about Phoebe."

"I get that, but you came back to me multiple times and still left. Why am I supposed to believe that this time is different?"

Dan caught my hand, his large grip engulfing mine. He twined our fingers while he mulled over my question. It felt too nice, too right. And the urge to reject it was strong.

"You're right, I was an idiot who didn't think about what my actions did to you." He rested my hand against his thigh on top of the blanket and sighed. "I should have talked to you back then, made a plan, told you how I felt. Maybe then you wouldn't be looking at me like I'll vanish before your eyes."

I glanced away, biting my lip to stop the agreement on the tip of my tongue. He was right, communication would have changed it all. It wouldn't have made it any easier, but at least I would have known where we stood.

He tugged on my hand, drawing my attention back to him.

"I'm here to stay. Before I knew about Phoebe, it was all you." He smiled, the light in his eyes weak. "I was losing my mind trying to get in touch with you."

They were pretty words that made my heart sing, but they were just words.

"Why did it take you nearly five years?"

He winced. "The band kept growing after we got signed. It felt like we didn't stop moving, didn't stop touring." His eyes dropped to our twined hands. "For at least a year, I couldn't think about anything else. I woke up, did a sound check, played, crashed. And then we woke up in a new city and did it all over again."

My brows climbed. "I think you're forgetting a couple of crucial moments in between all that."

"Okay, so there was a lot of alcohol in between. I was young, stupid, and on a high, okay?" The words flew out of him in a self-loathing rush. "We finally got home and I woke up. Everything was different but not you, not this incessant need to see you, to know that you were alright."

His fingers grazed along my cheek as he stared into my eyes.

"It took me too long to come home. I know that, babe, and I regret it every single time I see the hesitation in your eyes. Or the intelligence in Phoebe's." He tucked a strand behind my ear, leaning in until he pressed his forehead to mine. "Just give me a chance to prove I'm awake, please? I'm not going anywhere and I'd be here even if we didn't share a daughter. Just let me help you, let me shoulder some of the worry."

Tears burned my eyes and I shut my eyes, willing them back. I might be a fool but I really wanted him to mean it. Hell, I needed him to mean it.

I opened my eyes and stared into his cautiously optimistic gaze. Any hope of saving myself from future heartbreak evaporated. I'd been delusional to think I could have parts of him and not others, to think I could protect myself. There was too much history between us, too much passion, real and remembered.

The easiest course was acceptance.

"Fine. Prove it."

CHAPTER TWELVE

With a grip on the back of my neck, he tugged me towards him. His lips slammed against mine, devouring my moan. Somehow I ended up in his lap, straddling him, my work skirt bunching up around my waist, and my aching sex pressed against the hard ridge of his cock. Between the fabric of his boxers and my underwear, there was barely anything separating us. His hands gripped my waist, urging me to ride him.

"I didn't mean like that," I gasped when he released my mouth to trail open mouth kisses along my jaw and down my neck. He hit a particularly sensitive spot on my neck and I shivered, my hips kicking forward and giving him exactly what he wanted. We both groaned with the sensation.

"I know, but I can barely think straight when you look like this." He bit his lip and his gaze dropped, roaming over my twisted blouse. The material was snagged in my skirt, pulling the fabric tight across my chest. "And that blouse has been screwing with my head for the last couple of hours." His hands coasted up my sides as he glanced up at me, the fire in his eyes sending a hot flush up my body. "I'll take my time wooing you again, babe, but right now, we both need to come," he whispered, his voice loud in the silent yet tense atmosphere of my flat.

My eyes snagged on Phoebe's bedroom door. *What if she wakes up and we're...* I chewed my lip.

"I can be quiet," Dan said, a clear challenge in his voice.

I lifted a brow. "And I can't?"

He pressed his lips together, refusing to comment, but his eyes gave him away. They sparkled with amusement.

"Using my competitive nature against me isn't cool."

"Is that what I'm doing?" he asked, his voice high despite his attempt at conveying innocence.

I shook my head at him, my lips twitching no matter how hard I tried to look stern.

His eyes softened as he took in my indecision. "She's out cold, babe." His hands coasted along my bare thighs, barely touching yet driving all of my focus on the movement. "You know how she is when she's ill, does she normally wake up a lot through this?"

I pursed my lips. "No."

Dan nodded, but removed his hands from me. He held them up and speared me with an intense look. "Then you choose. If you want to take the edge off, so the bite of need is more manageable, we can do that." His lips curled up on one side when I didn't move. "Or you can slide your gorgeous ass out of my lap and sit on the other side of the room while we watch TV."

My breath caught at the gravelly sound of his voice, dragging across my nerve-endings. If there was a choice in there, I didn't hear it.

His brows rose. "What's it going to be, babe?"

"Fine," I breathed, slamming my mouth back to his. "But we —" Kiss. "Have to —" Nip. "Be quiet." He groaned as my tongue flicked against his lip, his hands settled on my ass, pushing the fabric of my skirt completely up, so his fingers pressed against bare skin and lace.

He trailed open mouth kisses to my ear. "Good with me." He pulled me towards him, grinding me against his erection and urging me on again. "I wasn't the screamer."

Before I could comment, he jolted forward and stood with me in his arms. My legs wrapped around him and I clung to him.

"How about a little warning, next time?"

Dan's brows climbed. "Did you want me to fuck you on the sofa?" He stopped in the doorway, mischief dripping from his whispered words.

"No, no. Bedroom is good," I said in a panicked rush. I did not need to scar myself or Phoebe with that visual.

Grinning, he set me down in the bedroom and disappeared back into the main room. I frowned at him until the lights started to turn out and understanding dawned.

He emerged from the darkened hall and quietly shut the door. When he turned back to me, his face was set. He threw something on to the bed, his focus never wavering from me.

"Once we start this time, we aren't stopping," he warned as he prowled towards me. All I could do was nod. "No changing your mind. You're mine." He stopped in front of me, barely touching but close enough that I could feel the heat of him through my clothes. "Understand?" he asked, his voice deep and gravelly with desire.

"Yes," I croaked.

His smile was triumphant as he dipped his head to catch my lips. His strong hands caught my hips, pulling me into him as he went to town on my mouth.

Kiss.

The sound of my zipper sliding down rent the tense air.

Lick.

My skirt fluttered to the ground. His hands coasted over my lacey French knickers and up my sides. I bit back a moan at the feel of his calloused fingertips dragging along my skin.

Nip.

Cool air hit my exposed stomach as he rid me of my sensible work blouse. My hands roamed the naked, toned ridges of his back with wonder. He'd filled out a lot since we were last together. The thought of his strong body above me sent a rush of liquid heat to my core.

Suck.

My blouse and bra had barely hit the ground when he pushed me back onto the bed. He stared down at me, sprawled out almost naked on my forest green sheets — *okay, so maybe I bought them because of him*. His eyes blazed as he lowered himself to his knees and pulled me to the edge of the bed.

He still wore his boxers. I tried to sit up, and he pressed me back down with a firm hand between my breasts.

"Dan, what are you doing?" I dragged my lower lip between my teeth and his eyes traced the movement hungrily.

"Reminding myself how sweet you taste."

He pressed soft, open mouth kisses to my stomach, setting butterflies free inside as he worked his way down. He hooked my underwear and tugged it down my legs. His lips followed the material's path, tracing a vein down my inner thigh, the bristles of his beard scratching deliciously against the sensitive flesh.

When he pressed my legs wider apart, making more room for his broad shoulders, my core clenched tight. When his fingers pressed between my lips, I jumped. Chuckling, Dan pressed another kiss to my inner thigh.

"Relax, babe, I've got you," Dan whispered before his tongue parted my folds and my back bowed.

He lapped at me, moaning as he did, adding even more sensation to the mix. I fisted my hands in the sheets, unable to control the restless shifting of my hips. Dan pressed a hand to my stomach to still me. Then he sucked on my clit, and I had to press a hand to my mouth to quiet my moans. His wicked laughter vibrated through me.

Not content with making me squirm, his fingers joined the party, delving into my hair and grazing against a bundle of nerves that swept sweet lighting through me. It charged through my lower back and up my body, pickling my brain with pleasure. He added another finger to the mix and increased the pressure, driving me over the edge so fast I had to bite my hand to stop myself from crying out.

Dan wiped his face on the sheet and stood up, a satisfied, purely male smile on his face. All I could do was stare up at him as he stripped out of his boxers. My eyes traced the lines of his body with interest, snagging on his hard cock. It strained against his stomach, begging for attention.

I sat up, reaching for him. He caught my hand and pressed it behind my back.

"Right now, I need to be inside of you, babe," he whispered, his voice low and hoarse.

Dan pressed a kiss to my lips and urged me back until my head hit the pillows. There was absolutely no part of me interested in arguing. My hands raked over his torso, grazing with my nails.

He settled over me, dragging the head of his cock teasingly against my centre. My hips shifted and my legs wrapped around his hips, pulling him tighter against me. The glide of him against me was almost my undoing. In that moment, I would have let him do anything. Thankfully, he still remembered how to be sensible. He pressed one more kiss to my lips and pulled back, fumbling around the bed, searching for something between the folds of material.

When he unearthed his wallet, I remembered the thing he'd thrown when he came back in.

Suited up, he returned to me, the furnace of desire still burning in his eyes. His hands coasted up my body, loving me the way his eyes did.

He positioned himself above me and caught my lips in a

deep, wet kiss before pressing himself against my entrance. "Are you ready?"

At my nod, he drove into me. Despite the fact I was soaking for him, I winced, and he stalled. He pressed his face into my neck and groaned.

"You're so fucking tight, babe," he whispered against me.

"I know." I blew out a frustrated breath.

He lifted his head and pierced me with a hesitantly hopeful look. "How long has it been?"

"Since I last had sex?" I asked stupidly. We'll blame the endorphins from the orgasm still messing with my brain. I wasn't dodging *at all*. His nod was short and sharp. I pressed my lips together while I tried to figure out the best way to say it. Why I was hesitating was anyone's guess. What guy wouldn't be ecstatic to know you'd only ever had sex with them?

A smile bloomed on his face as he studied me. "Since we…" He swallowed. "Not since we made Phoebe?" The smile broke into an outright grin when I nodded.

His mouth caught mine in a sloppy kiss. When he pulled back for a breath, his entire face was lit up. "I'm going to make you come so fucking hard," he whispered before his lips met mine again.

Gradually, the tightness eased, and the lack of movement started to irk me. I shifted my hips, driving him deeper. He groaned against my lips and pulled back. He drove in again and again, edging deeper with each thrust, striking nerve endings deep inside me that made keeping quiet next to impossible.

"I told you," he panted between kisses. "You were always the screamer."

"And you liked it," I muttered around a gasp. "Now stop teasing me about it and remind me why I kept you around for so long."

He chuckled, slowing his thrusts. "That's easy. You loved me."

"I was thinking of the other reason." I gripped his ass, urging him to keep moving.

"Sure you were," he drawled.

Thankfully, he took the hint, slamming into me so fast that my core clenched deep inside. Pleasure twisted, edging me closer and closer to the edge until I bit down on his shoulder to stop myself from chanting "yes," at him.

Smirking, he slowed down, and I almost wept.

"What are you doing?" I growled, my heels digging into his ass, trying to force him to go back to the deep, hard, mind-blowingly hot movements of a second ago.

His shifted position, driving into me with shallow thrusts that hit an unexpected sweet spot. I gasped.

"Say you're mine," he demanded.

I shook my head, unable to think past the pleasure beating through me.

"Mel." He thrust again, another shallow angle that made my breath catch. "Tell me you're mine," he growled, pressing his forehead to mine.

There was no escaping his determined gaze. It burned through me as efficiently as his short, sharp thrusts.

"Dan," I groaned, shifting my hips to try and force him deeper.

This time, he stilled, his chest rising and falling as he caught his breath. "Don't make me say it again, Mel."

I scowled at him. "You're impossible."

My fingers pressed against his ass, urging him to keep moving. He didn't budge.

"I prefer determined." He gathered my hands and pressed them into the pillows at either side of my head. My core twisted, and a rush of heat coursed through me. His brows rose. "Say it."

"I'm yours."

It was just two words. Two tiny words. They shouldn't pack a punch. Yet any tension I'd been holding on to seeped away with how *right* they felt.

His smile was instant. Happiness glittered in his eyes as he drove into me, again and again. He ground his pelvis against my clit with each deep thrust and my eyes just about rolled back in my head.

"Say it again," he demanded through gritted teeth.

"I'm yours," I gasped around an intense jolt of sensation.

Dan slammed his mouth on mine, swallowing my cries as he worked me higher and higher. Pressure coiled inside of me, forcing me towards the edge. His grip tightened on my hand as he followed me over. He buried his face in the pillow beside my head, muffling his own shout.

He leaned back, a sweet, satisfied smile tugging at his lips and his eyes shining with contentment. "Okay so maybe we need to work on the being quiet part."

"Just a little."

Grinning, he lifted himself off me. "Give me twenty minutes, and we'll get some practice in."

I chuckled as he rolled away to dispose of the condom. All I could do was lay there, staring at the ceiling, mostly stunned. Why had that felt so right, so easy?

CHAPTER THIRTEEN

"Mel, wake up."

I blinked up at Dan, my eyes heavy with sleep. His hair stood on end, but he was far more awake than me. He'd put his black boxers back on but his bare and deliciously defined chest was on full display, distracting my already fuzzy brain.

Once Dan had fallen asleep, the worry for Phoebe got to be too much. Now I was sprawled out on the navy armchair in the corner of her room. I'd fallen asleep alone, with my feet on the matching footstool. At some point, she must have woken up and crawled into my lap. Phoebe's tiny body rested against me, a blanket of heat that negated the need for the throw I'd wrapped myself in.

"Why don't you go sleep in your bed, and I'll watch Phoebe for a bit?" Dan asked, his gaze bathing me in his concern.

He tucked his hands under Phoebe, and effortlessly lifted her from my lap. Her head rolled into his shoulder, and she buried her face against his chest. It was quite the sweet picture, her tiny body contrasted against his broad shoulders and thick biceps.

I rubbed at my eyes and sat forward. "What time is it?"

"Just after six," Dan said as he placed Phoebe back in her bed.

"I have to get ready for work."

I stood up, stretching out the kinks in my back.

Wait, I couldn't go to work. Not with Phoebe in this state. She was still hot with fever, and the moment she woke up, she'd ask for me.

"Work from home, today, babe," Dan whispered, his back to me. "I can stay to help with Phoebe, if you want." He tucked Phoebe in, his big hand smoothing her hair back with care.

Gah! I'd never tire of seeing that.

"Don't you have your own stuff to do?"

"Ryan's going to jig things around, so I can take a couple of days off." He turned back to me, studying me in a way that bared all of my secrets. I couldn't argue that I was fine, he could read the bone-tired lines of my body far too easily. "Text your boss, and go get some sleep."

"Okay." I sighed. My gaze rested on Phoebe's innocent face. "But will you wake me if she needs me?"

He caught my arm, tugging me towards him until he could wrap his arms around my waist. He tucked me beneath his shoulder and guided me towards the door. I turned my face into his chest, absorbing the peculiar but glorious feeling of his strength wrapping around me. There might have been a covert sniff or two as well. What? Even sleep-mussed, the man smelled divine. Musky and spicy, all at once. Like comfort and home, easing the tension holding me still.

In my half-asleep state, I enjoyed his attempt to take care of us both. Something I'd normally brush off. But in the soft early morning light, I didn't have the energy to do it. Stopping my hands from caressing his bare skin was hard enough.

Dan led me into my bedroom and straight to my rumpled side of the bed. He didn't have to tell me to lie down. One look at my pillow and my eyes burned with tiredness again. Every inch of me ached from sleeping upright in the armchair, and I felt heavy.

I lay down, burrowing my face into the pillow and shut my eyes. The soft duvet fell against me, the heavy weight of it helping to push the sleep on.

"Let me look after you, for once," Dan whispered close to my ear. He pressed a kiss to my forehead before retreating. I didn't have long to wonder why those words left a pang in my chest. I was out like a light.

※

I woke to the muffled sound of Phoebe crying in the next room. The clock on the bedside table said it was just after 8AM.

Definitely time to get up.

Stopping in the open doorway, I leaned against the frame, my breath hitching in my throat. Dan cuddled Phoebe in his lap. He wore his clothes from yesterday, which were at least now clean, but he still looked rumpled. His head was bent low, whispering to her as he rocked her. Her sobs lessened with every passing second.

My kid hated being sick and she hated missing nursery even more. I'm not sure where she got the outgoing genes because it definitely wasn't from me. I'd happily go days without seeing other people, and I'd always been that way. At this moment, she would want nothing more than to get dressed and go play with her friends.

"How's her fever?" I asked Dan, my throat tight with emotion.

He glanced up at me, concern in his eyes but not panic. Compared to last night, it was a huge step forward. And I appreciated it. Handling her when she was ill had always been difficult. Everything else usually had to stop. Not because she demanded all of my attention but because I forced it all on her.

What? I didn't enjoy feeling helpless.

"I don't know," Dan whispered, his hand pressed to her forehead. "She doesn't feel as hot as yesterday, but it's not…"

I nodded, relief sinking into my bones.

If it hadn't have started coming down, we would have been hospital-bound. She liked that even less than being stuck at home with me.

Dan's gaze caressed my skin as he assessed me. It wasn't heated — considering my hair was a matted mess and my skin probably an unsightly shade of white, it couldn't be. No, this was the concerned look of a man who knew me far too well.

"How are you feeling?"

I shrugged. "Fine. Nothing a shower won't fix."

"Then go shower, and I'll make you some breakfast."

Surprise made me straighten up. "You don't have to do that."

"I want to." His smile was tight as his focus dropped back to Phoebe. "I'll set her up on the sofa first?" It was a question but not. There was no real uncertainty on his face or in his voice.

Could it actually be this easy?

I'd always thought it would be hard, slotting into someone else's life again, especially as an adult with responsibilities and so many habits, both good and bad. But the way he handled my baby and tried to take worries from me, he made it feel like it could be easy.

The question was whether I believed it. And whether or not it would last.

Dan stood, lifting Phoebe with ease. He approached me, his face soft.

"I'll grab her duvet and pillow for you." I jumped out of his way, rushing to the bed and gathering all the fabric up in my arms.

He lay her down on the smaller sofa and I handed over her pillow, then the duvet. Our gazes caught and our hands brushed as he accepted them. It was all so… domestic. And terrifying.

"Could you lower the blinds?" I asked, backing away, my eyes skittering around the room, avoiding him. "The sun will wake her up as soon as it rounds the building."

He nodded and moved to do just that. I didn't wait—I escaped to the shower while his back was turned.

※

Work had been crazy busy all morning, and I'd barely moved from the breakfast bar, barely said two words to Dan. But then he'd mostly stayed out of my way. He'd spent most of the morning sitting on the sofa, watching Phoebe. I'm not sure she noticed him. Her despondent eyes were fixed on the TV.

Yes, I caved. I always did when she's sick. It had been the only thing to make me feel slightly better about being stuck on the sofa when I was a kid. Plus, I didn't have it in me to deny her when it was my fault she suffered from tonsillitis in the first place.

A steaming plate slid across the counter towards me, jolting me from my thoughts. I looked from the plate of wonderfully fragrant curry to Dan.

"When did you learn to cook?" I asked, unable to keep the wonder from my voice.

"About two years ago." He scrubbed his hand across his beard, his expression turning sheepish. "I got a bit tired of takeout and ready meals."

I nodded as he handed me a fork.

"Thank you, but you didn't have to." I dug into the curry all the same.

"You haven't drunk water in two hours," he said, disbelief colouring his words. "Why would I trust you to eat lunch?"

He wasn't wrong. I tilted my head, conceding defeat.

"Is it always like this for you?" he asked, genuine curiosity blanketing his features.

I glanced up from my plate, pausing in my efforts to devour the food without moaning. Jeez, he really had learnt to cook.

My brow furrowed as I tried to figure out his meaning. Phoebe, work, food. He could have been referring to any of them.

"Is work always so busy you forget to get up and move? Or even hydrate," he said, reading the confusion on my face.

"Pretty much." I shrugged, it was just normal for me these days. "Some days are worse than others. "I'm trying to get ahead on a couple of campaigns, but the existing ones keep catching snags."

He frowned. "What does that mean?"

"Depends on the situation. Sometimes, it's an influencer going off the deep end and needing removing from the campaign with as little input from the client as possible." I shovelled another forkful of curry into my mouth and chewed, biting back the groan on the tip of my tongue. Swallowing, I continued, "Others are simpler—tweaks to language, altering graphics that aren't performing, adding unexpected strings to the whole campaign." I shrugged, enjoying the way his eyes remained fixed on my face, his interest clear as day in those green depths.

Dan's gaze jumped to Phoebe, her attention rapt on the TV and the colourful cartoon playing. Something akin to admiration flickered across his face when he glanced back at me.

He shook his head, the admiration quickly replaced by guilt. I frowned.

"How did you do this on your own for so long?"

To anyone else, he'd look no different, but I could see it. His shoulders had slumped slightly and his mouth pinched with displeasure. At himself.

I pushed my plate aside and reached across the island for his hand. Grasping it, I made sure I had all of his attention focused on me.

"I didn't tell you, Dan. There was nothing you could have done." Reminding him of that fact when we were starting to get on was maybe a bad move. I couldn't let him do it though, blame himself. "Plus, I wasn't alone. I had the girls and my mother."

He fixed me with a hard look. "Did you actually ask for help?"

Glancing away, I bit my lip. "A couple of times."

Dan tugged my hand, drawing my gaze back to his. His brow quirked, telling me he didn't believe me.

I shrugged. "When I had to."

"Why am I not surprised?" He shook his head, a wry smile curling his lips.

"Because I'm a stubborn, prideful idiot?"

He chuckled at that and the tight pressure in my chest eased.

"Yeah, that sounds about right." The amusement faded as quickly as it came. He leant towards me across the island. His green eyes caught mine. "I hate the fact you had to go through this alone, but I'm here now, so please ask for help when you need it, okay?"

I took a deep breath, dragging the air into my lungs like it would make the words easier. It wouldn't. There were women who did exactly what I did and they never failed to look perfect and coifed, never stressed by the pressures of parenthood or the job. Why couldn't I manage that?

"I won't think any less of you, Mel." Dan squeezed my hand. "You'll still be the fearless love of my life."

I smiled, despite the L-word. My chest filled with warmth,

but before I could figure out how to respond, my phone rang. It vibrated across the counter and I snatched it up just as Phoebe started moaning.

Dan glanced towards her sharply, before turning back to me.

"Take the call, I've got it."

I bit my lip for a second and considered him, the phone continuing to vibrate in my hand.

"Seriously, Mel, I've got this."

I forced the tension to drain from me and nodded. "Try and give her more Calpol and bribe her into drinking something."

"Sure thing."

He pulled the bottle from the fridge as I answered the phone. Walking calmly around the island, he chattered to Phoebe, trying to distract her.

"Everything alright, Dylan?" I asked, holding the phone to my ear while turning in my seat to watch them.

Dan crouched in front of Phoebe. His fingers smoothed over her tangled red locks. She stared back at him with a self-pitying look I'd seen on his face far too many times when he got sick or a hangover hit him. Their white faces matched so closely. And the sight of them both together, that soft, patient glint in his eyes, it caused my chest to tighten with unintelligible emotion.

The man was settling into our lives seamlessly. I just had to hope he knew what he was doing, because I wasn't sure I did.

CHAPTER FOURTEEN

It took two days for Phoebe to shake her latest bout of tonsillitis. Work were unsurprisingly sympathetic about my working from home through it, but by Friday afternoon, I was itching to get out of the flat.

I loved everything about my space. Lock me in with a sick toddler for two days, however, and it lost its soothing atmosphere.

With Phoebe at my mother's for a sleepover, I finally caved to Dan's date requests.

Dan went home to change into something nicer than a t-shirt. I took that as a hint that it was time to wash my hair and wear something hotter than leggings. For the first time since the auction two weeks ago, I got dressed up, straightened my hair, put on heels, and was ready to leave the flat.

"You look incredible," Dan said when I opened the front door at seven PM.

His eyes roamed up and down my body, the heat growing the longer he studied me. I loved that look in his eyes. I knew I looked great. The green dress skimmed my curves and my heels accentuated my legs. But it had been so long since someone appreciated me.

He wore dark jeans and a button-down shirt that pulled tight across his biceps and shoulders. It was my turn to devour him. He'd been lanky in school, gradually filling out in uni but not like this. All that muscle just made him look bigger, more man than 'boy.' Rugged, with his short beard and artfully unruly hair. The laugh-lines circling his eyes also added to the overall grown-up effect.

I'd loved him as he was back then but here and now, it was hard to tear my eyes away from him.

Dan cleared his throat as he stepped into the flat. "Was Phoebe okay going with your mam?"

"She bounced out the door." My lips curled up remembering the contrast from a few nights ago. Unlike Wednesday night, I felt calm, optimistic. I took a deep breath, enjoying the feeling. "She's fine, and they know what to do if she starts feeling unwell again."

He nodded and his features relaxed. Standing in my entryway like this, it reminded me of a first date. And then the nervous jitters made themselves known, making my breath shaky and my smile a shade on the awkward side of forced. He clocked it quickly, but he didn't comment beyond the amused twinkle that entered his green eyes.

"Shall we get going?" He held out his hand, his easy grin having a calming effect.

"In a second." I glanced back down the hall, dragging my lip between my teeth.

Once I'd gotten ready, I'd started unearthing old photo albums. Next would come organising the huge library of videos I had painstakingly saved to an external hard drive. I should probably wait until we got back, but surely he'd love it.

"I have something to show you."

Catching his hand, I tugged him down the hallway to the sound of his deep chuckles.

"What is it?" he asked, impatient as always.

"Just wait."

We turned the corner into the kitchen, and he couldn't fail to notice the baby pink photo album sat in the middle of the counter. I dropped his hand as we neared and stepped away from him. His eyes were fixed on the book with open curiosity and confusion.

I pushed it towards him. "I've taken a lot of photos over the years, but these are the ones I got printed—the best."

His gaze moved between me and the book. Beyond the curiosity, I couldn't read him. He wasn't reaching for it like I thought he would. Why was that?

"I've got a hard drive with all the others, and a bunch of videos," I said, trying to break the silence and the growing tension. The nerves came back in a rush, causing me to babble. "But I figured we didn't have long before dinner, so this would do. I caught pretty much everything."

The hush descended again and I stared at him, scrambling to figure him out.

His hand slowly landed on the book. Lifting the cover, he lowered his head, focusing on the images as he flicked through and freeing me from his intense stare.

What the hell had I done wrong here?

Dan stopped flicking through the pages, coming to rest on a picture of Phoebe at her second birthday party. She wore a huge grin, her green eyes were crazed and fixed on the massive chocolate fudge cake lit up on the table. I'd had a heck of a time cleaning her and the flat after that one.

His thumb rubbed over her achingly familiar face. The two of them looked so alike. If we compared baby pictures, I'd bet he had looked like her as a toddler. Would it be cute if I asked, or would it just upset him?

When he glanced back up at me, something had shifted. His face had darkened, emotion warred in his eyes.

"I missed so much," he whispered, a hard edge entering his voice. "So many firsts."

"There'll be loads more."

There was plenty of time for him to play the overprotective father.

"Like her fourth birthday party is a couple of weeks away." I dragged a hand through my hair. This was not going the way I planned. "If you'd like a repeat of the fudge cake incident, I'll get one."

My mind chose to remind me of the damage — brown sticky crumbs embedded in the rug and smeared over my white walls. The day I discovered Phoebe could definitely not handle sweets. She'd run around the flat like a lunatic. It had taken hours to clean everything, and I was still finding the sticky residue months later.

"But you're on clean-up duty," I said, trying to lighten the mood. It didn't work.

"It's not the fucking same, Mel!"

I jumped. "I know, but it would be a first for you," I said, choosing my words with care. "And that's what matters. She's nearly four, Dan, not eighteen. There's loads of time."

He cut me with a dark look. "And if you'd had your way, she could have been."

Okay, so he had me there.

"Her first steps, her first words, the newborn smell…" He snapped the book shut without breaking eye contact. "All gone. Pictures will never give me the experience."

How had we gone from two days of domestic bliss to this?

"It wasn't all roses and bloody sunshine, Dan. I wasn't playing happy family without you. It was hard, and I would *never* do it again."

"Never lie to me or never have another kid?"

My nostrils flared. "It's hard to lie to a person I didn't see or speak to." I shook my head at him, a heavy weight settling in my chest. "I meant I'll never have another baby alone."

"You didn't have to have the first alone."

I stepped towards him around the island, anger fuelling me. "Is that so?"

"Yes," he grounded out, staring down at me with a stubborn set to his jaw.

"Okay, let's play the hypothetical game," I snapped, stopping inches from his solid chest. I tilted my head back and narrowed my eyes. "You went back to Glasgow and actually took the call. I delivered the news. And then what?"

"We would have been together." He didn't hesitate, just made that sweeping statement like it was fact.

My brows rose. "Where exactly, Dan?"

"In Glasgow, of course."

I snorted. "Try again."

"We would have gotten a flat and figured it out."

"You're not thinking this through." I placed my hand on his chest. The muscles jumped but it did nothing to soften his features. "We were too young, we had no money. You were focusing on the music and touring every chance you got."

His jaw shifted, not backing down an inch. "We would have made it work and we wouldn't be fighting right now."

"Stop being so flipping delusional," I snapped, pushing him slightly. He didn't so much as rock back. "I was terrified. Do you think I was going to leave my mother and my best friends to be with you?"

"Why the hell not?" he roared. Shaking off my hand, he started pacing tight angry circles from the living room to the island.

"You weren't reliable."

He scoffed. "You don't know that."

I quirked a brow. "Don't I? Where were you for my first ball?"

"I had a gig."

"But you promised you'd go, didn't you?"

A shrug.

I'd locked the date into his calendar months in advance, picked out my dress and bought the tickets. It was all set up. The week rolled around, and he was nowhere to be found.

Radio silence. I'd held onto my optimism until the day of the ball, when pictures of him on a stage the night before somewhere in the north of England started to surface.

"The trip to Croatia we planned between second and third year?"

He bit his lip.

We'd booked everything — correction, I'd booked everything. The month before, he dropped me a text — *a text* — to tell me he couldn't go. The band had landed a big tour in the US.

"How about my graduation?"

Silence.

"You decided to meet some stranger in London to jam, isn't that what your text said?" I asked, my voice dry.

"It wasn't a stranger," he muttered, his gaze sharp as he stopped on the other side of the counter. "It was a label exec, who signed us, and it was pretty fucking important."

I nodded. "To you, yes. But my graduation was a first, and you made it miserable. I'll never get that day back."

His jaw shifted as guilt flickered across his face, but it was there and gone in the blink of an eye.

"What are you trying to say?"

"There was no way in hell I was going to move four hundred miles away from my support network for a man who couldn't keep the most basic of commitments."

Dan growled. "We're not talking about some event or a holiday here." He rounded the counter and came towards me again. "It would have been different with her."

Yes, Dan, remind the woman you claim to love that she wasn't enough to keep your attention, but a baby would have changed it all. Great idea!

"Do you actually think you would have been present for her second birthday party?"

His nod was sharp. "I would have, and you took that from me."

"Oh jeez." I sniggered beneath my breath. "Think back for a second, will you? Where were you that day, Dan?"

He frowned.

"You were in LA, playing the Troubadour."

I watched him, waiting for the realisation to hit.

But his anger wasn't fizzling out. He was still glaring at me, grinding his teeth.

"If you'd given me a chance, I might have —"

"No! You're still driven by the music now, but back then, you were consumed by it."

I had to put an end to this. It was bloody draining, rehashing this as if it would achieve anything. I crossed to him, getting into his personal space without hesitation and stopping with inches between us. Staring up into his eyes, I allowed all the hurt to pour out. I plastered it across my face and let him see it all.

"If I'd given you a chance, you would have left me alone with a newborn. I would have been in a foreign city with no friends, no family, and no job. It was hard enough, Dan. I don't think my life would look anything like it does right now and I'm almost certain we wouldn't be talking."

He shook his head hard, staring into my eyes without a drop of uncertainty. "That's ridiculous."

"Oh really?" I drawled, a warning in my voice. "You think I'm just a pushover you can mess around and I'll always be waiting?"

"I didn't mean it like that."

"Didn't you?" My brows climbed. "If you'd left me with Phoebe in the first year, I would have grown to hate you. We wouldn't be talking. What is ridiculous is you getting pissed at me right now for looking after our best interests."

His features didn't soften. If anything, the tension in his shoulders ramped up. How was I going to stop this?

"I showed you the photo album so I could share some of

the good memories with you." I gestured to his rigid form. "I definitely didn't want to start an argument."

He studied me for a long moment with something calculating in his eyes. I held my ground but I was tired of this.

I slid my hand into his hair and pushed myself up onto my toes. I pulled his head down towards mine, claiming his lips before he could resist.

For a second, he didn't react, didn't respond or so much as acknowledge that I was kissing him. And then he broke, tilting his head to deepen the contact. His hands caught my hips, dragging me forward until I was flush to his hard body.

It wasn't a soft, forgiving kiss. I tried to start it that way, but he quickly took over. It was hard and fast and full of pent-up emotion. I didn't wilt beneath the force of it. Instead, I gave back even more, funnelling my own frustrations and pain into it, trying to communicate the years of heartache he'd caused me.

His hand dragged down my back while his other hand gripped the back of my neck and angled my head. Warmth spread through my body at the contact. So what if it was rabid?

CHAPTER FIFTEEN

Our hands roamed, mine slipping under his shirt while his dragged down my body and grabbing my ass. The bulge of his erection pressed against my stomach, hard and demanding. My feet left the ground and I wrapped my legs around his waist, gasping at the press of him against my aching core.

The moment he put me down on the island, I went to work on his shirt buttons, desperate for unfettered access to all that glorious skin. The counter was freezing beneath me, but it stood no chance against the inferno he was stoking. He wasted no time, tearing my leggings and underwear off. My dress was up around my waist and there wasn't so much as an inch of me that cared. It went over my head so fast the cool air hiding me was a shock, I shivered.

His lips left mine, pressing open mouth kisses along my jaw and down my neck. I squirmed as he licked, nipped and sucked on the tender skin just below my ear. My fingers tugged impatiently at his shirt. Getting it open was the easy part, getting it off wasn't so doable when his hands were pressed hard against the worktop beside my thighs.

My bra strap slipped down and his mouth followed. I

stopped caring about his shirt. Before I could register my bra falling away, his mouth was on me, sucking hard on my nipple and firing white lightning along my nerve endings. I moaned, my head falling back and my hands tunnelling into his hair, silently begging him not to stop.

Dan pulled back. He stared down at me with a dark, heated look in his eyes. His gaze dropped to his hands, pushing my legs wider. He tugged me forward, until I was on the edge of the worktop and had to lean back on my hands to stop myself falling into him. Without so much as pausing, his fingers swiped across my soaking wet core, flicking against my clit with one quick exploratory movement that had me collapsing back on the counter with a cry.

The glorious pressure disappeared, and I whimpered. I tried to sit back up but he held me in place with one firm hand on my stomach.

"Don't fucking move, Mel," he growled as the sound of his zipper rent the air, followed by the crinkle of the condom wrapper. My body clenched in painful anticipation, and I did as told.

The broad head of his cock dragged against my opening, and my breath stilled. I ached for more. His rough hands caught my thighs as he surged forward, filling me in one move. I gasped at the overwhelming pressure of it, struggling to catch my breath and adjust. He pulled back before I was ready, grazing against so many hotspots. I couldn't stop myself crying out his name as he slammed back into me, catching my clit as he bottomed out. Pleasure surged through me so fast I was useless to contribute.

Not that he needed my help.

He gritted his teeth as he pulled out. Sweat beaded on his body. There was a fire in his eyes that thrilled me, like he couldn't imagine stopping, couldn't imagine holding anyone but me. But despite all that, he looked far too in control. On his next thrust, I squeezed around him, desperate to push him over the edge as fast as he was driving me there.

"Shit," he gasped, his eyes going wide. "Don't do that."

I smirked and did it again. He released a shuddering breath and fixed me with a devious look. His pace picked up, hitting my clit with every thrust.

"Fuck, Dan, I'm…" I fell apart so fast it was embarrassing.

It was his turn to smirk as he pushed me further back on the island. "On your knees," he demanded, slapping my thigh lightly.

"I'll get on that once my body reforms." My eyes fell shut as I focused on just breathing.

My eyes flew open as his hands tucked under me, simultaneously turning me and making room for himself on the surface.

"I said on your knees," he growled, climbing up onto the island. Glass shattered against the kitchen floor and we both froze, frowning.

My vase lay in shards on the tile, water pooled around them while the flowers just looked sad and limp from the fall. *Oh well.*

Muttered a quick "sorry," as he helped me onto my knees. His fingers dug into my flesh while his knees forced mine further apart. He pressed into me slowly this time, testing the angle while I braced myself with every last ounce of energy I could muster.

"Please don't push me off the counter," I whispered beneath my breath.

He chuckled, hearing me. "I'd catch you before you hit the ground."

I gasped again as he surged into me, triggering aftershocks from the last orgasm. My core squeezed tight in response and he groaned, his grip tightening on my hips. Instead of slamming into me as I'd expected, he started slow, drawing out every single pulse of pleasure sweeping through me and keeping me perpetually on the edge of all-consuming bliss. Keeping myself upright was a chore. My body shook, and my eyes wanted nothing more than to roll back into my head. It was intense and I *needed* more. I pushed back against him, urging him on, but he stilled me fast.

"Dan, please, I can't take any more," I whimpered, lowering to my elbows.

He blew out a harsh breath as the angle deepened our contact. For a couple of moments, he lost control, pounding into me, building the pressure until I was gasping, right on the edge.

His frantic movements slowed, and I growled his name.

He chuckled, caressing the skin of my hip. "Promise me something, and I'll give you what you want."

"Anything." The word flew out of my mouth with very little thought.

"We're done keeping secrets from each other."

Beyond Phoebe, I had never kept things from him.

"Promise me you'll be honest with me from now on, Mel." His fingers tightened again, dragging me up and down his length with deliberate, torturous movements.

"I promise," I gasped. There was no need to think about it. It's what I intended anyway.

His grunt of satisfaction vibrated through me, making every inch of me tense. He powered into me so fast and hard my knees slid along the counter with each move. His grip tightened on my waist, holding me in place, driving me closer and closer to my breaking point. Fingers pressed against my clit, shattering the last of my control.

"Fuck," Dan growled as he broke, surging against me.

Spent, I slid down on to the counter and rested my head in the pillow of my arms. *Who cares if it's freezing?* I'd have to be capable of feeling it to begin with, and my body was busy going up in flames.

Dan lay down on the counter next to me, his breath

coming in shuddering gasps. I rolled over, my shoulder brushing against his as I flung an arm over my eyes. *Breathe. In. Out.* He turned on his side, tugging me into him until he could bury his face in my neck.

"So much for dinner," I joked, almost wheezing.

Dan sniggered, the noise muffled by my skin. I dropped my arm as he lifted his head. Mirth shone in their depths, easing the last of the tension. "Didn't I tell you that part of the plan?"

I grinned. What an idiot.

"I'm never going to be able to look at my kitchen the same again." I'd need to seriously deep clean before I cooked anything.

He took in the scene we'd created.

"Shit!" He straightened. "I'm sorry about your vase."

I sat up and shrugged. "It's fine. It was cheap anyway."

He gripped the back of his neck, frowning down at the mess. "I still should have been careful."

Thanks to our rush, he was still fully dressed and his feet were safe from the shards littering the floor.

"There's a dust pan and hoover in that cupboard." I pointed towards my tall utility cupboard at the edge of the kitchen area. I eyed the small pool of water spreading across the floor. "You'll probably need a mop too."

"Okay, just don't move." His fingers glided across my naked calf as he turned away.

It was an innocent touch, but it apparently didn't take much to relight the fire.

He sprang into action while keeping a watchful eye on me.

Tension seeped into him as he cleaned. He kept giving me side-eye when he didn't think I was looking. There was a question on the tip of his tongue, I could see it in his pursed lips and rigid back. If he was struggling to ask, it couldn't be good. I braced myself for the worst.

"If you could go back and do it again, would you do it differently?"

I'm not sure what I was expecting, but that wasn't it.

I stared at him, wishing I could give him what he wanted. But I couldn't. Had I lived the last four years with him running off to pursue his career, leaving me behind without a second thought... it would have destroyed me. I wasn't an optimistic ray of sunshine right now, but I wasn't drowning, either. I'd built a good life for us.

I cleared my throat, shaking my head reluctantly. "I don't want to hate you in any version of our lives."

Those words smoothed some of the hard edges from his face, but he didn't relax. He glanced down at the floor, trying to hide the flash of pain from me.

"You don't trust me," he whispered, setting the mop aside and picking up the wireless hoover. Anything to avoid eye contact.

Why did he have to ask loaded questions when I couldn't reach him? "Not yet, but we'll work on it."

His brow quirked, the disbelief clear in his eyes.

"Not *yet*," I repeated, enunciating the words with care. "If you keep showing up, the day will come."

He pressed his lips together, displeased with the answer. I thought it was pretty giving of me. Impatient sod.

"What do I have to do to get to that point?"

The hoover dangled from his hand, forgotten as he waited for my reply.

"Don't mess up."

He frowned. "How the hell am I supposed to do that?"

He wouldn't like the answer one bit but there was no other way. I wouldn't accept anything less.

"By putting us first."

He nodded, his expression vacant, absorbed in thought. The hoover clicked on and he scoured every inch of the kitchen and living room for shards. The fact he was so thorough without my having to ask gave me hope. Maybe there was a chance for us yet.

My stomach flipped at the thought.

I was going to be so disappointed if it failed, but I couldn't hold back anymore. I didn't want to.

When the floor was clean and safe, he returned to me, his face set in neutral lines.

"I have a vague plan. Do you want to hear it?" He returned without hesitation, leaning towards me. His hands rested on the counter beside my thighs, tantalisingly close.

My breath caught in my throat. Every inch of me tensed at his nearness.

I nodded, unsure of my voice.

"First, we order food."

I released the breath. That I could do.

"Next, we fuck until neither of us can keep our eyes open," he whispered, his voice low and full of promise. My sex ached at his words, and I shifted on the counter, trying to ease it. Smirking, he continued, "Then, I'm going to spend every waking moment proving to you that things have changed."

Could it be that easy?

"How does that sound?"

I cleared my throat. "Perfect."

His smile lit up his face, right before he threw me over his shoulder and strode into my bedroom. I was a giggling mess when I hit the mattress but the amusement soon fizzled out as he got started on point two.

CHAPTER SIXTEEN

"If you keep cooking for me, you'll never be allowed to leave," I said the next morning, wandering into my kitchen.

Dan stood at the stove, shirtless, flipping pancakes with finesse.

"Maybe that's part of my master plan."

I wrapped my arms around his waist and pressed a kiss to his shoulder blade. "This is the second time now and you haven't burnt a thing."

Chuckling, he turned away from the stove and tucked me into his side. "It's been years since I burnt the casserole at your mam's. You have to let it go someday."

I pursed my lips. "Pretty sure you destroyed more than a casserole." I rested my chin on his pec and grinned up at him. "If I remember correctly, you were banned from the kitchen for every single Sunday dinner after you burnt the gravy too."

"It's liquid. I have no idea how you burn gravy," he scoffed, the amused twinkle in his eye softening his words.

"My mother doesn't agree with you." I patted him on the chest, my eyes dropping to the bubbling pancake in the skillet.

He slipped the spatula under the drying batter and flipped it. Perfectly golden on the bottom. "If Phoebe sees you flipping pancakes like that, you definitely won't be allowed to leave."

I nabbed a pancake from the prepared stack and stepped away. He shook his head at my impatience while I pulled out a stool and settled in for the show. I drank him in. The rising sun caressed his naked back and set his auburn hair on fire. He hummed happily to himself as he worked through the last of the batter. He really was something. How I'd gone five years without him was beyond me.

"When does your mother normally drop Phoebe off?" He placed the stack of pancakes on the island and turned back to grab plates, cutlery and drinks for us. I wasn't lying when I said he'd never be allowed to leave. A girl could get used to this.

"Around six, but I have to meet the girls at one." We had the entire morning to ourselves. What a novelty.

He grinned at me. "What shall we do with ourselves?"

I eyed him. "I can't tell if you're genuinely asking or if you're going to drag me back to bed."

"I'm never going to get enough of you." He reached for my hand across the worktop we'd fucked on last night. My eyes stuck on his huge hand engulfing mine. *Has he cleaned the counter?* "But right now, I feel like we should get out of this flat and enjoy the morning, just us two."

"Do you have anything in mind?" I asked, distracted as I tried to figure out if the island looked shiny because of the surface and the sun or because he'd wiped it over. I really couldn't tell.

"We could go ice skating." He tugged on my hand, pulling my attention back to him. "You never did answer my text asking if you'd been, and the rink is still open, so we could…"

"That sounds great." I nodded before my eyes fell back to the counter. "You did clean the island this morning, right?"

Silence met my question and I glanced back at him.

"Having trouble concentrating, remembering what we did here last night?" His voice dropped, the gravelly edges vibrating through me with little effort. My eyes fell shut and I shivered. "You need to stop with that look. I've no issue destroying breakfast."

My eyes popped open to find his green gaze fixed hungrily on my lips. "You can't possibly want…" my voice trailed off as he quirked a brow at me. Okay, so yes, he could. I swallowed hard and glanced away. "Ice skating sounds great. I haven't been since before Phoebe."

He squeezed my hand, but I refused to meet his gaze. I didn't want to see the sympathy or the pain there. We were having a nice breakfast, and all I was going to do was enjoy it. The past could stay far far away.

His fingers rubbed circles into the back of my hand while we ate. They were feather light but his rough fingertips against my already sensitised skin… oh my, did they captivate all of my attention. By the time I'd cleared two pancakes, I was squirming where I sat.

The sound of his stool scratching against the tile drew my head up. His eyes were on fire as he walked around the island with a determined set to his face.

"What — what are you doing?"

His hands slotted under me, lifting me from my seat. "Dan, what are you doing?" I asked again as my arms wrapped around his neck.

"First I'm going to fuck you in the shower," he said, his voice even deeper than before. My core squeezed tight at the promise on his face. "Then we're going to go have some fun on the ice and try not to break my wrist again."

My lips curled up at the reminder. "That'd be best. Ryan might murder me."

"He might." Dan nodded, his gaze fixed on me. "But I'd

still strap on a pair of blades to see your eyes light up under the rink lights."

"You say the sweetest things."

He lowered me to the bathroom counter, his eyes smouldering as he pressed his forehead to mine. "I'll say some more if you lose that robe."

I didn't need to be asked twice.

※

"Can you stop doing that?" Dan demanded as I circled him again.

"What?"

He scowled. "You know what, you teasing minx. Stop with the spinning."

"But it's fun."

"You're making me dizzy."

"Oh, fine." I chuckled, falling into line beside him as we rounded the rink again.

"Why is it you're still a natural on ice, while I can't keep my balance for more than a couple of minutes?"

I pursed my lips as I turned on the edge of my blade to face him. Skating backwards, I made a show of scanning every inch of him from head to toe.

"I have no idea," I drawled, a teasing smile begging to destroy the effect.

"Half the ice hockey team are six foot or above, and you don't see them falling on their asses."

"They practice for who knows how many hours a day." I shrugged, enjoying the feel of the cool ice arena air on my skin and the burn in my thighs as I worked to propel myself backwards. "Babe, you're a musician. Bending your knees isn't exactly second nature."

"I know," he grumbled, pulling the most adorable pout. I might have seen it on Phoebe's face once or twice. "I would just like to not feel like I was in danger of injuring myself every time I bring you here."

My grin softened. "You don't have to bring me skating. We can do other things together." I turned again until I was gliding along besides him. I took his hand slowly, careful not to upset the delicate balance he'd managed to find. "If the risk is too much, we can stick to dry land-based activities."

"No. It was a fluke. It won't happen again." He picked up speed, determination fixed on his face.

"Okay but be careful when you bend for —"

He hid the ice with a grunt, landing on his ass instead of his hands, thankfully.

"Okay, that was an improvement."

Dan glared up at me.

"What? It was." My voice echoed around the busy arena. "You fell like I told you to. No broken bones."

"My ass doesn't agree with your assessment."

I grinned. "Now you need to remember how to get back up."

Grumbling, he shuffled onto his knees and gingerly placed a blade on the ice. It slid straight out from under him. I watched as he tried again. One of the hockey skaters wearing a staff jersey stopped behind him, waiting to see if he needed to step in. This time, Dan powered back to his feet. The steward nodded to me and took off around the rink at speed. My hair ruffled as he blew past.

"Show-off," he muttered, glaring after the guy with obvious envy.

I bit my lip and held out my hand. "So does this mean you won't be helping me corral Phoebe at Winter Wonderland?" I asked as he twined our fingers together.

Fear widened his eyes. "Has she been on the ice?"

I nodded, somehow holding back my grin.

Dan groaned. "Am I going to be the odd one out in this family?"

The word struck a shiver of pleasure through me. "Nothing some practice won't fix."

He fixed me with a deadpan look. "Are you forgetting the number of Saturdays I spent in this place with you? No, practice is definitely not going to help."

"You didn't *have* to spend all those weekends here."

"Then I'd have lost a day a week with you." He squeezed my hand until I met his soft gaze. "It was worth every bruise."

"You still would have seen me six days a week." My chuckle faded fast as I stared up at his serious face. "But I definitely loved that time with you. It was very memorable." I pressed my lips together to suppress the grin trying to overtake my face. Grinning would not make him happy.

"Right," he drawled, his eyes shining with laughter. It faded fast as he caught sight of the clock on the score board. "Shit. I'm going to be late."

I glanced from the time to him, confusion creasing my face. "Why? I thought we had the morning."

"I have to see my mother."

"Have to?"

"Yeah, standing date." He scrubbed a hand across his face. "I was having fun."

I snorted. "Liar."

"Alright, I was enjoying you." The light evaporated from his features and my heart hurt at its loss. "But I really do need to get going."

"That's fine." I nodded, guiding him across the centre of the ice to the exit.

I twisted as we approached, stopping myself before I could crash into the boards. Dan wasn't so lucky. He turned as he slammed into it, catching the edge of the glass to keep himself upright.

"One day, you're going to let me teach you how to stop." I eyed him as he stepped off the ice.

"You already tried, babe. I fell every single time."

He took a seat on the bench and started unravelling his laces while I grabbed our stuff from the locker.

"Yes, but that's why you need practice. You repeat until you don't fall."

Dan shot me a drool look as he tugged the first skate off. "Have we forgotten that I need my hands operational?"

"Yes, I know it's hard to play bass without your fingers working."

He leaned towards me. His lips caressed my hair as he whispered, "I was thinking more about you falling apart around my fingers last night."

My sex throbbed at the reminder and heat crept up my face. "Dan," I hissed, turning into him. "Don't say things like that in public."

"Why?" He pulled back, grinning. "No one can hear us."

"That's so not the point."

His eyes flashed hot as he tucked my hair behind my ear and leaned in again. "You're hot when you're flustered, babe."

Despite myself, I leaned into him. His breath tickled against my neck, setting me on edge far too quickly.

"Don't you need to get to your mother's?" I half gasped as he pressed a kiss beneath my ear.

He hummed. "Don't remind me."

"She already hates me. Let's not give her another reason." I stood, trying to shake of the desire he'd unleashed with such simple words.

"She doesn't hate you."

My brows shot into my hair. "She has a funny way of showing it."

"I take it you aren't coming with me?"

"No. The less time I spend with that woman the better for us." I shuddered at the thought of subjecting myself to her snide comments again. The day would come, but I needed to be mentally prepared. I needed to have Phoebe wrapped up in a bloody soundproof bubble first.

She'd once accused me of being nothing but a distraction, and the reason Dan got a B in his English A level. Let's just say it was the nicest accusation to fall from her lips.

"That's going to be kind of hard, considering she's Phoebe's grandmother." He turned his back on me, placing his skates on the bar for return. The way he said it was casual but I could see the tension radiating through his shoulders.

"I'm not saying she can't have a role in Phoebe's life." I crossed my arms, guarding against the memory of her shrewd mean eyes. "She just needs a personality transplant before she's allowed within twenty feet of my baby."

Dan turned back to me with a frown. "What does that mean?"

"How the hell can you ask that?" I demanded, lowering my voice as we marched out of the rink. "Do you not remember the horrid things she used to say to me? The cutting way she used to look at Freya?"

"She's been fine with me since I got back." Confusion blanketed his features and I tutted.

"Dan, you're her favourite. Of course she's been on her best behaviour."

"That doesn't mean she'd act that way with Phoebe."

I caught his hand and stopped outside the rink. He stared down at me, confusion still clouding his eyes. "I'm asking you to take it slow, Dan. Phoebe is young and impressionable and I don't want someone whispering nasty crap in her ears."

"My mother wouldn't do that."

"What the hell do you call what she did to me?" I asked, my tone sharp. "Just healthy conversation?"

"Fuck. I know, I'm sorry." He dragged a hand down his face. "It's just hard to deal with. I don't know how to handle it."

"Hey, look at me." I tugged at his hand, uncovering his eyes. He stared down at me with uncertainty. "You don't need to handle it right now. I'm just saying it's something we need to watch out for, so if I refuse to go see her, it's not me refusing to do things with you. I'm protecting myself and Phoebe."

His fingers caressed my cheek. "Okay, we'll take it slowly."

"Sounds like a plan."

He pressed his lips to mine in a brief kiss and groaned. "I guess I better go face the music."

CHAPTER SEVENTEEN

"I thought you had practice today," I said when I spotted Dan standing outside my building on Sunday afternoon, after I'd let Phoebe run riot around the local park.

He'd left us last night at my insistence. I wasn't ready to explain the change to Phoebe. Seeing him now, looking so delicious, made me regret that decision. He looked incredible, even if he only wore jeans and an old band shirt. The worn fabric hugged every muscle lovingly. The way my tongue wanted to after Friday night.

"Finished early."

Dan caught Phoebe as she launched herself at him, tugging me forward until I fell off balance. Apparently her harness worked both ways. His arm snaked around my waist, catching me before I could fall headfirst into the box shrubbery surrounding the flat.

"Now, this I could get used to," Dan whispered. His smile was blinding and smug, but oh, how I wished it would never leave.

I chuckled, patting his hard chest. "You may have to."

He sobered, staring into my eyes with weighted meaning. "There's no 'may' about it."

"Kiss," Phoebe shouted, clapping her hands and making us both jolt.

Dan held her in one arm and she leaned against his chest.

"We're married now. Kiss."

"Phoebe." I groaned. My head dropped forward until my face pressed against his shirt. Dan sniggered.

"We're not married, munchkin," Dan said, an equal mix of patience and amusement dripping from his words.

"So you lied to me?" she asked, the incredulity clear in her voice. I didn't need to lift my head to see her quirked brow. The kid had disdain down to an art.

Silence followed her question, and I took it as my cue to get moving. Regretfully, I stepped out of Dan's grasp and fixed my daughter with my own no nonsense look.

"How about we finish this upstairs?"

I didn't wait for a response. Instead, I opened the door and led them into the elevator. Phoebe chattered incessantly on the way up about anything and everything. Dan took it all in his stride, despite the curveball about lying. I wasn't sure how to solve that one. Hope she forgot?

When we got into the flat, she wriggled against Dan, demanding to be put down. He lowered her but it wasn't fast enough for her.

"I'm not glass, Daddy," Phoebe muttered. "Put me down."

I snorted. Dan shot me a dark look.

Phoebe raced into the living room, her question completely forgotten in favour of toys. I guess that solved that for now.

"She's got too much of you in her," Dan said, following me into the kitchen. It was my turn to shoot him a dark look.

"What's that supposed to mean?"

Dan held up his hands in apology, his eyes widening. I turned away, intent on making tea. Or doing something equally consuming with my hands other than shaking him. Too much of me. As if.

"She's feisty is all I meant." Dan turned me towards him. His eyes were soft with apology but he wasn't done. "She looks so much like me, and then she says something like that or lays you out with a sardonic look." Wonder painted his features, his lips curled at the edges and moisture shone in his eyes as he considered it. I was rapt. "She's incredible. Like you."

I leaned into his chest. "Keep talking."

❈

An hour later, we'd had tea, and Phoebe had managed to trash the living room. Toys lay strewn across the floor yet again.

"Put your toys away, Phoebs," I ordered, my tone stern and unyielding. She glanced up at me with pursed lips. "Now. We're going to the shop."

"Biscuits?"

I rolled my eyes. "If you put your toys away, I'll buy a packet of bourbons."

She scrambled off the floor and started throwing toys into boxes. The noise level increased but at least I wouldn't be in danger of stepping on a pony when we got home.

"Something funny?" I asked when Dan chuckled softly next to me.

He shrugged. "Neither I nor Freya needed that much bribery."

Freya was his sister. She was four years younger than him and had escaped Wales not long after him. Only she refused to return under any circumstance. The pair of them were like night and day. Freya with her poker straight blonde hair and serious demeanour and Dan with his auburn curls and cheery disposition.

I narrowed my eyes. "Is this another jab at her personality being all me?"

He pressed his lips together, refusing to answer, but his eyes gave him away. They shone with mirth.

"Because if it is, need I remind you that you want access to my bed?" I whispered, lowering my voice so Phoebe definitely wouldn't hear us.

"Punished for speaking the truth." He shook his head in mock sadness, amusement creasing his eyes. "What is the world coming to?"

I grinned at him. "My house, my rules."

He nodded, all serious — it was a front, but one I was enjoying. Before I could call him on it, Phoebe cried out.

"Are you okay, Phoebs?" Dan asked, shooting around the island. His long strides ate up the open floor space until he scooped our sobbing toddler off the ground. "What happened?"

She sniffled into his neck but didn't answer.

"Where does it hurt?" Dan met my gaze. Panic stared back at me.

"She'll be fine." The words were for him more than me. I'd seen far worse than a fall on the living room floor.

I skimmed my hands along her legs and feet while Dan held her against his chest. His body was rigid yet his hands were gentle where they cradled her. This man.

She whimpered as my fingers passed over her right heel. She'd probably trodden on one of her toys. I'd gotten far too familiar with her ponies in the last year. They'd wrung a number of late-night expletives from me. The culprit sat at Dan's feet, innocently pink and white.

"Can I see?" I smoothed my hand over her short hair.

"Is it bad?" Dan asked, concern tightening his features.

I shook my head, but his question set Phoebe off even louder. He had the sense to look sheepish when I glared at him.

There was a red mark on her foot but not a lot else. I rubbed my thumb over the spot and she quieted. She lifted her head before turning to face me, her eyes red and puffy but dry.

"Is that better?"

With her lip caught between her teeth, she didn't look so sure, but she nodded.

"Have we learnt our lesson about leaving toys on the floor?" I asked, my brows risen.

"Yes," she whined before burying her head in Dan's neck again.

"Good. Ready to go to the shop?"

When she turned back to me this time, her eyes lit up with excitement. She wriggled to escape Dan's hold and nearly landed on the pony again.

"Careful." Dan guided her away from the plastic torture device.

"Sorry," she mumbled, dodging the pony and skipping past me.

"Phoebe, have you forgotten something?" I called after her, turning to watch her progress.

She stopped at the kitchen counter and turned on her heel. She returned to us with a pout but dutifully picked up the pony and dropped it in the toy box. I could only dream that it would stay there.

"Good. Now, go grab your shoes and we'll get going."

Phoebe stomped away, leaving me to deal with Dan. He looked kind of annoyed. With himself, I hoped.

"I overreacted, didn't I?" he asked like he already knew the answer.

"Just a bit." I shrugged. "I was the same. You'll figure it out."

He scrubbed a hand down his face. "And if I don't, she'll play me."

"Don't be naive." I snorted, patting him on the shoulder in mock sympathy. "She's already playing you."

He growled. "Not helpful."

"Yes, it is." I turned my back on him and followed Phoebe.

"Explain," he said, chasing after me.

I spun on my heel to face him, not bothering to hide my glee. "She's too busy playing you to try it on me anymore."

His eyes widened. "Son of a —"

I cut him off with a look.

❋

I'd expected shopping with Dan to be hard for some reason, but we hadn't even entered the shop yet and he was already surprising me.

"What?" he asked in response to my bewildered expression.

My eyes fell to the trolley. It had a child seat built in. So why was I surprised? I hadn't asked for it. We hadn't discussed the practicalities of shopping with a speedy toddler. He just did it.

I shook my head. "Nothing."

"Okay then," he drawled, eying me like I had two heads. I couldn't blame him, I'd be giving myself side-eye too. "Shall I grab Phoebe while you get the bags?"

My brows drew tight. How did he…

Nodding, I put a pin in the thought and moved around to the boot of the car.

"I don't need that," Phoebe said when Dan helped her out of the car and tried to place her in the trolley.

"Is that so?" Dan asked, humouring her but not caving against her wriggling body.

She nodded hard. "Yes. I'm a big girl."

"And big girls don't ride in trolleys?"

Phoebe shook her head. "No. We walk." She wriggled

again, trying to catch him off guard. Thankfully it didn't work.

Bags in hand, I leaned against the open boot and watched them. I could see the cogs working, I just had no clue where he was going with this. It was… fascinating.

Dan frowned. "That's too bad. I loved riding around in these."

Her eyes narrowed. "You lie."

"Nope." He patted the handle bars. "Best fun I had at your age."

"Really?" she asked, slow and unsure.

"Yes." He tried to set her down in the seat but she resisted, pressing her feet against the seat. "Trust me, munchkin. You'll have fun."

She pursed her lips. "Shopping is never fun."

"Tough crowd." Dan chuckled before leaning down to stare Phoebe in the eye. "Stick with me, kid. That's about to change."

Unconvinced, she sank into the seat. Kicking her feet against the metal frame, she stared up at Dan. Her expression dared him to prove her right.

I followed them across the car park, shaking my head at the pair of them.

❄

Phoebe squealed as Dan raced the trolley down an empty aisle. I rolled my eyes and turned back to the pasta. I spent my days telling her not to run. I should probably be annoyed that Dan was degrading all that training, but the look on his face. It made my chest ache in the sweetest way.

"Again," demanded Phoebe, her voice high pitched. She clapped her hands, drawing my attention back to her. "Again, again, again."

Dan chuckled before glancing back at me in the middle of the aisle. His brows rose in question, waiting for me to stop him. I shook my head, a smile playing at my lips that he wouldn't fail to notice.

The damn man was winning and I didn't have any resistance left to fight him. Truthfully, I didn't want to.

Taking my silence as agreement, he raced her back down the aisle towards me.

"Whee," Phoebe screamed.

They skidded to a halt next to me. Dan's eyes shone as brightly as Phoebe's.

"Having fun?" I asked, dropping a package of pasta into the trolley.

He grinned. "I don't know." He leaned down until he was at Phoebe's level. "Are we having fun?"

"Yes," she yelled. "Again." The metal of the trolley rattled with her foot slamming back against the frame.

Dan glanced at me from the corner of his eye. It was sly, making me both suspicious and in danger of losing my heart.

"Maybe in a little bit," Dan said.

Phoebe pouted in fully expected fashion.

"There are too many people around now." With a finger beneath her chin, he lifted her gaze to his. "Okay, munchkin?"

She sighed. "Fine."

I bit my lip, struggling to contain the laughter.

"Where next?" Dan straightened, turning his attention on me.

I'd never seen him so carefree. Even when we were kids. He was always trying to look after one person or another. Me, his sister, his mother. With Phoebe, he seemed to shake off some of that pressure. I hoped it never ended.

CHAPTER EIGHTEEN

"Nanny!" Phoebe shouted, distracting me from the scrolling through my mental to do list of all the things I still needed to get done tonight.

Someday it would get easier.

And if I kept telling myself that, maybe I'd believe it one day.

Phoebe's feet slammed against the back of my chair, and I didn't need to glance in the rear-view mirror to know she was struggling with her seat belt.

"Look, Mammy, it's Nanny."

"Yes, I see her."

My mother was waiting for us when I parked the car in the carpark beneath our building. She was leaning against her four-wheel drive and straightened up when I shut the engine off. Phoebe mercifully stopped singing the sea shanty the nursery had decided to teach them today. It was probably going to be stuck on a loop in my head for the next few days.

"Nanny, I made slime," Phoebe called through the open car window. "Wanna see?"

"Not again? Maybe we should save it for the weekend,

cariad," my mother said, a perfect yet awkward smile plastered to her lips while concern pinched her brows.

"Good choice." I chuckled, throwing the car door open.

Phoebe unbuckled herself and jumped through the space between the front seats. She scrambled out of the car and into my mother's arms at record speed.

"Phoebe, we've talked about this." I shook my head as I locked up the car, closing her window in the process. "You need to wait."

She ignored me, too busy leading my mother towards the elevators and filling her in on all the gooey details of her experiment. My mother, on the other hand, heard me clear as day, and her lips twitched.

By the time I got upstairs after collecting all mine and Phoebe's things from the boot, my mother had the kettle on, and Phoebe was on a rampage.

"Mam, have you seen my doll?"

A pony went flying over her shoulder as she searched the boxes.

"Didn't you take it to daycare, munchkin?"

I placed our bags on the floor and unzipped her backpack. It didn't take much riffling to determine that there was definitely not a beat-up doll in there. Phoebe stood over me, chewing her lip. Somehow, I needed to tell her she'd forgotten it and avoid a tantrum. *Easy.*

My mother watched me with a sympathetic light in her eyes. "Phoebs, why don't we have some tea while your mam looks for it?"

She edged towards my mother slowly, her green gaze fixed on me the entire time with worry. *Me too, kid.*

I got the daycare on the phone. My mother needed an extra special Christmas present for her perfect timing. There's no way I'd be avoiding a meltdown if she hadn't been here.

My shoulders almost sagged when they confirmed it was at

reception waiting for Phoebe tomorrow. Some quick sweet talking got them to let me pick it up tonight.

It was only when I hung up and Phoebe came barrelling at me again that I realised how unrealistic that plan was. I didn't have the energy to cart her back out the door, and if I went she'd insist on coming.

"Is it there? Do they have it? Can we go?" she said in a mangled rush, bouncing around my feet with far too much energy.

"Just give me a second, Phoebe." I pushed her back towards my mother and pulled out my phone. "I'm working on it."

Mel: Can you do me a huge favour? Phoebe left her doll at daycare. She's going to be a nightmare without it. Will you go grab it? They're going to hold on for half an hour.

The dots danced immediately and I sank back against the fridge door. My teeth sank into my lip, gnawing as I waited for his reply. What if he was in the studio or had plans? I couldn't really expect him to drop everything to pick up a doll.

Dan: No problem. I'm on it.

I released a shuddering breath.

Mel: Thank you. Thank you. Thank you.

Dan: I'm getting the feeling this thing is important.

Mel: You just helped me avoid Phoebe activating her nuclear button. You're my lifesaver tonight.

Dan: Glad to be of service. I'll bring it to you in about an hour. See you later, babe.

"Daddy's going to pick it up, munchkin," I called from the kitchen, still leaning against the fridge. It was the only thing keeping me upright.

Phoebe finally stopped biting her lip. Her shoulders sagged back to normal level and she nodded. "Okay. I'm going to go play," she said in a perfectly normal voice.

I frowned at her as she wandered into her bedroom. "Well, that de-escalated fast."

My mother chuckled. "You used to be like that."

I fixed her with a droll look. "Oh great, so I'm to blame for yet another problem."

"I wouldn't call it a problem." She walked towards me, amusement creasing her features. "Just entertaining."

"For you, maybe," I grumbled.

"Sit down before you fall down." She pushed a steaming mug towards me. Her amusement dried up fast as she considered me. Worry creased her brows and pinched her lips.

"I'm fine," I said before she could ask. I did as told, taking a seat at the island.

"You don't look fine," she muttered, fixing me with narrowed 'don't bullshit me' eyes. "You look like someone dumped a world of responsibilities on your shoulders."

I shrugged. It wasn't *not* true.

"It was just a difficult day at work." I picked up my tea and sipped carefully, testing the temperature.

She took a seat across from me. "I think it's more than that."

I stared into the cup and mumbled, "What if it is?"

"Then I'd offer to help. Again." She caught my hand, squeezing until I glanced up at her. "I've got more time now. There's no reason for you to do all of this alone."

"I'm not doing it alone." It sounded like a robot had taken over.

We'd had this conversation so many times. I already relied heavily on her help. She went out of town for a month, and I'd crumbled into a mess. I wasn't living with my head in the clouds. Some days, juggling my job and Phoebe alone was hard, but it was my life and I just wanted to get on with it.

But now, I had Dan.

It didn't have to be as hard as it had the last couple of years. Yes, I was feeling a little overwhelmed today, and the need to get my laptop out and check that I'd actually sent that last email was a nagging buzz in the back of my mind, but there was a light at the end of the tunnel.

"You only just retired. Enjoy it."

She shook her head, prepared for the same old argument. "I can enjoy my retirement *and* help you." Another devious glint entered her brown eyes. "In fact, I've got far too much time on my hands now. Your father is driving me insane. You'd be doing me a favour."

I stared at her, deadpan. Try it on someone else.

"What! He is," she said, her pitch raising. "If I have to hear the same piano chord one more time, I swear he'll come home to find the piano missing parts."

Amusement squeezed my face. She'd need to take parts from multiple pianos if she really wanted to silence him. He had a baby grand, an upright, and various electrics. He'd retired nearly ten years ago, due to arthritis in his hands, but he was determined to keep up his skill level.

"I could babysit another couple of nights in the week, give you a chance to date." She absently turned her mug on the worktop, her gaze fixed on me, pleading. "I could give you a hand in the mornings. Or ask your sister. Ella's on her way back from Argentina. She's going to have some free time on her hands until she decides being home isn't exciting enough."

"She's really coming home?" I hadn't seen Ella in two years. My baby sister graduated from uni and took off travelling the world.

Mam nodded, her lips quirking slightly at the excitement in my voice. "She'll be home on Wednesday."

"I can't wait to see her, but I'm not going to rope her into my chaos while she's figuring things out. Can you imagine? I'd chase her away, favourite niece or not."

"I doubt that."

"I really appreciate the offer, Mam." I sipped my tea, stalling for time to figure out how to say what I needed to without hurting her feelings. "It's probably crazy of me to deny help, but I want those moments with her."

Phoebe chose that moment to barrel into the room. She ran towards her toy box in the living room.

"Slow down," my mother and I shouted at the same time. We shared an amused look, chuckling at ourselves.

Phoebe slowed to a walk and continued into the living room. She tore the top off the box and started pawing through them.

I cleared my throat, drawing my mother's attention back to me. "If I need the extra help, if something comes up, I'll ask for it." It was a promise I intended to keep and she nodded, accepting it without argument. "I just don't want to lose that time just for the sake of a break. I'd feel like a crappy mother."

"That's understandable." She smiled. "Just remember to look after yourself."

I finished my tea and kept quiet. What did that even mean in the grand scheme of things?

Take it easy at work? Unlikely with my workload.

Take time for myself? Spending more than a day away from Phoebe filled me with so much guilt and worry. It was hardly refreshing.

No, I just needed to keep moving forward. Things would get easier eventually.

※

My mother had gone home by the time Dan knocked on my door. I'd expected him to turn up with the doll, but he had gone one step further. He pressed a kiss to my lips before brushing past me with a massive bag of deliciously scented Mexican food.

Phoebe rushed out of her room as soon as she heard Dan's voice. "Doll?"

We both laughed.

"Hi to you too, Munchkin." Dan knelt down in front of her.

"Hi. Now, doll." She held out her hand.

He handed it over with a flourish that she didn't appreciate it in the least. She took the doll from him and raced back into her room.

"Thanks for doing that." I stepped into his arms when he stood back up. A hug from this man was exactly what I needed.

"Anytime, babe." He squeezed me tight, the combination of his height and body heat settling all of the frantic energy generated from my day.

Minutes ticked by as he just held me in the hallway, rocking softly to a beat in his head. It was glorious.

"Are we going to eat or what?" Phoebe demanded, breaking the relaxing atmosphere.

We broke apart, sheepish yet contented. I just felt lighter as I followed him into the kitchen. Helping Phoebe into a chair, I couldn't help but study him, completely at home in my kitchen, in my life. With the warmth curling around my heart, I was starting to believe he'd be different, that he'd changed.

Dan allowed Phoebe to talk his ear off for an hour, smiling sweetly at me across my small dining room table while we ate. That look had nothing on the flutter in my stomach his reading to Phoebe inspired.

Now, with the hyperactive toddler down for the night, we settled on the sofa, a throw blanket covering us both as I settled into his side. Some nineties sitcom played on the TV but I couldn't care what it was. I was too busy just enjoying the feel of him holding me.

"Do you want to pick something?" Dan asked, his voice low and intimate in the darkened flat.

I glanced up at him, resting my chin on his chest. "Are you going to hassle me for my choice?"

He gasped. "I've never —"

I covered his mouth, grinning. "No lies, remember."

"I'm not lying," he muttered behind my hand.

"Oh really?" My brow rose. "Don't you remember whining all the way through Mamma Mia?"

He shook his head, removing my hand. "I don't know what you're talking about. I was the perfect boyfriend. I'd never moan about your favourite film."

My other brow rose.

"You said Sophie was a meddling piece of work."

"Oh yeah." Dan nodded, memory clouding his eyes. "I still stand behind that assessment." He grinned down at me. "In case there was any doubt, I meant the fictional *and* the real Sophie."

"Don't repeat that near her." The man had a death wish. Sophie was anything but meddling. I mean I was the one who'd sent Nia on a blind date with the guitarist from Lover's Knot.

He tutted. "Only an idiot would say something like that to her face. I value my life."

His fingers smoothed up and down my arm. On the screen, Sophie got caught out for lying to her fiancé. The flat was silent but for the TV, and we were buried under a blanket, cuddled up. *I could get used to this.*

"What are you doing tomorrow night?"

"Probably catching up on work." Like I did almost every night. "Why?"

"Have dinner with me."

I nodded. "Okay. Are we cooking or ordering in?"

"No, Mel, I don't mean here." He sat up and turned to face me. "I mean let me take you out."

Was he going to dress up again? He'd looked so hot in his dark jeans and button-down shirt, his neatly trimmed auburn beard and broad shoulders keeping him firmly on my temptation radar. It was the straightest edge I could ever expect that rock star to get.

I frowned. "I can't. Phoebe…"

"We'll get someone to babysit."

My frown didn't budge. "With less than 24 hours' notice? It's not that easy, Dan."

"Okay, but let's ask before we disregard it?"

His eyes implored me to go along with him. Sophie would have work functions and Nia would be busy with edits. I couldn't ask either of them with no notice. I texted my mother.

My jaw dropped when her reply came back.

Mam: No.

Mel: But today you said you wanted to help.

Mam: I do. If it was anyone but him.

Mel: Mam!

"What is it?" Dan asked, eyeing my phone.

"She said no." My voice was flat with shock. "I didn't think she knew the meaning of the word."

Dan slumped back against the sofa. "I told you she hates me."

"She doesn't ha — she's just not used to you being back yet."

His eyes narrowed on me. "You're saying that to make me feel better."

I hummed noncommittally and focused on my phone again. "I could ask Nia to watch Phoebe on Friday if that works?"

"Yeah that'd be great, but I'm not letting this parental disapproval thing go." He fixed me with a hard look. "She will love me again."

I snorted. "If anyone needs to moan about parental disapproval it's me. No way has your mother changed her opinion of me."

He dragged a hand across his face, groaning, while I fired off a text to Nia.

"I have no idea what the woman thinks. She's turning into my worst nightmare."

My phone pinged before I could dive into that statement.

"Nia's offering up a sleepover."

Dan's face lit up. "Sounds perfect. Phoebe'll love it."

I laughed. "Don't you mean you'll love it?"

"That too." He tapped my hands. "Now tell her yes before she changes her mind."

"But…are we actually going to leave the flat? Because if we're not, I'd like to know in advance."

No use curling my hair again if we'd be ripping each other's clothes off before I even set foot outside the flat.

He rolled his eyes. "Yes. I can keep my hands to myself." My brows rose and Dan sighed. "Fine. I'll meet you at the restaurant. Safe enough?"

CHAPTER NINETEEN

"Did you find it okay?" Dan asked as I stopped at his table in a tiny Italian restaurant in the centre of town. He stood and pressed a chaste kiss to my lips, his fingers lingering on my hip longer than appropriate for a very busy but intimate restaurant. I hadn't seen him in two days, so I couldn't care less.

I'd missed him.

So had Phoebe. It had become her new favourite question. Breakfast. Where's Daddy? Nursery pick up. Where's Daddy? Dinner. You get the picture. I refused to see it as a portent of our future, and instead focused on how cute it was that my daughter had turned into a daddy's girl so fast.

"Yeah. Although, I didn't realise until tonight that the maps app could guide you through the arcades." I sat in the chair the server pulled out and shuffled in. "I'll never get lost in the Castle Arcade again."

"Yes, you will." Dan snorted.

I glanced around the restaurant, taking in the atmosphere. I'd walked through this arcade so many times over the years, but I'd never spotted it. It had a two-window front with pretty black trim that had adorned the shops for decades. An old mahogany counter sat at the back of the room, containing a bar and the pass for the kitchen. Three rows of tables spread out from the big windows to the bar. Lantern lights hung above each table, giving off just enough light to highlight the food but leave the rest of the room in muted shadows. It had such a cosy, intimate atmosphere. It wasn't hard to understand why Dan wanted to come here.

A bottle of white wine already sat on the table. Dan started pouring me a glass before I could even comment on the fact he knew my favourite. What else had he picked up while I wasn't paying attention?

"How did you find this place?" I asked, almost whispering.

Every table was full, a mixture of families and couples. All of them talked in hushed tones, contributing to the intimate vibe of the place. I loved it.

"Ryan's girlfriend worked here in uni. She brought us when we first got back." Dan reached across the table and took my hand. "All I could think about was sharing it with you."

The soft light in his eyes made my heart sing. If I still had doubts, they melted away under that look. His grovelling helped too, of course.

"It's beautiful."

He squeezed my hand, his lips curving slightly at the edges before he ducked his head to read the menu.

"Do you still hate balsamic vinegar?" he asked, scanning the card on the table in front of him.

"You don't?" My brows climbed at the question. Neither of us had liked it growing up. Too much bite for me.

"I might have been shown the light." His voice held an uncertain quality that made my lips twitch.

"I'm not sure this will work," I said, a teasing note in my voice. I shook off his hand and sat back in my chair. "We're so different now." I broke before the last word had fallen from my lips.

He gestured to my face. "You can't even keep a straight face saying that."

"Give me a break." I picked up the glass of wine and took a sip. "Your curious child used up all my acting abilities this week."

Dan chuckled. "What did she do this time?"

"Just the insistent questions about where you are." Amusement tugged at my lips. "I think it's safe to say she loves you."

The laugher faded from Dan's face, leaving behind the raw, insecure man I'd once known.

"Thank you for that," he whispered, his voice hoarse. He took my hand again, turning it so my palm faced up. His fingers danced along my life lines, both tickling and soothing. "And what about her mother?"

My thoughts shuddered to a halt. "What about her?"

Dan bit his lip, considering me before he said, "Does she love me?"

I swallowed, hard. I didn't want to think about the L word. I was perfectly happy with our pace.

But those warm fuzzy feelings reared their head, tutting at my ill-constructed facade. It was an inescapable fact. If I didn't love him still, I wouldn't have let him get as close as he had. There wouldn't have been any temptation, and our relationship would be straightforward, nothing more than co-parents.

I wouldn't be petrified of his ability to break my heart again.

His expression softened as he took in my reaction, seeing beneath the mask to the truth I didn't want him to see.

"It's fine." He squeezed my hand, leaning forward across the table. "Sorry I haven't been around in a couple of days," Dan said, moving the conversation away from us and my uncertainty. "If you want, you could bring Phoebe to the studio one day after nursery. Show her why I'm not around?"

I agreed, just as much for myself as for Phoebe. Just the

thought of the way his fingers moved over the strings and the bulge of his biceps had me clenching my thighs together to quell the ache.

Who was I kidding with this L word panic? I was a goner.

❄

"We need a game plan," Dan announced while I dug into my pasta.

"For what?" I asked once I'd swallowed.

"To win your mother back." He stared at me without an ounce of amusement. He meant it. I put the fork down and settled in. "Madeline used to love me, she will again. I just need help."

I groaned. "Please don't say it like that."

He chuckled. "Okay, I was the son your mother never had. She can't hate me forever."

Wincing, I muttered, "Somehow, you just made it worse."

His face scrunched up in disgust. "I'm not the one who interpreted an innocent fact like that!"

Fair.

"Now seriously. Game plan."

"Just give it time."

"Mel," he whined. "I don't want it to take time. I want the smiles back now."

I laughed, my face softening as I took in his desperation. "Show her you're here to stay."

"Yes, yes, but how?"

"Be the doting boyfriend and father at Phoebe's birthday next weekend." I turned my wine glass as I got lost in thoughts of all the things *I* wanted him to do, never mind my mother. "Put smiles on our faces. Take pressure from me." I chewed my lip. "If you could stop me stressing, I think she'd forgive pretty fast."

His brow rose. "Why are you stressing?"

My smile was not a happy one. "It's hard, being a parent and working my job. It's full on and time for just quiet relaxation is limited."

"Okay, so when things are stable with the band, you could quit if you wanted."

I stared at him, unable to judge from his blank poker face if he was serious. "Dan, you don't…"

He held up his hand. "I don't mean right now or next year. Money is starting to flow more freely, and if we keep climbing the charts like we have been, I'm pretty confident it's not going to be a thing we have to worry about pretty soon." He threaded his fingers through mine, his green eyes loving as he roamed my face. "I'm just saying that the option is there if you wanted to cut down hours or quit entirely one day in the future."

How was I meant to react to an offer like that? Say thank you and nothing more, or argue why it would be a bad idea?

Because it would be a bad idea. I'd be bored out of my mind and go stir crazy. It would make our lives easier, sure. I'd be able to travel with him when he toured and any fear of him leaving me behind would evaporate. That was no real solution though. I'd just lose myself in his world, following where he went with no life of my own.

"Thank you for the suggestion, but I don't want to stop working. I just need things to calm down a little." I smiled at him, leaning back in my chair. "You're already helping with that. Just you being here has taken some of the pressure off me."

"Yeah? How so?" He leaned towards me, his elbows resting on the table as he avidly watched me.

"Well for one, Phoebe's so focused on playing you, she's forgotten to work me."

"That's not funny."

I hummed and picked up my fork. "Anyway, you'll win my mother over easily. I won't be so lucky with yours."

"I'm not so lucky there either." Dan scrubbed a hand across his bearded jaw. "If I'd figured out how to mellow her, I'm pretty sure I'd have my sister in the city."

And just like that the teasing atmosphere evaporated.

"I'm sorry, Dan. I wish I could give you advice, but I was always out of my depth with your mother."

"I know. Sometimes she's too much for me, too." His smile was small and it didn't reach his eyes. "At least you always tried."

"Yeah, for the little reward it gave me." I snorted, trying to lighten the mood. "Do you remember when I bought her a Lush box for Christmas?" I shook my head. "She acted like I was trying to poison her or something."

Dan chuckled. "That was an entertaining dinner."

"Yes, it was, but I was so glad it was all take-out. After comments about poisoning her, I'm not sure I'd trust her not to try it on me."

"It's sad that you're not the first person to say that." All amusement dried up again as his shoulders sagged. "She wasn't always like that. I remember her before dad left, you know? Yes, he wasn't the best guy, but she always managed to make sure Freya and I were happy."

My heart ached for him. It was next-level messed up to yearn for a time when his dad was shouting at them and accusing his mother of cheating on a weekly basis.

In a way, it gave me space to feel sorry for his mother, but every time I reminded myself of that, she'd bite at me. It was like she could sense it or something, striking out at some imagined weakness.

"Then he left. She became obsessed with her image." Dan's voice cracked and drained his glass of wine. "She wants the best for me, but having Freya so far away, refusing to return her calls… she thinks it reflects badly on her, and it drives her crazy."

If I had been Freya, I would have gone further than

London. I'd have run to Australia and never picked up the phone again.

"She thinks people in our town look at her like she caused it." His laugh was bitter. "She doesn't see that she *did* cause it."

"I'm sorry it didn't get better over the years."

He shrugged. "Thank you, babe, but I'm not a teenager any more. I can't fix her. All I can do is hold on for as long as I can stomach. Focus on the happy memories before they fade, you know?"

I nodded. It's what I'd been doing with my dad for years. Hope was still a living, breathing thing inside of me when it came to my dad even though I knew he would never change. Telling Dan to give up what I held on to would be hypocritical.

Plus, I seriously fucking wanted his mother to turn over a new leaf. I wanted her to play a part in Phoebe's life. If she was still the viper I remembered from my teens, trying to cut me off at the knees every time I started to feel good about myself or my life, well she wouldn't be getting within ten feet of my daughter.

❄

The waitress set a single plate of chocolate fudge cake on the table between us, giving Dan a brief smile, her eyes tracing him with barely veiled interest. I leaned back in my chair, rolling my eyes. A gesture Dan caught.

He thanked her, picked up his glass, and took a sip, his eyes never leaving mine.

When she'd given up and wandered back to the bar, he placed the glass on the table and picked up his fork.

"I'll take courage in your jealousy." He dug into the cake without pausing to wait for me.

My brows climbed. "One, I wasn't jealous." I grabbed my fork and cut into the rich chocolate sponge. "And second, what's with this single dessert business? Pretty sure I didn't agree to sharing."

Dan chuckled. "I thought it would be romantic."

"Romantic?" I scoffed, my voice rising as I battled with his fork. "Do you not remember the last time you tried to share a dessert with me?"

"I'm sure you can avoid stabbing me tonight."

I pointed my fork at him, mildly threatening him with it. "I wouldn't be so sure." I pulled the plate towards me. "The years might have mellowed me but let's not expect miracles."

"Do I need to roll up my sleeves?"

My eyes dropped to his forearms. He was teasing, but who the hell would say no to an offer like that? Not me, that was for sure.

"That would be a good start." I shook my head. "Ordering one dessert. I thought you knew me better than that," I muttered, mock disbelief dripping from my tone.

Dan slowly placed his fork on his napkin, never breaking eye contact. There was a teasing glint in his eyes still despite the serious set of his lips.

"Oh but I do know you, babe," Dan drawled. He caught and held my gaze, mesmerising me. His fingers traced featherlight along my other hand, focusing all of my attention on him. "If I'd ordered two, you'd have made yourself feel guilty for it. Now you can enjoy dessert and blame me for tempting you."

Okay, so he wasn't wrong. I might have very little control around sweets. Like zero. The fact the cookies I made with Phoebe lasted a couple of days was nothing but force of will to set a good example. I may have also made sure the batch was big enough to hide my late-night raids.

"Besides, if I'd given you the choice, you would have refused your own and then stolen mine." His brows rose, daring me to deny it. I couldn't. We'd been down this road far too many times. "Wouldn't you?"

"Thank you for ordering dessert," I said by way of concession.

I placed another forkful of the gooey goodness in my mouth. Only just holding in the moan, my eyes fluttered closed as the sweetness exploded along my taste buds. Dan's fingers tightened on my hand, drawing my attention back to him. He was staring at me with heated interest.

He leaned forward, his lips curling at the edges. "Now back to this lack of jealousy bullshit…"

Before I could answer, a shadow fell across our table.

"Oh my god, are you Dan Lloyd?" A young-looking girl asked, her eyes wide and alight with excitement.

Another girl, her complete opposite in build and colouring stood just behind her, chewing her lip like she was uncomfortable. *You and me both.*

"You are!" She slapped her friend's arm when Dan glanced up at them with a hesitant smile. "I told you it was him, Jen. We're huge fans."

"Thanks," Dan said, his voice level but not right. Every inch of him had turned fake. He kept glancing from me to the door, the waitress taking someone else's payment.

"I'm sorry to interrupt your dinner but we were wondering if we could get a selfie with you. Our other friends didn't want to come out tonight and they're going to be so jealous when we tell them." Her grin widened. "Pictures will make them even more jealous."

Dan chuckled, the sound off to my ears. "Sure, but let's take this fast. We've got plans."

The girl's ice blue eyes cut to me with an edge I really didn't like. Her face was all perfect angles, and she had the air of someone who knew she was pretty but was still too young to understand that was almost worthless. People always figured you out if you were nothing but a vindictive pretty face.

Dan pushed his chair back and stepped towards the pair

of them. He plastered a smile on his face and let them take their pictures.

When they were gone, he collapsed back into his chair with a deep exhalation. "I don't think I'm ever going to get used to that."

I tracked the girls as they returned to their table, giggling to each other.

"I thought you'd be used to it by now."

"Not here. At gigs, it's a given, and you brace yourself for it." He dragged a hand through his hair and shook his head at himself. "I must sound like such an idiot. Moaning about attention when it's all I've wanted since I was a kid."

"Sometimes it's not the getting what you want that's unnerving, it's how it manifests." I assessed his strained features as I picked up my glass. "You wanted attention on the music. They're fixating on you instead, and you're uncomfortable with that. I can't imagine it only happens in Cardiff though."

"No but getting stopped in a restaurant or on Queen Street isn't normal. For Kelly Jones maybe, but not for me." He leaned towards me across the table and dropped his voice. "I'm the bassist, Mel. They're meant to look through me, not stare at me like they wish I were wearing less clothes."

I snorted, thankful that I hadn't chosen to take a sip of my drink in that moment.

"Babe, get used to it. They're always going to look at you like that. You're in a band." I forced my amusement away and narrowed my eyes at him. "Just make sure they're only looking. You're mine, and I'm even less interested in sharing you than I am this dessert."

I tugged the plate towards me.

His smile bloomed slowly as my words registered. "Good to know."

CHAPTER TWENTY

Opening the flat door to silence was a surreal experience. I don't know why. I'd been home without Phoebe plenty of times, but something about walking in with Dan's hand in mine just heightened the tension between us.

"Do you want a drink?" I shook off his hold and headed down the corridor, my heels clattering against the wood, charting my path.

He caught my hand again before I even reached the kitchen, spinning me into his chest and pressing me against the hallway wall. My breath caught at the fire in his eyes.

"No, I think I'd rather have you instead," he said, his voice gravelly. His head lowered, and need uncurled in my stomach. That's all it took — a look — and I was his.

My hands fisted in his shirt, pulling his lips to mine before he could decide to torture me with a detour. I needed to taste him. Now.

His fingers dug into my hips, pulling me closer while our kiss deepened. My body itched for the feel of his, pressed against me, skin on skin. The craving was so strong, I would have had no chance of fighting it if I'd wanted to. Luckily, I was in complete and utter agreement.

I started working the buttons on his shirt. The hallway wall was just as good a place to fuck as any other spot in the house. As long as it happened soon.

Before I could get even three of them undone, he picked me up. My legs automatically wrapped around his waist and my hands tangled in his hair, tilting his head to deepen our connection. I braced myself for the bite of the wall against my back.

It didn't come.

Instead, air ruffled my hair as he moved through the flat. The door to my bedroom squeaked, swinging open with a thump against the dresser. Dan climbed onto the bed and placed me in the centre. I didn't release my hold on him, tugging him down until he sprawled out on top of me chuckling.

This time felt different.

Our hands wandered, gliding over fabric and under clothing, subdued desperation in every touch. The last couple of times we'd been frantic, mindless with need. Now, however, I could luxuriate in the buzz his rough fingers sent through me as he pushed my dress up. Lean more fully into the thrill of having his big body on top of me, caging me in and protecting me at the same time.

Something had changed.

I didn't know what it was, but I didn't care, really. Too content to enjoy the sensations and the slow build.

Our clothes landed in a pile on the bedroom floor and soft kisses quickly turned to nips and groans, once heated, over-sensitised skin pressed against the other. Before he could get too comfortable in his control, I pushed him onto his back. He took it without a word of argument. His heated eyes dipped, taking in my naked body with interest as I sat on top of him.

There was urgency in the way he gripped me, in the glide of his hands up my thighs. I bit my lip, shifting until his bare cock grazed my entrance. He surged up, almost pulling at my hips mindlessly.

"Mel," he groaned.

My smile was teasing as I shifted again, dragging my centre along his length. Begrudging understanding entered his eyes as I did it again.

"Two can play at this game, babe." His deep voice grated across my senses, increasing the slickness between my legs. "Are you sure you want to play with fire?"

I ignored him, repeating the movement instead and somehow managing to almost drive myself over the edge. My eyes fell shut, and a moan fell from my lips as a wave of pleasure swept through me. Dan took advantage of my distraction and flipped me back onto my back.

Grinning, he caught my hands and pressed them above my head. "Now, let's see how you like being on the receiving end of slow torture."

He pressed the broad head of his cock against me and I couldn't help but shift, lifting my hips into him. He shifted away, and my core clenched, desperate for him. He repeated my own move, only he applied more pressure. I was shaking within seconds, tumbling over the edge I'd backed away from.

"Do you want more, babe?" His breath caressed my cheek before his lips crazed along my jaw.

"Need you," I panted before hooking my legs around his waist and trying to draw his cock closer to where I needed him. Operative word being tried.

"More it is."

"Dan, no." I gasped when he released my hands and shifted down my body.

His chuckle vibrated through me as he latched onto my nipple, driving the already sensitive nub tighter. Giving me no time to catch my breath, his talented fingers smoothed down my stomach. They grazed my core, pressing firmly as he opened me, pulsing against my clit.

I melted beneath his attention. The pressure built fast, and by the time he slid one, two fingers inside of me I was already on the edge, ready to free fall.

"Still think teasing me was a good idea?" Dan asked, raising his head from my breast. His distraction didn't offer a reprieve, his free hand continued to tease me, rubbing and pinching the sensitive flesh, making me squirm beneath him. "I'm waiting for an answer, Mel."

What had he asked?

I shook my head.

"I'm nearly there." My hips shifted, restlessly searching for the end. "Please, Dan."

Smirking, he caught my lips as he drove his fingers into me. On and on it went until all I could do was cling to him. I cried out as he crooked his fingers, sending a sudden surge of sensation up my spine and throwing me into one of the most intense orgasms of my life.

He pressed open mouth kisses against my cheeks and jaw, worshiping me in ways that brought tears to my eyes.

"Have you learnt your lesson?" he asked, teasing my entrance with his throbbing cock again while he sucked on my earlobe.

I pressed my face into his neck and I licked at his salty skin, nipping him the way he had me and eliciting a moan.

"Never going to happen," I whispered against the column of his neck before sucking on the spot beneath his ear.

His hips jolted forward, entering me in one swift movement that stole both our breaths. He pounded into me, mindlessly for a couple of seconds before reality set in and he slowed to a stop.

"Well played," he panted against my lips.

I swore as he pulled out of me completely, but then he took a condom out of my bedside drawer, and I cared a lot less that he'd stopped. We weren't ready for another Phoebe.

We'd covered a lot of ground in the last few days but there was more still to do before we got that comfortable.

When he dropped the foil package on the bed, I frowned. "What are you —" My words trailed off as he lowered himself down my body, meeting my questioning gaze with mischief in his eyes. "You don't need — Dan, no, I need you inside me now."

He didn't listen. Instead, he pressed my thighs further apart, making room for his broad shoulders. All argument died on my lips at the first flick of his tongue.

Shit.

He was going to ruin me for anyone else.

Who the fuck was I kidding? I didn't want anyone else. Never had.

"I'm never going to get enough of you, babe." His words vibrated through me and something inside me twisted, pouring liquid heat through me.

For what felt like hours but was only minutes, his tongue, lips, and teeth worked me, driving me to the stars and back again. I was a shaking, moaning mess by the time he crawled back up my body with satisfaction dripping from him.

"You're... you're evil," I whispered as he pressed a kiss to my cheek.

"I can do it again, if you want." His head started to dip and I caught him, locking my legs around his waist so he couldn't move.

"If you don't come inside me in the next couple of minutes, I'm going to make you sleep on the sofa."

"Now, who's evil?" He chuckled. He smoothed a hand over my thigh, the teasing light draining. "I can't do as you ordered, unless you let me move."

Hesitantly, I unlocked my ankles and let him go. Amusement and desire mingled in his eyes, while he slid the condom on.

This time, when he teased my entrance, he followed

through, pumping into me with one quick thrust of his hips. I gasped as he stretched me, filling me in ways only he ever had.

Our eyes caught and held as the pressure climbed inside of me. Having all of his attention focused on me was something else. It prevented me from hiding, threw my true feelings at me faster than I could process them. Between our moans and the slap of flesh, one thing became clear.

I was deluding myself.

I thought I could protect myself from repeating the past, but when he looked at me like that, with utter focus, like nothing else mattered, I had to face facts. I was a goner.

And then his pace slowed and he angled himself until he dragged across every live wire inside of me. He rocked in and out of me, deliberately catching them with each pass, snatching my breath and my sanity while staring down at me with love in his eyes.

The pressure built until we were both mindless. Any sense of pace went out the window and he pounded into me, driving us both higher, until my body couldn't take any more. I broke first, my body calming as wave after wave of pleasure coursed through me. He pressed his face into my neck, groaning while he powered through the pleasure, dragging out my orgasm.

His teeth sank into my shoulder and he cried out with his own orgasm. His hips continued to work me even as he slowed, playing havoc with the aftershocks and preventing me from catching my breath.

My hands smoothed up and down his back, holding him to me. It felt like he'd torn me apart and put me back together, whole again. My heart pounded in my chest while my mind raced with the implications of this development.

I loved him.

What the hell was I meant to do now?

CHAPTER TWENTY-ONE

I woke to a pair of little hands tapping my cheek.
For a second, it was just a normal morning, with Phoebe eager to get up and play. Then, reality set in with the press of the cool duvet against my naked body and the quiet sound of Dan's even breathing on the pillow next to mine.

Nia was meant to keep her until I picked her up. Had I forgotten to tell her?

"Wakey time," Phoebe helpfully sang in my face.

Gingerly, I sat up, holding the duvet to my chest while my other hand hovered at Phoebe's back in case the movement tipped her off the bed. It was too early. I didn't need to see a clock to know it. Dan had woken me at least twice through the night and it was still pitch-black when I fell asleep the last time. The light filtering in around the edges of my blackout curtains and the open door was too muted for anything later than 6 AM.

"Nia?" I called.

Dan groaned next to me.

"Yeah?" Nia called back from somewhere outside my room.

My robe lay across the armchair in the corner. It was too

far for me to grab it without flashing Phoebe or taking the duvet from Dan. I didn't really want to explain to the toddler why I was sleeping naked for the first time in her life.

"Phoebs, could you grab my robe please?"

She tilted her head, considering my request. "Do I get potato waffles if I say yes?"

Dan chuckled. I glanced at him sharply, and he pressed his lips together before covering the smirk tugging at the edges with his hand.

"I'll think about it."

Phoebe crossed her arms and stared at me. If I ever doubted she was half of my DNA, that defiant expression would cure me of it immediately.

Phoebe's gaze travelled between us. Dan had gotten his laughter under control and just lay there, sleepy and unhelpful.

"I thought we couldn't have sleepovers until we're married," Phoebe said, her small face screwed up in confusion.

"I'm working on it, munchkin," Dan said, his tone teasing but oddly serious.

Phoebe turned her head towards him. One brow quirked. "Try harder."

It was my turn to snigger. Dan shot me a stinking look before he shuffled up the bed into a seating position. The duvet lay across his lap, thick enough to hide any morning wood.

"Do you want to help me?" Dan asked without an ounce of humour in his tone.

Phoebe's face lit up, and my mind raced. He couldn't possibly mean it. He'd been back in my life for just over three weeks and we'd only been on the same page for a week. Or so I thought. I don't care how much history lay between us, if I didn't rush into marriage when I got pregnant, I wouldn't be bloody rushing now.

He must know that.

It had to be just for her benefit.

"Why did your auntie bring you home so early?" I asked Phoebe before she could answer Dan.

Phoebe turned back to me with her lips open in a tiny O. Her forehead creased as she thought back. She gave up pretty fast, shrugging. She scrambled off me, bouncing into the small space between Dan and me.

"Can I have waffles, Daddy?"

Dan's lips twitched but somehow he kept it together. "If you do what your mother asked, maybe."

Silence followed his response and I didn't need to see Phoebe's face to know she was trying to stare him out. *Good luck, kid.*

"Nia, a little help," I shouted.

She appeared in the open doorway with her eyes shut. I shook my head.

"You can open your eyes, you div."

"Are you both decent?" she asked, ignoring me.

"As decent as a duvet allows."

Nia nodded and opened her eyes.

"I've got to say, when you said you were going on a date, I did not expect this outcome." Nia's lips twitched as she took in the oddly domestic scene with wide eyes.

I glanced at Dan sheepishly from the corner of my eye.

Wait.

"You're lying," I muttered, staring at Nia's wide innocent expression. "James told you. You've been pretending all week."

Nia snorted. "Of course I knew." She gestured to Dan, amusement creasing her face. "He spilled to James the second he got home last weekend."

Dan's mouth opened and closed as he considered us. "It wasn't a secret."

Nia's brows rose. "Whatever you say." She stepped into the

room and picked up my robe. "Anyway, I've got a last-minute commission, so I need to get down to the beach," she explained as she dropped the robe in my lap.

I quickly shrugged into it, tying it off at my waist. Climbing out of bed, I scanned the floor for Dan's boxers.

"On the other side." Nia nodded helpfully towards the foot of the bed.

"We'll talk about it later," I promised, walking around the frame.

"Oh, yes, we will," Nia sang, turning away as I handed Dan his boxers. "I'll have Sophie briefed and ready to grill you. Don't you worry about a thing." Nia's grin was huge and her eyes almost glowed with unrestrained glee. She was going to enjoy grilling me far too much.

"I'm not sure that's necessary."

Her brows climbed, but she wandered out of the room without another word. To be fair, I had nagged her for details on her own relationship. It was probably payback time.

"See you at lunch," Nia called from the hallway before I could come up with a response. The door shut behind her seconds later.

"A little help here, babe," Dan said, his voice strained with uncertainty.

I turned back to them to find Phoebe leaning closer, her small hands resting on his pecs and her nose almost touching his.

"Phoebe, how about giving Daddy a second to get up?"

"Fine," she grumbled, shuffling back. "When do I get waffles?"

"I didn't say you could have waffles," I reminded her.

She shook her head. "You lied to me, so I get waffles," Phoebe declared, before crawling over Dan and dropping onto the floor.

Phoebe stomped past me and into the living room. Dan sat up, his face creased with amusement.

"Can't really argue with her logic."

"Can't argue with her…" I spluttered. My hands landed on my hips as I considered him. "We didn't lie to her."

His brows rose.

"Okay so maybe it was a small white lie but we do not negotiate with wily toddlers."

Dan slid to the edge of the bed and started getting dressed. A gruff grumble escaped his throat. It sounded suspiciously like, "Whatever you say, babe."

❄

Phoebe got her waffles.

The morning passed by quickly while Dan had an imaginary tea party with her and I dealt with a work emergency. It was only the sound of the front door opening and closing that clued me into the passage of time.

"Nanny!" Phoebe shrieked, dropping her fake teacup on her little table and abandoning Dan. She raced towards the door like a rocket.

"Slow down," I called, not bothering to rush after her. My mother would catch her before she tripped.

Speaking of the woman, she wandered into the living room and took in the scene with critical eyes. Dan straightened from Phoebe's tiny play chair, his back rigid and his face carefully blank.

"Daniel," my mother said, her voice cool, giving nothing away.

Before my eyes, Dan morphed into an uncertain sixteen-year-old desperate for my parents' approval. It was quite the transformation.

"Mrs Griffiths." Dan's voice squeaked, betraying his surprise. "It's nice to see you again."

My mother's mask broke as she frowned at him. "Is it?"

"Nanny, can we go to the park today?" Phoebe asked,

tugging at my mother's dress, completely oblivious to the tension surrounding her.

Dan glanced at me, his eyes begging me to help. When he'd left the first time, my mother called him a fool and told me I'd made a light escape. At the time, I'd completely disagreed. And then he started doing his vanishing acts. My perspective changed, and I could finally see things from her side. I mean she would know, right? She'd spent nearly thirty years with my dad, dipping in and out with little warning depending on what the latest band was doing on the road.

I studied Dan, searching for signs on his face that he would be exactly like my dad. I'd always thought he would be, but after the last few weeks, I wasn't so sure anymore.

Dan might just be different.

For Phoebe's sake, I hoped I was right.

For mine too. I couldn't take another heartbreak from this man.

"Mam, Dan's moved home permanently, isn't that great?"

She grunted, continuing to eye him.

"The entire band actually," I added, my upbeat tone struggling against the tense atmosphere. "And he's been great with Phoebe. I'm not sure I could have survived the last two weeks without his help."

Dan's nerves faded as he absorbed my words. "Do you really mean that?" he asked, his hope written plain across his face for all to see.

"Of course I do."

"And what happens when his band goes on tour next?" My mother crossed her arms, thoroughly unimpressed. "Is he going to make you ship off with him or will he just disappear for months on end like your father?"

"We haven't figured that out yet." I jumped in before he could make a bumbling attempt to talk my mother round.

"Don't you think you should have that figured out *before* you jump into a relationship with a flight risk?"

Dan sucked in a breath but wisely remained silent.

"No, Mam." I shook my head. "We're adults, and we can make our own decisions."

She pursed her lips.

"Seriously, Mam. We're good," I said, forcing the conversation to end. "Thank you for taking Phoebe today. I'll see you this evening."

With that, she turned her attention fully to Phoebe. The toddler bounced around her feet, firing questions a mile a minute.

"Are you ready to leave, Phoebe?" my mother asked, a genuine smile blanketing her features.

"Yes!" Phoebe shouted, stomping towards the door. "What took you so long?"

"Nanny, I learnt a song," Phoebe said, bouncing down the hall. "Wanna hear?"

"Sure, cariad," my mother dutifully answered.

"You might want to rethink that," I called after them, following them towards the door.

"That's lovely, but let's go get your things so we can start our day, shall we?" My mother suggested, holding out her hand for Phoebe's.

"Ice cream?" Phoebe asked, giving my mother her classic 'do it or I scream' look.

"You'll have to ask your Grancha," she said, passing the buck to my dad to refuse her. And he would refuse her. At first. Brown eyes identical to mine twinkled back at me. Devious woman.

"'Kay." Phoebe shoved her feet into her shoes while my mother plucked her coat from the hook.

"I'll have her back for the usual time?" Mam turned back to me, her brows risen but her focus on the space behind me.

"Sounds good." I knelt down and hugged Phoebe. "Be good for Nanny." She barrelled out of my arms, chanting ice cream at the door. I met my mother's concerned gaze when I stood up. "Everything's fine. You don't need to worry." The crease between her brows only deepened.

※

"Why does she hate me?" he asked again. It was at least the fifth time he'd repeated the question, and I had yet to get a word of explanation out. He kept turning his back on me to complete another lap.

"She just needs to get used to you being back."

"It didn't seem like a 'get used to me' thing, Mel." His brow quirked. "Why does she hate me?"

I sighed. "She thought I dodged a painful bullet when you didn't tear the city down looking for me." Crashing down onto the sofa, I continued, "And now you're back and she probably thinks you'll do it all again."

"All what again?"

"Leave me behind for the music with no warning."

He blinked. Seconds passed by while he digested that titbit. "That sounds remarkably similar to your concerns," he said, his voice tight as he scrubbed a hand down his face.

I mean, he wasn't wrong.

Wisely, I chose to remain silent on that leading statement. He already knew the facts, no need to repeat them like a broken record.

"Mel?"

I pressed my lips together and sat back.

Nope.

Not going to repeat it yet again.

We were making progress. Amazing progress. I was not going to be the one to derail that with reminders of our past mistakes.

When I didn't answer, he approached me, kneeling down between my legs until I couldn't escape his pleading eyes. I groaned and covered my face.

"Why does she hate me, babe?" he asked, pulling my hands away from my face.

"You know how my dad is, Dan." I shrugged, resigned to the ugly turn our afternoon might take. "She thinks you're just like him."

His brows creased in confusion. "But she's still married to him."

"I know!" I huffed, trying to lighten the mood. "I can't figure that one out either."

It didn't work. His face tensed, and I was at a loss for ways to ease it. There were zero easy answers to this problem. He knew it. I knew it. I wasn't going to pretend just to make him feel better now. It would be false and we'd had enough omissions and lies in our lives for a lifetime.

"Honestly, she'll come around."

"You don't know that."

"No, I don't." I shook my head. "But all we can do is prove her wrong."

Dan pursed his lips, just like Phoebe did when she didn't like an answer.

"How do we do that?"

"Prove you're going to stick around."

His face fell again.

"What! You're already doing it with me."

He sat back on his haunches. "I don't think she'll care that I make you dinner, entertain Phoebe, and give you amazing orgasms."

My lips twitched. "Well, she might care about the second one."

"What are we going to do?" Groaning, his head landed in my lap. "I can't take Madeline Griffiths hating my guts."

I chose to keep the salient fact that he shouldn't have broken my heart to myself. He didn't need to be reminded that he'd made his own bed with this one.

"If she sees how happy you make me, she'll come

around." I ran my fingers through his hair, massaging his scalp and trying to free him from the tension.

His head rose and he glanced up at me. "And do I make you happy?"

I bit my cheek, containing the grin that instinctively tried to take over. "Well the jury is still out on that one."

He sat back again, his brows raised. "I'm pretty sure you were very happy last night."

I tilted my head considering. "It was pretty good."

His eyes widened. "Pretty good?" he muttered. "It was more than pretty fucking good. Be honest."

I shrugged.

Last night had been amazing. But for the first time since my mother walked in, the tension had drained from him. A small white lie was worth that.

"Right, we need to fix that." Gripping my hands, he pulled me off the sofa and on to the floor. He rolled me under him with little effort, holding my hands above my head with a wicked grin that made my stomach flip.

CHAPTER TWENTY-TWO

The moment I walked into the backroom of The Hound, they pounced. Nia and Sophie started blasting questions before I'd even taken a seat, let alone poured a fortifying glass of wine. Dan had left me for rehearsal with the guys and it was just as well. I'm not sure I wanted to see their avid attention focused on him just yet.

"Are you actually together?" Nia grinned.

"What will you do when he goes on tour?" Sophie edged further forward in her seat.

"Can we double date now?"

"Is he mad you kept Phoebe from him?"

Nia frowned. "I guess it'll be triple date with Ryan and Alys."

Sophie glanced around, checking to see if anyone was listening before whispering, "Do we fully trust him now?"

"Has your mother seen him?" Nia winced at my nod. "Was it bad?"

One after the other, they fired questions at me, giving zero time for responses. I settled back in the booth and sipped my wine, content to let them wear themselves out.

"How does his beard feel against your thigh?" Sophie

asked, garnering a sharp look from both me and Nia. "What? I've heard it feels amazing but I can't imagine it's worth the hairy kisses." Her lips puckered like she'd tasted something foul.

There was a beat of silence while we considered her. Then Nia and I burst out laughing.

"Alright, it's not that funny."

My eyes watered. "It's kind of is."

"Oh, it definitely is," Nia said, blowing out a shaky breath. "Considering a personality transplant are we, Soph?"

She glanced away, crossing her arms. "I'm just curious."

That garnered another snigger from us.

Nia eyed me, her laughter fading. "Seriously though, how are you dealing with all this?" She twisted her wine glass as she considered me with concern. "It's a pretty big change to your life, right?"

I nodded before letting my head fall back against the leather of the booth.

"Fine, I think. It was weird at the start." Understatement or what? "I'm just taking it day by day. Phoebe loves Dan, so that helps."

"And do you?" Nia asked, an edge to her voice that drew my eyes to her. "Do you love him?"

I pursed my lips. It felt weird, admitting it to my best friends, when I couldn't let myself give Dan the same. But they were my best friends and here I was safe to say anything I wanted, even if it scared the ever-loving crap out of me. There would be no consequences of my admission.

"I don't think I ever stopped."

Nia's smile was sympathetic.

"You may not want to hear this," Sophie said, biting her lip. "But I'm just going to say it anyway. The definition of insanity is repeating the same action over and over again and expecting a different outcome."

It took a moment for her meaning to sink in, and when it did, I glared at her.

"That was not helpful," I muttered, raising my wine glass to my lips.

"Yeah, Soph, let's just get the facts before we proclaim it's all doomed." Nia's brow furrowed as she stared at our best friend. "Dan might actually be for real. I didn't think James was, but look at us now." She glanced back at me, her expression softening. "I wouldn't discount it yet. Enjoy it and give him a chance to prove you right or wrong."

I pulled a face. "It's the proving me right part I'm worried about."

"There's nothing you can do to guard against that, lovely." Nia shrugged. "Either he's got it figured out or he'll screw up. I'm more interested in what he does when he screws up, honestly."

I frowned. "I don't understand."

"Yes, you do." Nia rolled her eyes but explained all the same. "How he screws up and what he does with it will tell you how serious he is."

Sophie's head tilted as she considered Nia's words. "She's got a point."

"Not you too." I groaned. "Can we stop with the riddles please?"

Nia chuckled. "He has a habit of disappearing when things get hard or too distracting from the music," she said, speaking slowly in case I was having trouble keeping up. I was. "It's inevitable that something will go wrong, and when it does, how he reacts will be important. Will he lean into it, or will he fix whatever he screws up?"

"I wonder what he'll do if a surprise tour pops up." Sophie stared hard at the amber liquid in her glass.

"That's exactly what I mean," Nia said, pointing at Sophie like she'd nailed her point. "Will he talk to you first or will he just go? If he goes, then he's learnt nothing."

"And if he tells you, then the options will need to consider you and Phoebe," Sophie added, lifting her wine glass.

"And if it doesn't?"

"Then you'll have your answer." Sophie shrugged.

With those helpful comments swirling around my brain, we ordered food, and I tried to pretend like they hadn't affected me.

❄

We were halfway through our meals when the atmosphere changed in the pub. The noise level seemed to grow out front, the sound echoing down the hallway that connected the open main area of the bar to the small cosy section we favoured in the back.

"What the hell is that?" Sophie asked, her brow furrowed. She leant out of the booth, as if she could see around a corner and down a long hallway.

People all around us had stopped eating, too, their attention equally rapt on the doorway. It wasn't overly crowded. The back area never was. The usual Saturday clientele preferred to be up front with an easy view of the TV screens and the latest sports match. Those of us who didn't care for sports, or the loud cheering men in jerseys, favoured the quieter leather booths that lined the wall.

Someone shouted out front. Their voice cut above the ruckus but not enough to be heard clearly in the back. Moments later, the culprits wandered into the room wearing shellshocked expressions. James, Jared, Ryan, and Alys followed Dan to our booth. Jared and Ryan grabbed chairs from an empty table and dragged them towards us.

"Was that you?" I asked Dan as he slid onto the seat next to me. His arm wrapped around me and he pushed me tighter into the corner. My fingers smoothed along his chest without thought, trying to soothe him. His t-shirt was oddly stretched. "Are you okay?"

"Let's just say that was unexpected, and forget about it," Dan said, his voice unnaturally flat. His hands opened and closed against my side. I'd never seen him agitated like this.

"Or we accept that Matt is right," Ryan said, his voice shaking and anger darkening his eyes as he guided Alys into the seat next to Dan.

Sophie took one look at James's white face and scrambled out of the booth. He took her seat, moving in close to Nia so she could claim the end of the bench. He immediately pulled her into his side, burying his face in her neck.

"What happened?" Nia whispered to James, her words almost lost to the muted music.

"We were fucking mobbed," Jared muttered, collapsing into a chair. His head fell forward and into his hands as his shoulders slumped.

"It's fine," Dan said, still with the expressionless tone that set me on edge. "We just weren't ready for it."

"Ready for it?" Ryan scoffed, blowing out an agitated breath. "Man, I don't think I'd ever have been ready for that."

"Never." James lifted his head. His wide-eyed gaze fixed on the fabric above our heads. He swallowed hard. "Them clawing at me…" His gaze settled on Dan, haunted. "I'm never going to get used to that."

I'd seen enough music documentaries and been to enough gigs with screaming girls to understand some of what they were feeling. People had been pretty chill so far. I hadn't thought it would be an issue. How stupid. Their new album had just won a BRIT award.

How were we going to get them out of here without it happening again?

"What was Matt's offer?" I asked, directing the question to Dan.

He met my gaze but pressed his lips together.

"Security," Ryan answered instead, his voice deadly serious.

My focus jumped to him. He held Alys's hand tightly in his lap. His fingers rubbed in agitated circles as his knee jumped. Alys sat back in the booth, leaning her head against the cushion. She looked pale. Other than the auction, we hadn't officially met. Would it be weird for me to be concerned for her?

"You okay, Alys?" I asked, following my instincts instead.

She nodded her head but kept her eyes closed. "I just need a minute."

Ryan's hand tightened on hers before he glanced at James. "I'm calling Matt, and we're getting a detail."

From the way he speared James with a look, I expected him to argue. He took one glance at Nia and nodded. Ryan's gaze travelled to Dan next, who froze.

"There's no question really, is there?" I asked. "You need it. Accept the help."

He studied me, searching for something, but what?

"Why are you hesitating?" I glanced between him and the rest of the band. All but Ryan steadfastly avoided eye contact.

Ryan sighed. "Just tell her, Dan. We need to get this sorted."

He stiffened against me but one look into my eyes and the tension drained from him. Or at least the belief that he could keep whatever it was from me.

"Would you still trust me with you and Phoebe?"

I frowned. "What does Phoebe have to do with you getting a security detail?"

"I was worried it would be too much for you if we..." He shrugged.

My eyes widened as his meaning sank in. He thought I'd put a stop to us if I knew how crazy things were getting.

Having someone watching his back would make me feel better.

Dan watched me, his lip caught between his teeth and his eyes sad but accepting. He really expected me to run from him.

"I don't care how much attention you get." My hand cupped his jaw as I stared into his eyes with determination. "That was never on my list of concerns. Take the security. We'll all be safer for it."

"Oh, thank fuck." He blew out a breath and then his face lit up beneath my hand. His eyes shone with unshed tears as he pulled me into his arms and pressed a kiss to my hair while holding me tightly.

"Then it's settled," Ryan said, his voice deadly serious. "I'll call Matt now."

Just as he pulled out his phone, a tall, blond bartender appeared with a tray of drinks. He placed them on the table and handed Ryan a business card.

"From the owner," he said, nodding at the card in Ryan's hand. "There's a back exit we can get you out of, and when you're next coming in, give him a call, and he'll have this room cleared out for you."

I glanced between Nia and Sophie, both wearing equally surprised expressions that would mirror my own. That was a pretty sweet offer.

"Thanks, man," Ryan said, pocketing the card. He nodded towards us. "I'm pretty sure these three would pitch a fit if we tried to stop them coming here."

"Too right," Nia muttered, vehemence dripping from her words.

A low chuckle spread around our table and it was the first sign that our normal would return. Jared didn't react. He hadn't relaxed so much as an inch with Ryan's decree, but I'd never known him well enough to say why.

I'd always assumed that they were all dedicated and understood what being in a rising band meant. Looking at him, I had to wonder if that were true.

"Are you absolutely sure you're okay with the security?" Dan asked again when the door closed on the flat.

I glanced back at him. "I don't think being okay with it is really a factor, babe. You need it."

He followed me into the kitchen, his frown only deepening. "That's not an answer."

"Yes, it is. I want you safe." I pressed me hands to his chest, staring up into his tight eyes. "I want us safe. What you experienced today was unnerving, but what would it have been like if Phoebe was with you?"

"I can't stop imagining it," he whispered, his voice hoarse. He broke away from me, pacing the kitchen. "Fuck, why couldn't this happen later. Like next year. Or just not now."

"It means you're making a stir." My smile was gentle as I watched him. "People are starting to pay attention, and that's a good thing. It was going to happen one day. Today was the first. It may not happen tomorrow or next month, but you've seen what it can be like, and you can prepare now."

He stopped.

"It's a necessary evil of the life you've chosen. Are you going to quit music?"

"No," he breathed, his shoulders sagging.

"Then we'll adjust. We'll prepare Phoebe, hire security, and enjoy the quiet moments while we have them."

His smile was small, but growing. "That easy, is it?" His hands landed on my waist, tugging me into his chest.

"As easy as you want to make it."

He nodded before wrapping me up in a hug. I'd never seen the loveable giant shaken. I'd like to never see it again.

CHAPTER TWENTY-THREE

The next day, we decided that going out was probably not the best plan. Getting out had been fun, but we'd have to be blind to miss how much it shook the guys. Which was how I ended up with the entire band in my living room gathered around a tiny plastic table sipping from a toy tea set. Phoebe had batted her lashes and they fell into line.

"That kid has game and I need to learn it all," Nia whispered, awe filling her tone.

Alys nodded. "I mean I've got Ryan wrapped around my finger, but that was a higher level."

"Please, she came out of the womb with game," Ella, my sister, scoffed.

We were almost identical — mousy brown hair flowing down our backs and hazelnut eyes containing far too much wariness. Yet she was three years younger than me and sometimes it felt like she'd stopped ageing at twenty-one. It was in the way she handled herself, so carefree, so loving and open. Like my father hadn't damaged her, the way he had me. Sometimes I envied her.

Now she sipped her wine, her eyes twinkling as the guys scrambled to follow Phoebe's orders. Nia, Alys, Ella, and I stood at the kitchen island, holding our own adult sized mugs staring at them. With the tiny chairs, the guys' knees were almost up to their chins, but not a single one of them grumbled. Not even Jared. Phoebe took it all in stride, preening under all the attention.

"It's called parental guilt," I said, not taking my eyes off them. One of these moments, Phoebe was going to break out the dress up, and I'd need to be ready with the camera. "You should have been better prepared, Nia."

She snorted. "It's not like I could predict your daughter taking them all by the b—" She paused, glancing at me with a sheepish expression. Her voice dropped and she whispered, "you know what's."

"But you'll send me that one you took, right?" Alys asked, her eyes shining with mirth. "My dad will love it, and Emily won't believe me unless I have pics."

"Definitely," I promised.

"Let's face it, I'll be hijacking their Instagram account with it," Nia muttered, laughter rippling through her words. She turned to us sharply, a magical look in her eyes. "I *could* hijack their Instagram."

"Oh, their fans would love that." Alys chuckled before glancing at me. "But would you?"

As much as I got that music was a huge part of Dan's life, and one day, he would get snapped with Phoebe, the thought of knowingly putting her face out into the world had a hard ball forming in my stomach. I'd rather it be on our terms, not some fan or magazine, but did that moment really have to be now?

"It's too soon," I said, shaking my head.

Nia placed her phone back on the island and nodded.

I side-eyed Alys, pleasantly surprised with my new friend. Nia and Sophie had taken to her fast, but opportunities to hang out the last month had been slim. What I'd seen so far I liked a lot. The fact she'd clearly thought through the repercussions of putting Phoebe out into the world was oddly refreshing in the 'share it all' culture social media had nurtured.

"Thanks for checking, Alys."

"Of course." Her smile was genuine, lighting up her entire face. "I know the effect social media and their fans can have on a relationship. Wouldn't want it to get in your way."

Before I could reply, Phoebe tugged at my jeans. She grinned up at me, her eyes on fire with unspent energy. Uh-oh.

"Mammy, can I have chocolate milk?" she asked, twisting to look at the fridge behind her.

I bit my lip. She was hyper. Did I really want to add chocolate milk to the mix?

"How about some juice instead?" Dan asked, kneeling down next to Phoebe.

My shoulders itched with the feel of every single pair of eyes in the room focused on us. On Dan. I guess this was their first real sighting of Dan as a parent. Was it weird for them or cute?

"Nope," she said, the word popping on her lips. "I want chocolate milk."

"I don't think we have chocolate milk, munchkin." Dan glanced up at me for confirmation that I understood his lie. And it was a lie. There was a bottle in the fridge and he knew it. Smart man.

"I'm not a munchkin." Her brow furrowed as she shook her head distracted from her original request.

"No?" Dan asked, his lips twitching with barely contained amusement.

She pursed her lips, her eyes darting between us. "Munchkins are small. I'm not small."

Dan quirked a brow. "That so?"

"Yes."

"So if I tried to pick you up right now, I wouldn't be able to?"

Her lips stretched in a grin. "Nope."

I wasn't sure where he was going with this, but he was up to something.

"Okay, let's test that," he said and then snatched her off the floor, spinning her around. Phoebe shrieked, filling the flat with her laughter. The guys chuckled as they joined us around the island for real drinks.

"He's like a different person," Ryan said, nodding to Dan teasing Phoebe with the biggest smile on his face.

James nodded. "I didn't think I'd ever say it, but he makes a pretty good dad, right?"

Nia snorted. "More like he's just slapped you in the face with your own biological clocks, and you don't know how to deal with it."

"I'm pretty sure I know how to deal with it." James smirked, his gaze fixed on her. "C'mon, Shutterbug, let's make a baby." He approached her and she backed away.

"No. We've discussed this, and it's still no." Nia held out her hands, fending him off before he'd even reached her. "I'm only twenty-seven. Put it on ice."

Ryan raised a brow at Alys, and she glared at him. "Put that look away." She gestured to Nia. "I'm with her. Twenty-six is far too young."

"Definitely." Nia shuddered before glancing at me sheepishly. "No offence, Mel."

I chuckled. "None taken."

Hell, it's not the life I would have chosen for myself either. But hearing Phoebe's shrieks as Dan spun her around the room… my heart swelled. I might not have chosen it, but I wouldn't change my situation for the world.

"Still not a munchkin?" Dan asked, tilting Phoebe back until she almost hung in the air.

She shook her head hard. "No," she cried, giggling all the while.

Dan tutted and started spinning her again.

"Mam said you should break out the face paints, and see how the guys fare then," Ella reported, reading from her phone. From the excitement in her eyes, I'd say she agreed wholeheartedly.

The doorbell sounded over the raucous laughter of the guys. Dan paused in his teasing, his brows climbing as he met my confused gaze.

"Are you expecting anyone?" He nodded towards the hallway and the door beyond.

My mother usually texted when she was on her way over. My phone sat dark on the counter, no notifications waiting. This was an impromptu gathering, and other than Sophie, everyone was present.

Before I could reply, the bell went again. Frowning, I strode into the hallway. It was a Sunday so it wouldn't be the postman and I hadn't ordered anything that would arrive by courier.

"Maybe hold on the face paints," I said as I started down the corridor. "Let's not destroy my furniture today."

"No fun," Ella cried behind me.

I opened the door and immediately wished I'd checked the peephole. Glaring at me from the other side of the doorway was Dan's mother. A woman I'd purposefully avoided ever since Dan and I broke up. The first time.

"Annette," I said, my voice loud and projected for Dan's benefit. Or for mine, in the vague hope that he'd rescue me. "What a surprise!"

She looked me up and down. Her hair was a stark blonde, a shade that you only got from a bottle and too much time in the sun. Yellowed teeth flashed in a haphazard attempt at a smile that didn't reach her eyes.

"Mother trucker," Ella muttered in the distance. "Dude, the hell is your mother doing here?"

"Aren't you going to invite me in, Mel?" Dan's mother asked, trying to project an authority she'd lost over me years ago.

Did I have to?

"Mam, what are you doing here?" Dan pressed his hand to my back and I relaxed a fraction. The worried strain in his voice prevented me from rushing back into the flat to hide all the alcohol.

As if we were still kids.

The woman used to chain smoke like a pro but if her son so much as sniffed at a bottle of alcohol she'd go off. Back then, her erratic behaviour had struck fear in my heart. But then I was a teenager with a stable mother who didn't have to work two jobs and who wasn't the slightest bit neurotic. Even with my dad always on the road. Annette was a shade of humanity I'd never understood.

Her smile was awkward, like it didn't fit right. "You weren't answering my calls."

"So you turned up here?" Incredulity dripped from Dan's lips. "I gave you Mel's address for emergencies."

"What if it is one?"

The hope on her face gutted me.

She'd driven her only daughter out of the country, and her son struggled with his role as her bouncing board. I'd heard enough about it from Dan but seeing it, the desperation, was too much.

"Would you like some tea, Annette?" I asked. The words came out of my mouth, but I was disconnected from it, like someone else was speaking through me.

Dan tensed against me. His gaze burned into the top of my head and I could almost read his mind. *What the hell was Mel smoking?*

"I don't think that's necessary," Dan said, his voice tight. "She's not staying."

She didn't acknowledge him, just smiled shyly and pushed past Dan. I wouldn't take it at face value, but at least she tried.

"Did you have to invite her in?" Dan growled, shutting the door.

I shrugged. "What else was I meant to do?" I whispered, my eyes wide and my tone bewildered.

He considered me for a second then his eyes fell shut and he groaned, pinching at the bridge of his nose. "What is it with this weekend?" Dan muttered beneath his breath so that no one else could hear. His voice was strained with displeasure. "I didn't ask the universe for a bloody family reunion, did you?"

I patted him on the chest, partially comforting and partially mocking. "Guess it's time for Phoebe to meet her grandmother."

Dan blew out a breath, totally unimpressed with my apparent calmness at the situation. Little did he know, my heart pretty much stuttered at the thought of an afternoon with the woman.

❄

Silence engulfed my tiny flat. Well, except for Phoebe's oblivious chatter over her favourite ponies. The band stood around the island with the girls, their uneasy gazes fixed on the sofa where Annette sat. She was a hard woman to deal with. Happy and chatty one moment, on edge and depressed the next. You never knew what mood you were going to get her in.

Dan sat opposite her, his brows furrowed as he tried to engage her like the dutiful son he was. The fact was, neither of us knew how she would react to meeting Phoebe. She hadn't exactly been all that motherly to him and his sister, Freya, growing up. She expected you to do whatever you were doing right the first time and failure wasn't an option. Given her yo-yoing mental state it had been a confusing stance for us growing up.

The kettle clicked, breaking me from my thoughts. I opened the fridge and removed the milk. Nia slid another mug across the counter towards me.

I smiled in thanks. "Are you guys having refills?"

Nia pulled a face, and the guys tensed. I'd take that as a no.

"Maybe we should leave," Nia said, her voice lifting with an unspoken apology.

I couldn't blame her. She'd made an art of avoiding Dan's mother after she'd belittled her photography dreams when we were thirteen. Her own mother had just about exploded when she found out. Despite Nia's dad being a strait-laced asshole, her mother cherished and fed her kids' dreams.

The want to be that kind of parent was a pressure behind my eyes I couldn't ignore. And if she ever tried to put Phoebe down, I wouldn't cower. Adult me could take anything she threw and I'd be ready for it. I glanced at Phoebe, happily holding up colourful ponies, not a stress line on her young face.

"We can stay if you want us to," Ryan said, misreading my silence.

I shook my head. "Thanks, but it's awkward enough, right?"

They all nodded, relief filtering through their expressions.

"Go, it's fine."

"I'm going to stick around," Jared said, his gaze fixed on Dan's mother with narrowed eyes.

Ella glanced at him sharply. "No need, I'm here. We'll be fine."

Jared's focus shifted to her, and it was like he took her in for the first time. I braced myself. I'd heard enough stories. The man had grown into a massive manwhore.

Rather than the suave grin I was expecting, his expression hardened. "I'm staying."

"Geez, Jared. No need to fight her," James muttered, walking past him. "She'll share the tense atmosphere, right, Els?"

She crossed her arms, her brows climbing. "Do I have to?"

Chuckling, the rest of the band called their goodbyes and trudged out of the flat. Despite the driving need to get away, I joined Dan on the sofa. I handed out mugs of steaming tea with a forced smile.

"So how've you been, Annette?" I asked, trying for cordial but not quite masking the tremor in my voice.

She was just too damn unpredictable.

"I'd be better if I'd known I had a granddaughter," she snapped, trying to land a barb that would not land.

I shrugged it off without much effort. I wasn't going to tell her before Dan. Maybe not even after Dan.

"Mam," Dan warned.

"What?" she cried, gesturing carelessly with her mug. "It's true. I don't know how you can be so calm about all this, Danny boy." Her brows climbed as she assessed him. "I thought I raised you better than that."

Hot liquid spilled from her mug and onto the floor. Too close to Phoebe for my liking.

"Phoebs, come play with auntie Ella," my sister called from the kitchen.

She turned to Els with a puckered brow. Shaking her head at her, she stepped up to me, an uneasy look in her eyes I could do with never seeing again. I lifted her into my lap and only then did I relax. She leant into me, her legs resting across Dan's thigh which was pressed hard against mine.

"And to name her Phoebe, of all names." Annette shook her head, her mouth pulling in unpleasant lines.

Phoebe stiffened against me, pressing her face into my chest. She wouldn't understand what was happening, but she could read a room when she wanted to. I tightened my hold on her, squeezing her briefly.

"It's such a strange name," Annette continued.

"And Freya isn't?" I asked, letting too much bite into my words.

Annette smirked. Of course she bloody did. She thought she was getting to me. In a way she was, but not like she would be imagining. No, I hated the fact she was talking negatively about my baby girl as if she wasn't sat right in front of her.

"Freya's exotic."

I snorted. "Freya was the Norse god of love and sex. She was a—." I cleared my throat, my eyes dropping to my daughter's rigid body. "She liked men too much."

Annette's amusement fled, and her face darkened. I couldn't find it in me to care. The sooner she left my flat and my life the better. *Why had I invited her in?*

"Now listen you little slut —"

"Mam!" Dan roared. He stood so fast his tea sloshed down his jeans, splattering the floor.

Phoebe jumped in my lap and my heart plummeted to the floor. She pressed her face tighter into me.

Annette stared at her son with disdain. "Really, Dan. What did I teach you about raising your voice at me?"

"You taught us nothing." His voice shook with anger. "I spent years trying to tiptoe around you and your mood swings. Trying to protect Freya from the vile things that would come out of your mouth." He glanced down at me. Some of the tension drained from his face as he studied Phoebe. It was replaced with sadness. "I will not let you poison my daughter's life the way you have your own."

Annette's face slackened.

"I'm done," Dan spat. "Done playing the go-between with Freya, done humouring you. Take a good look at my baby, Mam, because you'll never see her again."

"Now, Daniel, you don't mean that." She stood on shaky legs. A sketchy smile tried to claim her lips but just wouldn't stick, as her eyes flickered between us. They stuck to me, an imploring quality in their depths that sickened me.

How dare she talk about us that way and expect me to stick up for her!

"Leave now." Dan's tone broke no argument.

The fight drained from her body and she left without a word. I found myself staring at the hallway while he saw her out, expecting her to turn around and start shouting or something. When he returned to me without an altercation, I began to feel the ache in my back. Had I been lying down, I might have curled myself around Phoebe in some useless attempt to protect her. Holding her wasn't going to buffer her from her grandmother's barbs.

Dan pushed the coffee table away and knelt before us. He pressed a hand to my knee while another caressed my jaw, staring up into my face with concern.

"She's gone," he whispered, an apology written in the lines of his face. "Are you okay?"

"Did you mean what you said?"

He tilted his head, his brow furrowing.

"That you're done with her?"

The confusion cleared quickly. "Yes, I'm not going to let Phoebe grow up with the venom she's capable of spewing."

My nod was stiff. "Good."

Dan's gaze dropped to Phoebe. His big hand smoothed down her back and she whimpered.

"Munchkin, what's wrong?" Dan cooed, his voice quiet but caring.

She shook her head, refusing to look at him.

His green gaze caught mine, his worry a gnawing presence.

"Let me try," I mouthed.

He relaxed marginally onto his hunches and tilted his head.

"Did Daddy scare you?"

Phoebe nodded against me.

"Because he shouted?"

Another nod.

"It wasn't directed at you, Phoebs." I squeezed her. "You know that right?"

She lifted her head and it felt like someone stuck a hand in my chest, squeezing my heart. Her eyes were red and she bit her lip. I smoothed her auburn hair back and tried to smile. Swiping at her cheeks like it would take away the sadness, I leant in, pressing my forehead to hers.

"He was looking out for you."

Phoebe glanced at Dan, her lip caught between her teeth.

"It's true, baby." Dan leant forward, his attention focused on her. "I got angry because someone was trying to hurt you. I'll never allow that."

He rested his huge hand on her knee. It took a moment but something about his earnest green eyes calmed her. She softened in my arms.

"Do you understand, Phoebe?" I asked, squeezing her briefly.

Her head tilted back until she could see my face. She nodded. "Daddy will always be here to protect me."

With that, she flung herself at Dan. My heart jumped into my throat, but he caught her without issue. He stared back at me, his arms wrapped tightly around Phoebe with a stunned expression that confused me for a second.

And then Phoebe's words sunk in.

His actions today, kicking his mother out, promising Phoebe he'd always look after her... they were a promise I wasn't sure he'd intended to make to either of us. But he had. It relaxed me in a way that weeks of his wooing had failed to achieve.

I took a deep cleansing breath and settled back against the sofa cushion with an unconstrained smile.

CHAPTER TWENTY-FOUR

"If you guys need to take a minute, I can stay and watch Phoebe," Ella offered half an hour later once Phoebe had started to uncurl from her shell.

Jared spluttered. "I'm here, I can watch her." He cut Ella with a scathing look. "You can go."

Dan and I shared a careful look. What the hell was going on with these two?

Ella turned on him. Her hands fell to her hips and the carefree energy my little sister was famed for evaporated before my eyes.

"You're not family. *You* can go."

"I'm even better than family." Jared sneered. "I'm chosen family, so don't let the door hit you on the way out."

Ella opened her mouth to snap back, but I was done with it. I needed some fresh air and a drink so if they were serious, they could both stay for all I cared.

"Jared? That's my sister. Watch your tone if you want to keep that family status."

Dan sniggered, but Jared had the sense to look sheepish. Ella just grinned, far too amused by his defeat.

"Sorry," Jared mumbled.

"Thank you for the offer, Els." I glanced at Dan, despite the amusement of their little fight, there was a strain around his eyes. Getting out would be a good idea. "If you're serious, we're going to take a walk or something."

She nodded. "Of course, I'll pull out the colouring books." Her eyes tracked to Phoebe who was happily playing with her ponies on the living room rug. "Promise, she won't notice you stepped away."

And even if she did, she wouldn't care. She loved Ella. Sophie and Nia were trying to compete for favourite auntie status, but I didn't have the heart to tell them they'd both lost to my sister ages ago.

Ella turned to Jared. "Sure you're staying? Isn't colouring beneath the rock star playboy?"

Jared just glared at her, arms crossed.

"There's something going on here." I gestured between them, my eyes narrowed. "I have no idea what, but I will figure it out."

Dan snorted. "I think it's pretty obvious, but right now, I'd rather get out the door than debate whether Jared was stupid enough to mess around with your sister." He placed a hand on my lower back and started guiding me towards the front door. "We'll be back soon guys. Phoebs, be good for your auntie."

I glanced back over my shoulder at my toddler. She was frowning at us but made no move to follow. It helped that Ella swooped in with coloured pencils before we'd even turned down the hall.

※

*D*an and I walked for ten minutes in silence. Every time I opened my mouth to say something, the words stalled on my tongue. I was really happy that he'd turned his mother away, but what if he took it wrong? What if he was regretting that heat of the moment decision?

As we wandered into the centre of the Bay, the area got busier with people out enjoying their Sunday night, despite the cold. The restaurants were lit up, reflecting out on the black water like a beacon. It was a sight I never grew tired of, whether I was viewing it from the flat or ground level.

Dan stopped outside my favourite restaurant and cocktail bar. "Shall we grab a drink?" He nodded to the quiet glass fronted building.

In the summer, the place was always heaving with people spilling out onto their patio. Tonight, there was a bitter bite to the air. Winter had well and truly arrived in Cardiff and no one was willing to brave the freezing cold hair driving in from the Bay. Candles flickered on tables and despite people speaking in hushed tones, their voices rose in a cacophony of sound. *At least we'd have privacy.*

"I thought you'd never ask." I smiled at him before leading the way up the steps to the front door.

We were seated and gave our orders quickly. Sat facing each other, there was no way to avoid the subject any longer. Well, I at least couldn't ignore it.

"I'm sorry it went downhill so fast."

Dan glanced up at me with a sad smile. "It was inevitable. I knew it wasn't going to be easy when she first saw you again, but I wasn't prepared for that." He pressed his lips together. That sadness overtook his expression as he reached for my hand. "I'm sorry she said those things to you. I shouldn't have even let her in the flat."

I gripped his hand and stared into his suspiciously shiny green eyes, imploring him to hear me. "Babe, I'm the one that invited her in, but the fact it turned to shit so fast is on her. Not you or me. We gave her a chance and she blew it."

He nodded, his smile turning rueful. "I know you're right. I just wish it could have been different."

A waitress delivered our drinks and we both took deep glugs of the alcohol before broaching the subject again. Well, at least I was using it to stall. Who knew if Dan had deployed the same tactic?

"Did you mean it?" I asked, the words falling from my lips slow and hesitant. He tilted his head in confusion. "That you were done with her?"

"Yes, I meant it." His voice was gravelly as he assessed me. "Does that scare you?"

"No, the opposite actually." For the first time since we left the flat, my smile wasn't forced or sad. "It makes this feel more real. Like you're in this for the long run."

"I am. I was before, but I get why tonight would be like a concrete line in the sand for you." He pressed his fingers against his glass, drawing patterns in the condensation absently. "I expected more from her. She knew how I felt about you, when we were in school and now, and still she attacked you." Moisture gathered in his eyes and he swallowed hard. "Attacked Phoebe, who would have embraced her if she'd just left her baggage outside the door."

Tears burned behind my eyes as I watched him try to hold his sadness in. "If we don't make a big deal out of it, Phoebe won't remember, and if you feel like trying again in a couple of months, we can."

He was shaking his head before the words had finished forming. "I appreciate the sentiment, Mel, but she doesn't deserve it. I just don't want her trying to tear Phoebe down the way she used to you. I'm sorry she did that to you and that I didn't listen to you. I never understood why she did it, and I still don't, but I don't want to risk it, do you?"

My smile was grim as I sipped my cocktail. "No, I don't want to, but I'd agree to supervised visits if you needed that."

My phone rang in my bag, interrupting us before Dan could respond. I pulled it out of my handbag with an apologetic look.

"I'm sorry."

Dan's brows furrowed with worry as he waited for me to answer it. It could have been Ella calling to say there was a problem, so I understood that look far too well.

I frowned at the caller ID before answering. "Mam?"

"Are you okay, Sweetheart? Ella called me." Concern dripped from my mother's voice.

"What is it?" Dan mouthed across the table, intrigue and confusion warring in his eyes. I shrugged.

"How much did Ella tell you?"

"It's Ella. What do you think?" My mother chuckled.

"She gave you a blow by blow?"

"Exactly. Annette's damn lucky I wasn't there." Anger vibrated down the line and my frown deepened. My mother rarely voiced her anger. "I'd have thrown her out the window for talking to my girls like that."

"I'm okay, mam. Better now she's not in my flat or anywhere near Phoebe."

My eyes were fixed on Dan, assessing him for the slightest reaction to my words. He didn't give one. He just sipped his drink, his head tilted towards me, trying to hear my mother.

"Dan did well." She sighed. "I might have been wrong about him."

"What did she say?" he mouthed.

"Later," I mouthed back.

"I can't tell you how happy I am hearing you say that." All of the sadness and agitation evaporated with those simple words. "I know he'll be really happy to hear it too."

She cleared her throat. "Could you pass him the phone? I owe him an apology."

"Sure." I held out the phone to Dan, my heart fluttering in my throat. "She wants to talk to you."

Dan's brows rose, but he accepted the phone. I sipped my drink while they talked. It was a quick call but with each second that ticked by the effects of the night melted away. He relaxed into his chair and nodded along with her, murmuring quiet agreements.

Oh, how the tables had turned. Now I was the one on the edge of my seat, trying to hear the entire conversation.

"What did she say?" I asked when he hung up.

He slid the phone across the table towards me, his face ablaze with happiness.

"I scored an invite to Christmas dinner. That's progress, right?" He grinned.

My mother guarded her Christmas guest list closely. Invited friends had to be vetted to make sure they wouldn't derail the festive cheer.

"That's huge progress. Did she apologise?"

He nodded. "She didn't need to, though. I would have done the same in her position."

I chuckled. "You've got at least two decades before you have to worry about that."

He scowled. "I had better have two decades."

"Okay, daddy, focus." I patted his arm, grinning at his pain. Welcome to my world. "Stop stalling and fill me in."

"We're patched up. Or at least, from the way she said it, I've earned a clean slate, so I'd better use it wisely." He scrubbed a hand across his jaw, his eyes twinkling. "I'll be honest, I'm a bit shocked."

"You and me both."

All the pieces were falling into place.

※

We were laughing when we returned to the flat. A complete contrast to the sombre way we'd left. Finding Jared sat on a tiny toy chair again, colouring quietly with Phoebe was an unexpected sight. For a second, I caught sight of Ella frowning at Jared from the kitchen. She stood there entirely oblivious to our entrance, leaning against the worktop, nursing a steaming mug of tea.

When she noticed us, she straightened. Her expression cleared instantly, replaced by a sunny welcoming smile that was almost her normal. It wasn't good enough to fool me—my sister was unnerved and Jared Michaels had something to do with it.

"Mammy!" Phoebe cried, rushing towards me. "Look what Uncle Jared helped me make."

Ella growled into her tea cup while Jared grinned at her. If she could see the picture, she'd have steam coming out of her ears. It was a stick figure drawing of five figures.

"Is this you?" I asked, kneeling down in front of Phoebe.

She nodded. "And that's you. That's daddy, and that's Auntie Ella, and Uncle Jared."

Ella stiffened. She glanced at me sharply, her eyes trying to drill through the paper. I angled it away from her. She didn't need to see Phoebe's interpretation of her relationship with Jared. In the image, his stick figure had his arm around her. There were arrows pointing to each of us.

"It's beautiful," I told Phoebe, holding the paper to my chest. "Why don't you go add it to your pinboard?"

She snatched it from me and ran off to her room.

I straightened and met Ella's narrowed gaze. "Thanks for staying, guys."

"No worries," Jared murmured, shrugging into his coat. "I'll get out of your hair though, so you can enjoy some peace and quiet."

"And thanks for calling mam, Els." I pulled my sister into a tight hug. "You have no idea how much that helped."

She squeezed me back. "Oh, but I do. I'm glad it went to plan."

Dan stepped in the moment I released her with his arms wide open. "Thanks for my Christmas dinner invite."

She grinned. "You're welcome. The distraction from my love life will be more than welcome."

We both chuckled.

When they'd gone, Dan started making dinner while Phoebe and I settled on the sofa with a film. *It could get used to this.* Dan kept catching my eye across the room, smiling like he had everything he needed in this one room. I knew exactly how he felt.

CHAPTER TWENTY-FIVE

I woke up Monday morning on cloud nine. Seriously, it felt like I was floating. Work passed by so smoothly that by the time 3PM rolled around and I had to pick up Phoebe, I could take the rest of the afternoon off without worry.

"Do you want to see where Daddy works?" I asked Phoebe when I picked her up.

"Yes," she shouted as I buckled her into her car seat.

I'd anticipated as much, warning Dan that we'd be coming before I'd even made the offer. An insecure part of me still held on to a worry that he'd change his mind about wanting us in his life. Thankfully, it was a lot quieter after last night.

Maybe I should have expected the ringing in my eardrums though.

When I pulled up at the studio address, I stared around the site with a frown. It was an industrial site. The building looked like a regular old mechanic's shop or something, covered in grey metal sheeting and broken up by only a heavy red security door.

I fired off a text to Dan before I unbuckled Phoebe, checking we were in the right place.

"Hurry up, Mammy," Phoebe demanded, bouncing in her seat, barely containing her excitement. "Daddy needs my help."

"Does he now?"

"Yes." She nodded, her expression stern.

"When did he tell you that?"

"When I tucked her in last night," Dan said, making me jump out of my frigging skin.

I turned to face him with a scowl. He sniggered at my expression, keeping himself out of arm's length.

"Want to make a noise next time?" I muttered, glaring at him still.

He smirked. "Whatever you say, babe."

Grumbling to myself, I pulled Phoebe out of the car. The squirming toddler reached for Dan immediately and despite his jump scare, I couldn't find it in me to be annoyed at her wanting to be near him. I'd had her for nearly four years, it was his turn now.

❋

*J*ared was laying down a drum track in the sound booth when we walked in. Ryan and James sprawled out on sofas in the room next door. Nia was focused on photographing Jared's grim-faced determination as he pounded his drum kit. The man was kind of terrifying when he focused like that.

Ryan and James glanced up from their phones when we entered, genuine welcoming smiles painted their faces.

"Oh, this is going to be fun," James murmured, his eyes dancing as he took in Phoebe's electric gaze.

It swept around the space, focusing on Jared's drums with an interest I didn't like.

"Why don't you give her a go on your bass, Dan?" Ryan suggested, spotting the same eagerness I had.

"Mel might wish she'd never brought her." James grinned, his gaze fixed on me with understanding. He shrugged. "My mother definitely wasn't happy when I picked up a guitar, but it was better than the drums I wanted first."

"So you're saying it could be worse?" I asked, amusement dripping from my words despite the lowkey dread.

I'd have to move. I wasn't rude enough to let someone play music in a flat. This lot probably didn't care, it was so ingrained in their lives, but I couldn't do it to my neighbours, even if I'd never met them.

Ryan snorted. "A lot worse." His gaze fixed on Jared, going ballistic in the recording studio.

Point taken.

"Give her the guitar."

They all laughed again. Dan smoothed a hand over my lower back as he passed. He caught my eye with something similar to an apology, but it wasn't one, because he didn't mean it. It would be impossible for him to hide that excitement. He wanted to share a part of himself with Phoebe. And I didn't blame him.

He settled on another sofa, placing Phoebe at his side while he picked up his bass. Resting it in his lap, he explained the instrument to her quietly. I took a seat in a spare armchair and watched them with a burn behind my eyes. Why did the sight of him playing chords for her make me teary-eyed? It was so sweet. My dad had never bothered trying.

At his insistence, she plucked at the strings, eliciting endless giggles.

All of us were distracted by her. Well, all but the sound engineer. He was steadfast in his concentration, which was impressive when some of her giggles were painfully loud.

Ryan's phone rang, breaking the carefree atmosphere. His entire body tensed as he answered it.

"Hello?" Ryan said, sitting forward.

Dan's gaze flew to him, and James turned in his seat so he could watch him with a disconcerting intensity.

"Yeah, this is Ryan." He glanced at Dan and nodded.

As if it was even possible, the tension ramped up in the room. What the hell was going on?

The drumbeat stuttered to a halt in the next room. I strained to hear the other side of the conversation, but I was too far away and the volume on his phone was set too low. The door to the sound booth opened and Jared joined us, followed by Nia.

"That'd be bloody brilliant." A smile broke across Ryan's face. "We'll be there."

He nodded at the guys and started to lower the phone, but the person on the other end wasn't done with him. Ryan listened intently as the guys exploded from their seats, absolute joy overtaking their features. Well, Dan and James's features. Jared leaned against the doorway with what I could only characterise as a gutted expression on his face.

I repeat: what the hell was going on?

Nia perched on the armchair next to me. "I'm assuming this means they got it."

"Got what?" I asked, my confusion audible.

"Didn't Dan tell you they were up for the The Kasey Show?"

I glanced at the man in question. He was dancing Phoebe around the room while James and Ryan looked on with huge smiles.

"No, he didn't say anything." It was huge news. A massive opportunity for them.

"That's weird." She frowned, her focus on James. "It's all they've talked about in here for weeks."

A live broadcast that millions tuned in for each weekend. Some of the greats had been on it over the years. I should be happy for them. I swallowed. "When is it?"

"Saturday."

Phoebe's birthday was on Saturday.

How could he film a show in London and be at her party? The answer was simple: he couldn't.

His face was lit up with joy right now, and I couldn't share an ounce of it. No, I was caught in a rerun of all my Dan-shaped disappointments. How on earth would I explain his absence to Phoebe?

"They need us there by three for sound check," Ryan said, pocketing his phone. "I'll talk to Matt about a hotel and car."

"And security?" Jared asked, with an uneasy quality to his voice that I couldn't figure out. He still leaned against the doorframe, his face grim.

Why wasn't he overjoyed, too?

Ryan nodded. "I'll move up their start."

Jared relaxed a fraction. Something wasn't right there. My gaze snagged on Dan, swinging Phoebe around the room. I had my own concerns to deal with.

"Isn't this great?" Dan stopped in front of me, grinning like a fool with my daughter mirroring him, having no clue that the excitement would lead to tears.

Someone had placed a lead ball in my stomach.

"Yeah." The word came out weak. I'd never been a good actor. The one time I even tried to take drama in school, I failed it spectacularly. A wooden, sweaty mess my teacher had called me. Faced with Dan practically bouncing at news that gutted me, I wasn't much better.

"We could have a weekend in London just us," Dan said, enthusiasm still dripping from him. He was so focused on the win he wasn't thinking.

"That's a lovely idea." I tried to smile but it felt all kinds of wrong. "But I've got Phoebe's birthday party all set up."

His brow furrowed for a second before his eyes widened. The pieces finally slid into place for him.

"Shit," he mouthed, mindful of Phoebe still dancing in his arms.

He glanced back at the guys, indecision blanketing his features. I braced myself. This was it. He'd made such a fuss about missing those important first moments in Phoebe's life. Part of me hoped he'd remember that and make the right choice. The other half knew it wasn't going to be that simple.

When he turned back to me, he was biting his lip, and I knew.

"It's fine," I lied, my newfound faith in him cracking.

"Mel."

"No, it's important to you." I took Phoebe from him, trying to smile to make the words believable. If I got into it now, I'd cry, and I refused to cry in front of his bandmates. "I get it."

I didn't.

"I should get her home," I said, not looking at him. "Let you guys get back to work."

"Mel," he said again, a crack in his voice. I ignored it, ignored the way it tugged at my heart.

With a lump in my throat, I got out of there. He didn't follow me, but then he knew me well enough by now to realise it wouldn't have done him any good. He'd made his choice. He'd chosen music over his family.

That's what he said we were, right?

A family.

Funny how it didn't apply when the music came calling. It was my dad all over again. He'd been made of pretty words and no follow through as well.

Tears slipped down my cheeks as I made my way to the car. Shouldn't have let myself hope. I knew better.

CHAPTER TWENTY-SIX

My phone vibrated across my desk. Dan's name lit up the screen, and I was paralysed. I didn't know what to say to him. He wisely chose to give me space Monday night and didn't try to stop by my flat, but now we were on day two of me dodging his calls, and it felt all kinds of wrong.

Yet I couldn't stop.

The screen went dark, and I slumped back in my chair. Dylan, Charlotte, and Lisha were out grabbing lunch. In work, I could put on a pretty successful front — everything was fine, I wasn't upset, I was just getting on with the job. If I'd gone for lunch, they would have grilled me and I would have broken.

Hell, I was dodging Nia and Sophie's calls for the very same reason. Talking about it would make it real.

Talking about it meant I had to do something about it. It meant I had to have all sorts of complicated, life-altering conversations.

So I dodged his calls.

Pretty sure I used to be braver than that. The old me wouldn't have hidden away. She shouted her demands and then shrugged when it didn't go to plan. Of course, I'd tried that with him once and it failed epically. He told me he was going to Glasgow, and I'd asked him to stay.

Not-so-spoiler alert, he didn't stay.

I frowned at the dark screen, twisting my lip between my fingers as I scrambled for some sort of solution. A decision. An action. Anything but this helplessness.

If I did nothing, we would fall apart.

And yet, what else was I meant to do?

Cave in and say it was all fine?

That would be a colossal lie. It wasn't okay. I was disappointed and dejected, that was the truth. Talking to him about it wouldn't eradicate that feeling. He'd still decided that a gig was more important than us.

And say I accepted it and let it go now, what about the next time?

With his career and the band's ambitions, there would definitely be a next time. So what I chose to do now would set a precedent.

I needed advice from the one person who had been through this. The sound of the phone ringing filled my ears as I locked myself in the staff toilets. Everyone was still out but I really didn't want company for this conversation.

"Hi sweetheart, I'm in the middle of something. Can I call you back in half an hour?" My mother asked, her voice distracted.

A sob broke me before she'd even finished speaking. I'd held it together since yesterday afternoon. I hadn't cried once since leaving the studio, and *now* I broke? Frustration swept through me, making my face hurt.

"Mel, what's wrong?"

I blew out a breath, willing myself to calm down. Swallowing, I tried to explain. "I don't know what to do, mam. He made such a big deal of missing Phoebe's life, but now he's going to miss her birthday party for a live show."

"Dan's got a concert on Phoebe's birthday?" My mother asked, her words slow and measured.

"Yes, and it's a huge opportunity, so there's no way he won't do it." I plucked some tissues from the box on the counter and dabbed at my eyes. "What do I do?"

"There's nothing you can do."

"Wh— What?"

"He's a musician, love. You knew how this would go." She sighed. "I don't know why you're upset about it."

My breath caught in my throat. "Because the man I love won't put me or his daughter first. He didn't even pause, mam. He completely forgot it was her birthday."

Silence filled the line, and the longer it went on, the stronger the tension headache at the back of my head became.

"Listen, you're not going to like what I'm about to say, but I have to say it."

I stiffened. My throat hurt as I swallowed. "What is it?"

"It doesn't get better," she whispered, regret lowering her voice. "You knew this day would come. You've seen it over and over again with your father. You should have been prepared, and I… I thought you were. The choice is to accept it or walk away from him forever."

Tears splashed down my cheeks as I stared at the lavender paint cracking on the cubicle doors. "I don't know what to do with that."

"I'm sorry, sweetheart."

I frowned, anger thrumming through me quick and fast. "You're not, though, are you? You didn't want me to get back together with Dan in the first place. You were glad when he didn't take my call all those years ago. Be honest, you're glad he's done this now."

A swift intake of breath was the only sound.

Moments ticked by, and I couldn't undo the damage,

couldn't claw the words back. Even if I could, I'm not sure I would have.

"There's no arguing with you when you're in this mood, Mel. So I'm not going to try."

She hung up and my eyes fell shut. Regret swept in hard. *I'm a fucking idiot.*

Doors slammed outside the bathrooms. The low murmur of voices floated down, signalling that my time was up. I needed to get it together and fast. Yet, the tears wouldn't stop flowing. I pressed tissues under my eyes to minimise the damage, but I shouldn't have bothered and just washed my makeup off. Concede defeat to the fact that my life was crumbling around me and I hadn't even had the pieces in place long enough to know what I was missing.

I shouldn't have said any of that to my mother. She didn't want me to get hurt, but I chose to give in to Dan. It was my decision to ignore the inevitable.

Just hadn't expected it to come so soon.

Somehow I got myself under control and was able to return to my desk without any curious glances from my colleagues. Well, from anyone but my work besties. All three of them studied me with narrowed eyes. Lisha opened her mouth to ask the question and I shook my head at her. There was a benefit to working closely with someone for so many years—they knew your tics. One look in my eyes and they all settled back in their chairs with a nod. Conversation turned to our latest campaign and I almost sighed, my relief palpable.

Now if only it were that easy to untangle my heart.

I was no closer to figuring it out when I had to collect a hyperactive toddler from nursery. What I should have anticipated was the redheaded giant camped out outside my flat.

He leaned against my door, his arms crossed and a grim look on his face. My chest hurt, just looking at him.

"Daddy," Phoebe shrieked, racing off down the hallway without thought.

His face lit up as she barrelled into him, hugging his calf. My eyes burned with tears at the sight of it but I had to harden my heart if I wanted to get through whatever was coming without breaking into pieces.

"Hey, munchkin, did you miss me?" he scooped her up into his arms, smiling like he didn't have a care in the world.

"Where were you?"

"I missed you too." He swept her up into his arms and turned towards the door, an expectant glint in his eyes while he waited for me to unlock the flat. "Did your mammy miss me?" he whispered into her ear.

I cut him with a sharp look as I pushed the door open.

"I think so," Phoebe said, her little voice deadly serious. "She keeps crying."

My back stiffened at her words. "Enough, Phoebe. Go wash up for dinner."

"But mammy…" she whined, holding tight to Dan.

"Now." My tone brooked no argument, and she pouted. At least she unattached herself from Dan's neck and let him put her down.

With her out of the way, I focused on pulling together dinner while he leaned against the wall. His gaze burned every inch of me.

"Why are you angry at me?" he asked after five minutes of my banging around the kitchen.

"I'm not." Slam.

His brows quirked. "Want to try that again, babe?"

"Why?" Bang.

"Because you've clearly got something on your mind, and it might help if you told me what it was." Despite his crossed arms, he wore a patient expression.

"I don't know what you're on about." Crash.

The plates drying on the rack clattered into the sink, cracking as they hit the porcelain, and I stopped dead. My throat closed up so fast I wasn't ready for it. Something about the sight of the broken remnants of my dishes swept under my defences. My eyes burned and I rubbed at them, willing the emotion to go away.

"Shit," Dan growled as I sniffled.

His strong arms wrapped around me, tugging me back into his hard chest. It was too familiar. I didn't want him to let me go.

"This isn't the best time for this, Dan. I need to get Phoebe fed and ready for bed." I shook off his hold and stepped away. "Please just go, we'll talk tomorrow."

"No."

I spun to face him, my eyes wild. "What the hell do you mean, no?"

"Exactly what I said. No. I'm not leaving." He crossed his arms and stared at me with determination my emotions couldn't handle yet. "You're trying to shut me out, and I'm not willing to let that happen. So I have an alternative suggestion." He advanced on me and I backed away, failing to escape him as he followed. "I'll make dinner. We'll get Phoebe ready for bed *together*, and then we'll talk."

Dan didn't give me a chance to argue. He poured me a glass of wine and guided me towards a stool at the island. Once I was seated, he went to work cleaning up the smashed plates.

I should have pushed him out the door. Pitched a fit and forced him out. I was capable of it. The anger was a sizzle just beneath the surface.

I couldn't voice it.

So instead, I sat there and watched him act like everything was fine, like he hadn't chosen his career over his daughter's birthday.

CHAPTER TWENTY-SEVEN

*I*f it hadn't been for Phoebe's constant chatter, we would have eaten dinner in awkward silence. Or not, if the fire in Dan's eyes was anything to go by. I curled up on the sofa while he tucked Phoebe in and read her a bedtime story. Seeing him squeezing his big body onto her tiny bed while she stared up at him with utter adoration would have broken me, and I needed my strength. He wasn't going to walk out the door without a fight.

"She's asleep," Dan said, his voice subdued as he joined me on the sofa.

I hummed in response. He took a seat next to me, turning so he could study me. My knees were tucked under me, and I leaned against the arm, angling myself away from him. It was too hard to look at him. All I'd feel was my heart cracking and I didn't want it. I wanted to be numb. *Why the fuck can't I numb myself like I used to?*

"Tell me what happened in the studio, Mel." He rested his arm across the back of the sofa, reaching for me but not touching. His eyes burned my skin as they traced my face. "You're avoiding me again, and I have no idea what I did."

"Are you doing the live show?" The words came out choked, barely making it past the lump in my throat.

"Of course we are. It's a huge opportunity."

I searched his face for some understanding of what that meant for me, for us. "Okay, and what about Phoebe's birthday party?"

His brow furrowed. "I don't know. I completely forgot it was the same day, babe, but we're talking about the Kasey Show. If we turn it down, we won't get another offer."

My laugh was hollow. His face tightened with concern. I wanted to slap it away. "Then go, Dan!" I threw my feet down on the floor and powered up off the sofa. "Go, have the time of your life. Enjoy your precious fucking music career."

"What does that mean?" He stood, following me into the kitchen where I poured myself another huge glass of wine.

I whirled on him. "You know what it means," I hissed. "You've spent the last month telling me it's different, but here you are, repeating history. What the hell is stopping you from doing it again?"

He scoffed, throwing his hands up in exasperation. "I'm not your dad, Mel. Painting me with his mistakes isn't going to help us."

"Then stop making his mistakes." I swallowed. "Stop repeating your own mistakes. I want to be able to share the important moments in my life with you. Phoebe will want that too."

"Last I checked, I was only going to London for a night." He paced towards me, closing the tiny distance I'd created. "I should have discussed Glasgow with you. I know I fucked up back then, but I was an inconsiderate teenager, and I learnt my lesson. The London show isn't that."

"You pitched a fit about missing important moments in Phoebe's life." I pointed to the photo album tucked between the cookbooks on my kitchen counter. "And now you're *choosing* to do it. I can forgive you doing it to me, but not her."

Dan sighed, dragging his hand through his hair as he followed me around the flat. "There's always compromise in this industry, babe. There'll be yearlong tours, months at a time on the road, and in studios who knows where in the world. You know this. We just need time to figure out what our lives look like when that happens."

"You've already decided how our lives will work?"

He shook his head, but his lips were pinched and he was holding himself with this cautious set to his shoulders. The fucker had mapped out my life.

"Don't lie to me."

"What will it take for me to prove to you that I'll be here, that I'll never leave Phoebe?"

Every time he specified that everything he did was for Phoebe, the crack in my heart widened. I just wanted him to love me enough to consider me before he chased after the next opportunity with a blind drive. *Why can't he understand that I need him to be here for* me*?*

"I'm not your dad. I'll always come home. I'll try not to miss big moments, but I can't control the music industry or the opportunities it decides to offer me."

"I can't deal with this right now, Dan." I spun away, pressing the heel of my hand to my forehead in the hope I could will the incoming tears away.

There was a shuffle behind me and Dan said my name. With my heart in my throat, I turned to find him on one knee and my stomach hit the floor.

"Please don't," I whispered, tears streaming freely down my face. I didn't even try to swipe them away.

"Melanie Griffiths, you're the love of my life." Tears shimmered in his eyes and I swallowed hard. "I can't imagine my life without you and Phoebe. Nothing was right before I came home. I need you in it. Will you marry me?"

I shook my head as I backed away. My back hit the fridge hard and I slid down it, my eyes fixed on the diamond glittering under the spotlights. When had he bought it? Why had he bought it? There was no way getting married would patch the holes in our relationship.

"I cherish our family, babe. I don't know why you'd doubt that."

I snorted at that. If he cherished us, he wouldn't be on his knees now, and he would have had a conversation with me before agreeing to the live show.

"You cherish Phoebe, I know." My voice hardened along with my face. "You don't need to keep repeating it. I believe you, but I can't marry you." Swiping my hands across my eyes, I forced myself back to my feet. "That would be the worst mistake we could make."

His mouth moved but no sound came out. Brows furrowing, he stared up at me. "I don't understand," he finally whispered as he climbed to his feet. "What do you want from me, Mel?" Dan demanded, his arms outstretched. "I'm here, aren't I?"

"For now."

"No, always. I love you. The last ten years couldn't change that, and nothing will now." His features hardened as he considered me. "So what if it's hard? We're together, we love each other, and we have a healthy daughter. All the rest of it can be worked out as we need."

"I don't," I said, my voice hoarse as I choked on the lie.

His expression slackened and every inch of him froze. He swallowed hard and whispered, "You don't what?"

"I don't love you."

He was shaking his head before I finished. "I don't believe you."

I crossed my arms and forced the pain away. "And I believed you were going to at least try and put me—and Phoebe—first. I guess we both lied."

Silence fell between us. His gaze roamed my face,

searching for a crack. I hoped he wouldn't find one. If he didn't leave soon, I'd crumble.

"We wouldn't work, Dan." The words came out soft, lacking the anger of a moment ago. Moisture burned in my eyes again, warning that it was only a matter of time before I broke down. "It's good that we know that now. We can focus on raising Phoebe without any of the emotional destruction our relationship would have caused."

He winced, but the fire didn't go out in his eyes. "I don't think you mean that. We've been good together the last couple of weeks. There's absolutely no reason we…" His jaw slackened as some devastating thought I couldn't read flitted across his face. "You don't think I'd be a good father…"

"That's not what I said." I frowned. "This is about us. Our ability to have a healthy relationship." I gestured between us, willing him to hear me, even though I could see him shutting down. "You're a great father. There's absolutely no reason you should doubt that. Phoebe is obsessed with you. I'm pretty sure she likes you more than me." I bit my lip as those last words left my lips. The look he gave me was anything but reassured.

"It would make sense, the fact you didn't try to tell me." His eyes were glazed over and despite the fact he was staring straight at me, he wasn't seeing me.

"I didn't try because you fobbed me off." Exasperation overtook me and I barely contained a growl. "We've been through this, Dan. It was the wrong time in our lives and I was terrified of having to live through heartbreak after heartbreak."

His lips thinned. "And now you're choosing that. I'm never going to understand this, am I?"

I almost laughed. He wasn't going to understand? Try being the person he repeatedly overlooked when it came to his career.

"Clearly not." I crossed my arms and glanced away.

This was pointless. We were just going round and round in circles, hurting each other in the process. If he still wasn't seeing things my way, he never would. I had a clear picture of how our lives would unravel if I gave into him and went along with his act first, think later approach. I'd end up alone at home with the kids while he lived the wild life on tour. There was no way I'd avoid turning into my mother.

"We're not getting anywhere here, so maybe you should go." My voice was nothing but a wisp of sound, but he heard me all the same.

I don't think I'd ever seen Dan look crushed, but that wide-eyed, pinched look would haunt my dreams. It made me want to claw back every word and pretend everything was perfectly fine, make believe that our lives wouldn't implode, leaving me resentful of him. I couldn't stomach hating him. That would be worse than living without him.

He was silent, as he let himself out. The moment he stepped out of sight, the tears flowed freely. They robbed me of breath. Gasping, I crawled into bed, fully clothed, and just let the pain take over. *May as well get it out now.* Before I had to face Phoebe's onslaught of questions in the morning.

CHAPTER TWENTY-EIGHT

"Where's daddy?" Phoebe asked the next morning as she tore a potato waffle to pieces. She'd looked at me with narrowed eyes when I placed the plate in front of her without having to nag for them.

I was feeling guilty, so sue me.

"Away."

"Away where?"

"He's going to London, munchkin."

"Kay." She nodded before placing a piece of potato in her mouth.

I sipped my coffee and willed her to eat faster. I'd been slow on the uptake this morning and we were going to be late. Yet I couldn't make myself rush her. My energy stores were drained from a night of crying into my pillow.

"See daddy at party?" she asked with the most innocent look on her face. It wasn't really a question. She wasn't expecting the answer to be anything but a yes.

"We should get moving, Phoebs." I turned my back on her and emptied my coffee in the sink.

I didn't want to tell her, didn't want to see her face crumble the way my heart had last night. Was that so wrong?

Ushering her out the door was the easy part of the morning. I allowed myself to believe it was all going to be fine. Then we got in the car. She pitched a fit for Rhiannon's music. I put it on without an argument. It was something I'd have to get used to, even if it cut me in two every time I heard their songs.

Anger and sadness mingled inside of me, neither of them trying to win the other over. They were just content to quietly torture me with what ifs and doubts.

What if I'd let it all go? What if I'd cancelled the party I'd spent the last two months planning? What if I had it all wrong and he actually did love me enough?

Maybe he truly meant the proposal and it wasn't a ploy to shrug off my concerns. Maybe he truthfully planned to discuss a plan for our lives that wouldn't involve me giving up everything I loved. Maybe, and this was the killer, maybe he had changed, and I'd let the best part of me walk out the door.

The doubts only made me angrier. Doubting myself was not going to help me get in front of the pain.

I dropped Phoebe at day-care and headed into the office, hoping that work would offer some kind of reprieve from the inside of my head.

No such luck.

The moment I sat at my desk, the girls pounced.

"Who do I need to maim?" Charlotte asked as I powered up my PC.

"No one." My voice was subdued, while I focused on the screen. One sympathetic look, and I might break.

Lisha hummed next to me. "Wouldn't be lying to your work wives, would you?"

"Yes, because we all know how badly that works out." Charlotte swivelled towards me. The burn of her gaze made it really bloody hard not to look at her.

Dylan sighed. "Mel, you know they won't stop until you spill it. Just get it over with before they get obnoxious."

Lisha gasped. "I am never obnoxious."

"Whatever you say, Lish," Dylan drawled. "It's not like you didn't spend an entire day trying to get the new marketing manager to dish all his secrets like you had a right to them."

"I'm going to pretend you didn't say that and focus on the fact that our friend looks like she spent the night crying." Lisha's chair slid into my space and her elbow landed on the desk in front of me. "Now, why don't you share the damage, and we'll see if we can help you feel better." It was impossible to not look up when she was that close, and she damn well knew it.

Their faces fell as I filled them in. By some miracle, I got through it all without breaking down and crying. Maybe I'd cried myself out last night and this was my reprieve. One could dream.

"That sounds horrible. I'm so sorry, Mel." Lisha's hand engulfed mine, squeezing.

"I'm sorry it didn't work out," Charlotte murmured.

"I'm confused," Dylan said, breaking the trend. Her brows were furrowed as she studied me.

"What's confusing about it? The man picked a gig over his daughter's birthday party." Lisha slid back to her side of the desk.

"Fine, that part is shit." She nodded but the confusion clouding her blue eyes didn't clear. "What exactly did you want him to do, though? We all know you well enough to know you'd never ask someone to give up something they love, so I know you weren't trying to get him to choose you over the band, but I don't understand what he was meant to do."

My throat convulsed before her words had fully registered. *Shit, I guess I'll be crying at work for the second time in a week.*

Charlotte frowned at her. "Honey, the fact his solution was to cancel a party she's spent months working on is the problem."

Lisha nodded. "Yeah, like don't just say things will work.

Put in the effort to make a plan that suits them both. I didn't hear any such thing. Did you?"

"And," Charlotte growled, "he's buggered off and left her to explain to Phoebe that he'd rather be on stage than with her on her birthday."

They continued on, but I couldn't pay attention, couldn't stop myself from zoning out. I don't think I even got my emails open, I just disappeared inside my head. They were all right and that just left me a confused mess with no sense of which way was up.

Did I want him to choose between me and the band? I didn't think so, but I couldn't see a way our lives could peacefully coincide while music was his first priority. Wasn't that the same thing?

I was no closer to an answer when Owen tapped me on the shoulder just before lunch. Somehow, I'd managed to get at least some light admin done.

"Can I borrow you for a second, Mel?" He nodded towards the conference room with a friendly smile.

I nodded and followed him into the glass-encased room. Purposefully choosing a seat that would put my back to the other room, I sat and forced a pleasant 'nothing to see here' smile to my lips.

"What can I help you with?" I asked when he spun his chair to face me and propped his elbows on the conference table.

Please say he hasn't noticed my lack of attention the last few days.

"Nothing in particular right now. I just wanted to check in and see how things are going." He settled back with that easy confidence that helped him win most deals. "It's been awhile since we caught up."

I nodded, my smile starting to fracture. *What the hell was going on?*

"The work from home flexibility seems to be working well.

Can't tell you how impressed I am that you managed to pull off the Michael's campaign." He tilted his head, his sincere eyes fixed on me. I usually found it endearing, but right now, it was setting me on edge. What was he trying to get at? "Most of the people in that room would have struggled with the campaign alone, especially with the curveballs you got thrown at the eleventh hour, but you just kept ticking through."

"Uh… thank you?"

He chuckled. "It's not a trick question, Mel. You know I've always seen incredible potential in you."

His words settled in my mind, reminding me of how strong I actually was. Heartbroken or not, I was still strong willed. I sat forward and pushed my shoulders back, embracing the piece of myself that had been missing all day. "Okay?" I couldn't take it anymore. "What are you trying to get at, Owen? I'm struggling to figure out where this is going."

"There she is." Owen grinned, his eyes lighting up with genuine pride. "I can tell something's wrong. From Lisha and Charlotte's hushed rants, I have an inkling that it's something to do with a certain red-haired musician…" I opened my mouth to say who knows what — reassure him that I could do my job— but he held up his hand and continued, "but I don't need you to confide in me. I just wanted to remind you that you're amazing at your job."

I blinked, still unsure of the entire conversation. "Thank you."

"You're still the most capable person on my team, so if I can make anything easier for you, just let me know." His gaze caught mine, holding me in what felt like a staring contest only I could almost feel him shouting at me to ask for something. "For example, if you needed to work remotely, on a prolonged basis, at any point."

I wanted nothing more than to sink back into the chair as his meaning sank in. Prolonged basis like…while Dan toured?

Fuck, my boss was trying to clear the path for me, and it was too late.

"That's quite a generous offer. Thank you."

His brows rose at my subdued answer. "You're welcome. Just make sure you take me up on it someday soon."

With that, he led the way out of the conference room while my heart pounded in my throat. I felt faint, sick even. *Had someone turned the heating up?* I collapsed into my chair and shrugged out of my cardigan, far too hot. *Would it draw too much attention if I rested my head on the desk?*

Shit, what was I going to say in a couple of months when he asked why I hadn't chosen to work remotely?

"What did he say?" Charlotte asked just as I decided it would be perfectly fine if I pressed my forehead against the desk while my heart rate slowed down.

Their faces scrunched up with sympathy as I explained Owen's offer. Could you call it an offer?

"Oh honey, I'm sorry."

Dylan frowned at her. "Why? Doesn't that make part of the problem better?"

My eyes widened as her voice ricocheted around the office and heads turned towards us. "Dylan, church voices, please."

"Sorry," she whispered, ducking down in her chair as her face flushed crimson. "It helps though, right?"

I shook my head. "I don't know." Hell, I was now more confused than I'd been going into the conference room and that was a feat.

"There's no rush for you to figure it out, Mel," Charlotte said, rolling towards me. "Owen won't rescind the offer, so if you decide it fits *your* plan then take it. If not, maybe still take it and enjoy a little working holiday."

"Yes, that's a brilliant idea," Lisha hissed, grinning at me. "You've got at least a year before Phoebe's in school, right? And your mam's retired now. She could go with you."

It would be an ideal solution for me and Dan, but would it

have changed anything if Owen had made the offer a week or more ago?

Dan still didn't get it. He'd decided to play the live show. He didn't ask my opinion. He expected me to get on with his plans, rather than make them with me.

CHAPTER TWENTY-NINE

"What a pleasant surprise," my mother said when I walked into her kitchen later that night. She sat at the table with a cup of tea and a book. One look at my red face and her smile evaporated. "What did he do now?"

I chuckled. It wasn't a nice sound. "What makes you think I'm here because of Dan?"

Her brows climbed. "Aren't you?"

"Yes, but it could have been something else."

"On a Friday evening when you'd normally be tucking that one in?" She nodded to Phoebe, sleeping in my arms. She tutted, pushing back her chair and standing. "Put her down on the sofa and I'll put the kettle on."

My gaze roamed the quiet house. "Where's dad?"

It was a stupid question.

"Having a jam session with some friends." She shrugged, clicking the kettle on. "He won't be back for hours."

My brain stuttered to a halt. My dad was in his late fifties, and still, she had to put up with this. I put Phoebe down on the sofa, tucking her in with a throw before I started spiralling too far to claw my way back. I didn't need her to wake up and see me crying my eyes out.

"How do you do it?" I asked when I returned to the kitchen. I didn't even pause for small talk. Answers were a thing I needed right now, whether they made me feel better or not.

"Put up with your father and his musical aspirations?" She gestured towards the table and handed me a mug of steaming tea.

"Yes. I need to understand it." I sat across from her and cradled my cup between my hands. It was too hot, but I didn't care. The heat was comforting.

She pursed her lips as she considered my question. From that alone, I knew I wasn't going to like the answer. And I still needed it.

"Habit mostly." She sipped her tea, her brows pinching as she made sense of her own life.

"How is habit the solution to staying with someone?"

Her lips curled as she lay her hand on mine. "Sweetheart, to you, he's the absent father who couldn't prioritise time with you." A secretive glint entered her hazel eyes and she glanced away. "To me, he's the man I chose. Obsessions and all. He's sweet, funny, and when I really need him, he's here."

"But he wasn't here." I shook my head. "Not really. I broke my arm, and he was on the other side of the world."

"I could handle your broken arm just fine on my own, thank you very much," my mother scoffed, tapping my hand. "I mean the big things. When I was struggling and in over my head."

"When was that?"

She hummed, thinking back. "You were four, when Ella went through her phase of having fits. He dropped out of a huge international tour that year."

I stared at her, surprise rendering me speechless. So he'd actually chosen to miss out on half of my life... well that stung.

"What I'm trying to say is that when things get really serious, he's here." She let go of my hand and picked up her tea cup, shrugging. "Plus I love him. I didn't want anyone else."

I shook my head, struggling to understand it. "But doesn't all the time apart annoy you?"

"In the beginning, maybe, but I got used to it," she said, her voice wistful. "It made my life exciting sometimes. Everything was predictable but him."

I rubbed at my temples, the pieces not quite fitting together in the way I wanted them to. Coming here was meant to clear the fog and let me see some kind of sense in all this.

Loving Dan enough to get through long periods of separation wasn't the problem. It was whether I wanted that for myself. Whether I wanted my life to come second for the rest of our lives, because as he'd already proven, I, we, would be second priority. It would be me home in the UK, raising our daughter, while he toured entire continents for months at a time.

I could handle the small things myself. I would be, and already was, perfectly capable of handling the day-to-day dramas. As long as he came home, as long as he called.

"I chose our lives, sweetheart," my mother whispered. She watched me closely with a sympathetic eye. "There were countless opportunities to train in his world, but I knew that life wasn't for me. You have to draw some kind of satisfaction from the job to make working on a tour worthwhile. I didn't have that, and it would have hurt us."

"What kinds of opportunities?"

She waved the question away. "What I'm trying to tell you is that just because I chose not to go on tour, not to look for a way to fit into that life, doesn't mean you couldn't try." She bit her lip. "If you want to."

Immediately I shook my head. "How could I do that with Phoebe?"

"Big-time musicians travel with their kids all the time. You wouldn't be charting new territory." She held up her hands. "It was just a suggestion. Not a practical piece of advice." She smiled. "See, even I don't have all the answers."

I chuckled at that.

My gaze trailed over the kitchen I'd spent most of my childhood life in. The space held so many memories, the ghosts of countless birthday parties, baking parties, laughter-filled dinners. Despite the challenges of my dad always being on the road, we'd been happy most of the time.

But more than that, this one room felt like home.

Even now, the corner was overflowing with the supplies for tomorrow. The cake Nia had picked up was already chilling in the fridge, and boxes of brightly coloured pony party gear sat in boxes, waiting for a little girl to flip her lid at the streamers and balloons we'd managed to source. Tomorrow, Phoebe would have a party just like Ella and I had had growing up, with family and friends filling every room in this big house, laughing and chatting over the spiked juice in the kitchen and children running riot under our feet.

Between my best friends, Ella, my mother, grandparents, neighbours who had seen me grow through some of the most awkward phases of life, I'd never truly been alone.

I wanted that for Phoebe.

Tiredness swept through me. Answers weren't a thing I was capable of finding right now.

"Can I stay here tonight?"

"Of course you can. Just..." she trailed off, biting her lip. "Don't hide from him, sweetheart. I know I was hard on him, but he seems to have made a real effort with you the last few weeks."

My gaze fell to the scarred wooden table top. "I thought he had."

"What happened?"

I couldn't remember how much I'd actually said before blowing up. She hadn't given even a single hint that she was pissed at me for yesterday. She should be. I studied her like I could crack her secrets if only I looked hard enough.

"What is it, Mel?"

"I'm sorry about yesterday." I slumped back in my chair, remorse engulfing me. "I shouldn't have said those things to you, and I didn't mean them."

She reached for my hand across the table. "You were upset. I know you well enough not to take anything you say seriously when you're in self-destruct mode."

My brow furrowed. "So you're not mad?"

She shook her head, a small smile playing at her lips. "No, I'm not, but thank you for the apology." Patting my hand, she nodded for me to go on.

To be safe, I started from the beginning. I filled her in on the live event and the proposal, and sympathy creased her face.

"I can't offer any solutions. Life with a touring musician was never easy, but building one with someone in a band will be harder. You're just going to have to figure out how or if you two fit in each other's lives."

If I can make anything easier for you, just let me know. If you needed to work remotely on a prolonged basis at any point.

Owen's words from earlier today floated through my mind.

"Would I be losing myself if I chose to follow Dan on tour?"

My mother pursed her lips. "If it was what you wanted and you were enjoying your life, then I don't see why."

"So that's not why you didn't go?" I asked, my voice low and measured.

She shook her head. "I just didn't want to. I wasn't big on music and the world was different. The internet was new, and remote working wasn't even a concept."

"Owen made me an offer today, but I don't know if I should even entertain it." As I filled her in on my conversation, she nodded along, sipping her tea. I couldn't read her, couldn't figure out either way if she thought it was a terrible idea.

"That was generous of him," was all she said.

"Mam, can you stop being cagey and tell me what you think?"

"Should I have spiked your tea?" A single brow rose.

I glanced down at the cooling liquid. "Maybe."

She sighed. "Look, I can't tell you what to do. It *is* a generous offer, and if you decided it was the right thing for you, I'm sure the other pieces would fall into place."

"But?"

"There's no but." She chuckled at my scrunched-up face. "Is it what you want? If Dan walked in here right now and dropped a sudden tour in your lap, would you be comfortable picking up and following him?"

"If he dropped it in a way that suggested I didn't have a choice, then hell no." My voice vibrated with a sudden wave of anger.

"And if he told you he wouldn't do it if you only said the word?"

"I'd go." I didn't even have to pause to think. Despite everything, the thought of him stalling his dreams for me still turned my stomach.

"Then I think you have your answer." She pushed her chair back and gathered our cups. "Did you bring a bag, or will you need to pop home in the morning?"

"We're good. I'll be up early to get everything set up," I said as I stood, too distracted to really pay attention to anything.

Was it actually that easy?

"Okay, is Phoebe sleeping with you or in Ella's room?" Mam asked, loading the cups into the dishwasher.

And was it giving up a part of myself if the answer was yes?

"I'll tuck her into Ella's bed."

I wandered out of the kitchen, not really seeing anything while my mind tried to finally find the solution to this puzzle.

Was it actually a solution if he kept trying to take the choice away? I didn't need to search hard for that answer as I carried Phoebe up the stairs. It would be a resounding no. But if Dan had been paying attention all this time… well, then the answer might be different.

CHAPTER THIRTY

People were far too punctual. The clock struck one, and the bell went. The morning had flown by thanks to a steady stream of tasks. Between my mother and I, we were like drill sergeants, directing Nia and Ella on set up while Sophie entertained Phoebe. We could have hired caterers but home-made buffets had always been the way in this house.

"Would it kill them to be ten minutes late?" My father grumbled, climbing down from his ladder and making his way to the living room's sliding pocket doors. "They won't go up in flames for tardiness. I should know."

I laughed at him as I hung the last banner.

"I dare you to say that to their faces," Ella called from the other side of the living room where she also balanced on a ladder trying to get the last of the pieces in place.

If anyone could scare them into being late, it was him. Even in his fifties, he cut quite the imposing figure. Growing up, he'd been the definition of a gangly musician, standing over six feet with his brown hair flowing down his back. He'd conceded that it was too much work a couple of years ago and chopped it all off. Until then, he'd rivalled me for unruly hair.

"I see?" Phoebe demanded from the other side of the door. For such a small thing, her excited voice carried clearly.

"All in good time," he said, blocking her view with his body as he fit himself through the small gap he allowed in the doors.

I stepped off the ladder and glanced around. It looked like the entire cast of My Little Pony had thrown up on my parents' living room and dining room. Balloons swayed and Happy Birthday banners fluttered in the breeze from the open window. *Note to self: close the window.* The coffee table had been removed, along with any other sharp edge we couldn't trust Phoebe around, let alone someone else's toddler.

"I think we're done."

Ella sniggered. "Sure you don't want to add some streamers while we're at it?"

I shook my head at her, my first real smile of the week playing along my lips. "Mam would kill us."

She shrugged. "We don't live here anymore. We could do it and then vanish out the bathroom window."

My lips twitched but I turned my back on her, instead surveying the dining room. The buffet was all set up with pony paper plates and cups. A white tablecloth, plastered in the colourful animals dropped the table, already laid out with more food than our guests could eat. We'd somehow managed to find meats with the print on it — that was either going to be a disaster or no one would notice. The cake waited in the kitchen for reveal time, and my mother's special adult's-only punch had been mixed and stored out of the reach of grabby toddlers.

Even if I wasn't feeling a hundred percent, even if I kept looking at the door, searching for a specific face every time it opened, it wasn't hard to enjoy the anticipation.

"Come on, let's get my determined niece in here before she takes the door down." Ella pressed a hand to my shoulder.

Her smile was careful but sympathetic despite her teasing words from moments ago.

I nodded and let her guide me to the pocket doors. My hands rested on the handles and I braced myself. I could hear my dad's bellowing voice waxing poetic to the family members on the other side like it was perfectly normal for him to be in the same space as his children for longer than half an hour.

"Ready?" Ella whispered.

I wasn't allowed to say no. So, I took a deep breath and flung the doors open.

❄

You could barely hear the music over the toddlers screaming at each other in play and the chatter of adults. The jungle juice was well and truly flowing ,and by the time everyone had helped themselves to lunch, most of the adults had that buzzed glaze in their eyes. *Maybe it was a bit too strong this year.*

I hadn't had a drop yet. I was too close to an emotional wreck to risk it. Knowing my luck, I'd have one glass and spiral. Nope, no jungle juice for this mother.

Phoebe was showing every single person she could her ponies, and while she was perfectly safe surrounded by all the kids from her day-care and my aunts and uncles, I couldn't stop watching her. She hadn't asked where Dan was this morning. I'd gotten so used to fielding the question, the lack of it unnerved me. Somehow it made me miss him more. How was that even possible?

"I think this might be your mother's best yet. Has she tweaked the ratios?" Sophie asked, snagging my attention as she sucked down at least half a glass of juice with a straw.

"No, no, no." Nia slashed her hand out, catching our attention and proving that she had well and truly crossed the tipsy line already. "There's something new in it. Can't you taste it?"

Sophie took another deep pull from her straw. Her eyes lit up, and Ella laughed.

"You're right. It's orangey."

They turned to us with a question in their eyes.

"Don't look at us!" Ella held her hands up. "We were on the decorating committee. Mam was on booze duty, and she guards that recipe from even us. Besides, you two were in the kitchen with her. Weren't you paying attention?"

"I was on childminding duty." Sophie pointed at herself.

Dan and I used to sneak off with a jug of it when my parents weren't looking. Didn't matter how cold it was outside, we bundled up and whisked our stolen booze away to the trees lining the property. I'd been looking forward to his reaction to seeing the stuff again.

"I don't believe neither of you have ever spied on her and taken notes," Nia said, deflecting the problem back onto us.

The pair of them turned to me, accusation replacing the question.

"Sorry, Ella's right." I shrugged. "I can't help, but you both do remember where the bathroom is if you feel the slightest need to bring it back up, right?"

Their noses wrinkled.

"Thanks for that visual, Mel," Nia muttered.

"Yeah, don't put me off my cake, please." Sophie glared at me. "I have a date with at least two slices today, and you will not spoil my fun."

Before I could reply, someone tapped me on the shoulder. I turned to find my father.

"Mel, honey, can I borrow you a second?" he asked, his tone low but insistent. His gaze bounced around the room, anywhere but at me.

I immediately sought out Phoebe. She'd settled in the

corner with the toys. Other kids surrounded her, and she looked like she was holding court. My heart rate slowed as I followed him into the kitchen, now that I knew it wasn't about Phoebe. Thankfully, the room was empty but for my mother, who leaned against the kitchen sink nursing a cup of tea.

"No jungle juice for you?" I nodded to the teacup in her hands.

"I'm pacing myself," she said, before taking a deep drink from the cup. Any bets it wasn't tea?

"I uh…" Dad cleared his throat behind me and I turned to face him. Regret was a shadow in his eyes.

Ella slipped in the door behind him, and I held out my hand to her. Something told me I didn't want to hear this alone. She took my hand and squeezed as we faced our father together.

His gaze danced between us and our mother. He swallowed and tried again. "I'm sorry I haven't been here a lot."

My mother cleared her throat, and his gaze jumped back to her. Something like fear flickered there. *Had mam told him to explain himself to me?*

"I'm sorry I wasn't here all that much when you were growing up. I'm sorry I missed so many important moments in your lives." He swallowed, glancing away for a moment while he tried to gain control of the emotion glistening in his eyes. "Most of all, I'm sorry I made you doubt Dan."

My jaw dropped. I'd never heard my father utter the word sorry once in my entire life. To hear it three times in less than thirty seconds was unnerving. My mother's lips were pursed, and I couldn't tell what was her and what was him.

"I didn't know how to be a dad when you were growing up. It didn't come easy to me the way your mother says it does Dan." He shook his head. "But that's no excuse really. I could have tried, but I was selfish. I missed huge chunks of your lives and we barely have a relationship because of it."

He stepped towards me, sadness and regret glistening in his eyes and a hesitation to his steps, like he expected me to turn away. I didn't think I was capable.

"I thought I missed my chance, honey." His gaze tracked to the kitchen wall, behind which we could hear Phoebe's excited screeches. "Then you had that gorgeous little girl and I saw it for what it was, a second chance. I can't do anything about the past, but I want to be here now, if you'll let me?"

"Honestly, I didn't need your apology, Dad." He winced, and I held up my hand. "Let me finish. What I need is for you to start acting like my father, to make me feel like you at least care about my life." I bit my lip as pressure started to build behind my eyes. "I also need you to keep making Phoebe happy. Not asking a lot, am I?" I said the last with a teasing lift, and everyone laughed, breaking the tense atmosphere we'd been building.

He nodded, his face wet with tears. "I can do that."

For the first time since I was little, I let my father wrap his arms around me. I'm not sure who held who tighter. When we separated, my mother had given up any attempt to stem her tears, and she joined the rest of us in a family hug.

Ella's smile was huge but watery when we all broke apart. My mother wasn't faring much better, and dad tucked her into his side.

"Pacing yourself, did you say, Maddy?" He chuckled when she growled at him.

With his arm around her, for the first time in so long, I could enjoy their love for what it was, without the stain of our failed relationship colouring my view. Instead of pain in my mother's eyes, all I saw now was love and joy, things that had always been right in front of me.

Things I wanted so desperately in my own life.

Phoebe's chatter grew closer, and everyone straightened. My mother dropped her teacup in the sink and stepped away from it like she hadn't consumed a cocktail of at least five hard liquors.

When Dan pushed open the kitchen door with Phoebe in his arms, my breath caught. Why wasn't he in London? They should have had soundcheck by now. He should have been doing whatever it is musicians do in the green room before shows.

Instead, he stopped in the doorway, Phoebe squirming in his arms. His eyes fixed on me and the hesitation in those green depths hurt. *I deserve that.*

My mother cleared her throat. "We'll give you two a minute."

"But don't take too long," Ella said, glancing between the two of us with narrowed eyes. "It's nearly cake o'clock, and I'm running low on sugar." She plucked Phoebe from Dan's arms on her way out the door. "Aren't we, Phoebs?"

"Yes!" Phoebe shouted. She pointed at us over Ella's shoulder, a cute little frown on her face. "Want cake."

Chuckling, my parents followed, leaving me alone in the almost silent kitchen with Dan.

"I wasn't sure if you'd want to see me." Dan stuffed his hands in his pockets. "But it didn't feel right to not be here."

"What about the show?"

"I was so miserable, the guys sent me home." He shrugged. A grain of amusement filled his voice as he edged towards me.

"I don't understand." Confusion made my voice breathy. "How can they do the show without you?"

Dan took another step. He was so close, my hands itched to touch him. I fisted them instead. *No, answers first.*

"They got a fill-in." His brow erased and the amusement faded.

I frowned. "That's a thing?"

He nodded. "Ryan suggested it Monday after you left, but

I was too much of a prideful sod to realise it was actually the perfect solution." Sighing, he took another step towards me. He was almost within reach now. "I'm sorry I didn't listen."

For the first time since I heard about the show, the tension inside me eased. He chose us. I bit my cheek, trying to hold back my smile.

"You're going to have to spell it out for me." I swallowed hard against the lump in my throat. Couldn't do anything about the burn of tears, but at least I could talk. "What does this mean, Dan?"

He stopped so close I had to tilt my head back to read his face. "It means I'm here, and if you still want me, I'd like to show you that it's not just a one-time deal."

"Not a one-time deal?"

His hands smoothed up and down my arms and I willed myself to stay strong.

"It took me a hot second, but I get it." He stared into my eyes and I couldn't look away, didn't want to. "I hate that you compare me to your dad, but I get it now, babe."

I pressed my hands against his chest, not pushing him away, just touching. I couldn't stop myself, I needed that contact badly.

"You're right, I was too much of an idiot back then to raise my head from the music. Apparently, I'm still not that smart. It's the only explanation I have for the fact I couldn't see that you needed me to be here for you before our family." He smirked as my eyes widened. "Yes, I finally got what you were saying all along." He stroked my cheek, his calloused fingers scraping against my sensitive skin while his eyes bored into mine, trying to communicate something that I daren't believe. "The music is great but it's not enough. Babe, there's plenty of room in my life for the music and you," a small smile quirked the edges of his lips and his eyes shone with unshed tears, "and Phoebe."

"We have to talk through decisions together. You can't just

decide you're doing something on the other side of the world and vanish without thinking about how it affects us." I sucked in a deep breath and stopped backing away. Instead, I closed the distance again. "It's bad enough that I remember, but her? I'm surprised I haven't had questions all morning about where you are and why she doesn't have presents from you. The fact she didn't say a word was even more heartbreaking." I pointed towards the living room, my eyes watering. "That little girl adores you. Don't ruin that, please." My voice cracked and I lost the battle with the tears. "There can be no half measures. You have to commit to her."

Pain shimmered in his eyes. "I know you turned me down because you think I wouldn't be a good dad," Dan said, wincing as he said it. "But I can't stay away from you, babe. I need you more than music."

"First, you're an amazing dad. Get that out of your head." He nodded, but he didn't look convinced. "I'm serious, Dan. You're doing great and you probably would have done great four years ago too."

A sad smile curled his lips. "But *we* would have suffered, right?"

"Unfortunately." I forced my face to gentle. "It's better this way." We did fine, just the two of us. I was strong enough to handle a full time job and raise Phoebe, even with her tonsillitis attacks. Yes, it would have been nice to have someone to share the ups and downs with, but it wasn't necessary.

He nodded. "Okay, then it's a good thing I'm not going anywhere." He leaned towards me, his expression deadly serious. "I'm not leaving *you* or her."

My brows climbed and my hands landed on my hips. "And what is that supposed to mean?"

One look at his hard determined eyes and my heart started galloping again. "It means I'm going to be here for you. I'm going to help you the way I would have from the start and when the music comes calling, we'll discuss it before I jump." His hands skimmed down my face, brushing my tears away.

Dan stopped so close his shoes nearly touched my toes and I had to crane my neck to meet his eyes. He leaned down, his forehead almost resting against mine. A hair's width separated us. My breath stilled and I braced myself for the feel of his hands on my skin again.

"So if I said no, you'd turn down a tour, even if the rest of the band really wanted it?" I asked, my voice hoarse.

"Yes," he said without an ounce of hesitation and my heart pounded. *Dare I hope he was serious?* "The guys might flip out, but they'd come around. If you needed me to quit, I'd do it too. It would hurt but I need you more."

Tears overflowed my eyes, but I didn't pull away, couldn't. "That… that means a lot, Dan." I smoothed my hand over his chest. "But I don't want you to give up something that's ingrained inside you. We'll figure out how to integrate our lives."

Surprise widened his eyes. "You're sure?"

I nodded, and an infectious smile overtook his features. His hand settled on the nape of my neck and his head descended. It happened so fast I'd have missed it if I'd blinked. His lips brushed against mine, delicate, soft, patient. Just a feather light caress, a reminder that I was his.

My arms wrapped around his waist, and I pressed myself tighter against him. Who would have thought I'd miss his kisses as much as the warm sense of safety he gave me?

I sighed against his lips, sinking into his hold. For a minute, I allowed myself to forget all the pain of the last few days. I fed all the anger, heartache, and stress he'd caused me into that kiss. The pressure amped up until we were gasping for breath.

Panting, we broke apart. I let my forehead rest against his chest while I recovered. He tilted my head back.

"So we'll see where this leads us?" he asked, smug satisfaction blanketing his features.

"Yes. That sounds like a plan." I chewed my lip, unsure if I should share the things I'd learned in the last few days. It didn't feel like there would be a better moment than this really. "I might actually have a suggestion."

"Oh?" His brows rose.

"My boss suggested I could work remotely for prolonged periods."

"That was generous of him." It took a moment, and then it clicked. "Does that mean you could come on tour with me?"

I'd barely nodded before he was spinning me around the room. Clinging to him, I couldn't stop laughing.

"That's fucking amazing, babe," he finally said when he set me on my feet.

"It's perfect until September, at least."

Dan frowned. "Why September?"

"Phoebe starts school. Plus, you have The Brightside tour, right?"

His smile fell for all of a second before an idea lit up his face again. "Yeah, but we could hire a tutor to travel with us." He nodded, the idea growing on him fast. "Loads of bands travel with their families, so why not us?"

It was exactly what my mother had said, and I guess the only way to find out if it worked was to try it. With Rhiannon going on tour for two years from May, it would either be the best solution or a nightmare. We'd adjust as needed. Knowing he would have quit for me, it gave me faith that we could get through anything as long as we communicated.

Some of his excitement drained. "Is that what you want?"

I wanted him in my life, always had. Seeing Phoebe grow up, with her dad within easy reach, would be a huge improvement. I didn't want either of us to be thousands of miles away from him. Remote working would mean I could keep my job, have all of those things, and travel like I'd wanted before Phoebe. It was a no brainer really.

"I love you." I chuckled as Dan's face lit up. "So if it means we get to be together and keep the important pieces of our lives, I'll go anywhere you want."

He squeezed me against his chest. "Say it again."

"I love you, Dan."

"Fucking knew it," he muttered against my lips. "I love you too, Mel. Always have, always will."

If my heart got any fuller, it would explode. He pressed yet another chaste kiss to my lips, and I was moments away from dragging him into the pantry.

Before I could make a move, he lifted his head. "Just to be clear, if I proposed again you'd…"

"Throw something at you."

"Thought so." Dan nodded. A sly look entered his eyes. "I'll just be patient and catch you where there's no throwable objects."

I chuckled as his lips descended and finally he kissed me like he meant it. Without breaking contact, I pulled him into the cupboard and shut the door. His head came up as the light snuffed out. Only a muted glow filtered in under the door.

"Do you need something, babe?" he whispered, his voice low, grating across every sensitive nerve ending that had missed him just as much as the rest of me.

"Yes." I brushed my lips along his jaw and he shivered. "You."

His fingers clenched against my hip and that was all the warning I had before I was plucked off my feet and plastered to his chest. We went wild, tugging at each other's clothes, hands sliding into the other's hair gripping tight, groaning at the feel of the other pressed so tight. The feel of him throbbing against my entrance made it all worse.

How no one came to check on the commotion was a shock I had no interest in questioning. Even more surprising was the fact that not a single thing fell from the shelves. We both came hard and loud. I'd be beet red when we went back outside but for the moment, I was content to just hold on tight and breathe him in.

"So does this mean I get to move in?" Dan whispered while we both struggled for air.

"You'd better."

EPILOGUE

Four weeks later...

"Are you coming to soundcheck today?" Dan pulled me back into his chest. He pressed a kiss to my cheek, and I melted back against him with a sigh.

Whoever said remote working was less stressful needed to take a good hard look at themselves. If anything, it was even crazier than it had been when I had to sit at my desk with the girls. The phone calls were almost endless, and I'd never tell Lisha and Charlotte, but I'd had to start screening them.

I turned in Dan's arms and hugged him back. This made it all worth it, though. We were two weeks into a surprise tour of the UK.

Had I expected us to have a little more quiet time at home before we were forced to put our plan in action? Absolutely.

Did I hate that we had a four-week tour in both the UK and Europe as a trial run between December and January? Definitely not.

We still could not believe how well timed it had been. Someone saw the guys on the Kasey Show and decided they were exactly what they needed to fill a hole in a multi-band travelling rock festival. The guys were sharing a stage with international Welsh sensations Marable, as well as a number of smaller British and American bands. The atmosphere was electric, at the venues and on the road. We had two weeks in the UK, a week off, and then we would fly out to Germany for another three-week leg across Christmas and New Year. Dan had been raving about Christmas in Germany, and now Phoebe and I would get to experience it.

"It was starting to look like you were going to pitch your laptop across the room."

I bit my lip. "Me? Never." Lies. I'd come close too many times to count. My team needed to learn some boundaries but we had plenty of time to work out those kinks.

"Whatever you say, babe." He slapped my ass, grinning. "Are you coming to soundcheck?"

I glanced back at my laptop, pinging on the desk in our hotel room. It started ringing, Charlotte's name flashing in the corner, and my decision was made. They were used to operating under their own steam. They did not need to run their every decision through me like they had been for the last two weeks.

"When do we leave?" I asked, flipping the lid down on the laptop.

Dan chuckled. "Ten minutes. Shall I grab Phoebe from Ella?"

With the short notice, there wasn't any time to find a care minder I'd trust Phoebe to. My sister had jumped at the chance of a break from what she called her boring nine-to-five. It was entertaining in more ways than one at times.

I nodded. "I'll meet you in the lobby?"

He paused on his way to the door, chewing his lip, when he turned back to me. "I'd rather you wait for me here. Graham said there were people trying to get into the lobby this morning." Concern creased his eyes. "I'd rather you not be down there if someone got in."

My heart fluttered. "They're just fans, Dan. What are they going to do?"

"Nothing. Hopefully." He pulled a face, unconvinced. "I'd just rather not risk it."

The attention on them had ramped up significantly in the last few weeks. It didn't help that we were sharing a hotel with Marable, but the fanfare wasn't entirely their fault. Their social media accounts had exploded, and the organisers had to upgrade the venues for each stop when the guys got announced. Plus, every time I ran into their manager, he seemed to be wearing a frown. Big things were brewing around Rhiannon and I couldn't be happier for them.

"Okay, I'll get changed and wait here."

Appeased, he headed out. I smoothed my hands down my yoga leggings. Probably best I didn't go to a gig wearing my home working gear. Dan might blow his cool if he caught one more guy staring at my ass.

❄

Phoebe bounced around the stage with the guys. She looked utterly adorable in her custom-made Rhiannon shirt and pink ear protectors. When she'd first run out, Ryan had been mid-lyric, and his bark of laughter had echoed around the venue. Every time he looked at her, he had a hell of a time getting through. The rest of the guys were at least able to keep playing, despite their laughter.

No, it wasn't the fact she kept shouting at them to play another song or kept trying to out-sing Ryan. It was the t-shirt James had made for her birthday. The front was a perfectly normal Rhiannon shirt, but the back said 'The first and best Rhiannon baby.'

Nia and Alys weren't impressed when she unwrapped it on the first day of tour. Phoebe and Dan loved it. The guys loved that it made their significant others uncomfortable, but also reminded them both that their time would come. *Rock stars.*

When the song came to an end, and the sound-techs declared them good to go, Dan stepped up to the mic. Even from the side of the stage, I could see the mischief glittering in his eyes. "Babe, can I ask you to marry me now?"

It was the third time he'd asked since we got out on tour. By this point, I'm pretty sure a couple of the bands had bets going. I'd spotted enough curious looks to be suspicious.

I'd gotten so good at this game, I didn't even have to pause to search for something. Instead, I automatically snatched a half full water bottle off the top of a flight case and threw it at him.

It sailed past his head without grazing him.

I'd gotten good at aiming too. The first time, it had hit him in the chest and left a bruise.

"Not today then." Dan nodded, his grin firmly fixed in place as he walked towards me. "I'll get you soon enough, babe."

My hands landed on my hips at the confidence in his tone. "Not if you keep doing it like that you won't."

I was only partially teasing. I'd say yes eventually. I just wanted us to settle into this new life before we added extra pressure on it. It got harder to say no each time he asked, but if he kept asking from a stage, he'd make holding out easier on me.

"Noted." Eyes sparkling with amusement, he tugged me into his chest. "I'll keep that in mind for the next one."

The guys laughed around us as they handed off their equipment to the roadies and filed out of the venue. We had hours to kill before the guys went on tonight.

From the corner of my eye, I spotted Ella glaring at Jared as he approached her. He stopped, holding out his arms, a look of utter exasperation on his face.

"What the hell did I do now?" he snapped.

"The roadies aren't your personal playthings, Jared." Ella shook her head, disgust curling her lip. "Try having a little respect for the women on the crew."

Everyone stopped, their gazes focused on Jared.

"I didn't —"

Ella's brows rose. "Oh really? So you didn't come off stage staring at Annie's ass?"

Annie being James's guitar tech and a very pretty blonde. Exactly Jared's type.

"No, I…" Jared's gaze shifted to Ryan. He stood off to the side with his arms crossed, taking in the scene.

If those two didn't get their shit together soon, they were going to find themselves locked in a room or tour bus together until they worked out their differences. They hadn't stopped bickering since the guys got back from London weeks ago and given that Dan now lived with me, they'd seen a lot of each other.

Tiny hands tapped my legs, distracting me from their face-off.

"I hug too," Phoebe declared just as she wrapped her arms around our legs.

Jared stormed out, the heavy security door slammed back against the concrete. The drama queen liked to make a good exit. He'd been finessing that trick ever since we got on tour.

Dan ignored the commotion and scooped Phoebe up. She shrieked with delight. "How about we treat your mammy to lunch?"

"Yes!" She clapped her hands. "Pasta."

Chuckling, Dan agreed with her. "We need to discuss our game plan, munchkin," he said as he clattered down the steps to the exit without me. "Your mam's a harder nut to crack than I expected." He glanced back over his shoulder at me, grinning like he couldn't wait for my reaction.

"Mammy!" Phoebe frowned at me. "Stop being silly. We need to get married."

I shook my head as I followed them. Life on tour with those two was definitely interesting. Intense sometimes but I wouldn't change a thing.

Turn the page for a bonus epilogue with Dan and Mel. I usually reserve this for my mailing list but this is easier in print. Plus, it's just nice to have it all together, right?

BONUS EPILOGUE

"Babe, are you two ready?" Dan called from the living room of our suite.

Phoebe sat in front of me on our bed, her arms crossed and a determined furrow between her brows. My baby girl turned five today, and she'd already seen more of the world than most kids twice her age. Yet, to take one look at the tantrum building in her green eyes, you'd never know.

"No. I'm gonna need a minute," I shouted back, crossing my arms and matching Phoebe's stare with my patented 'don't fuck with me' mam look.

We'd been on the road since May with The Brightside, bouncing between a tour bus, stadiums, and hotel rooms. Seven months of constant travel would be a lot for a normal person. Apparently, my daughter had decided today was her breaking point.

"Put your dress on, munchkin. You don't want them to start on the cake without you, do you?"

My only reply was her lip jutting out as her pout deepened.

Oh geez. I was not prepared for this when I rolled out of

bed this morning. We were meant to go to a cake shop uptown, but given it was raining heavily enough for a lake to form on the roads outside our hotel, it was a wash out. We were improvising with everyone gathered in our suite with cake and balloons and hastily organised hotel canapés. I didn't want to know how Matt, Rhiannon's manager, got the hotel to organise it with such short notice. Nothing short of black magic or bribery, I'm sure.

The door opened and I caught a pair of identical green eyes.

"Everything alright?" Dan asked, his brows furrowing to match his daughter's.

"Not really." I gestured to her. "She won't get dressed."

"What's wrong, munchkin?" Dan shut the door and knelt in front of Phoebe. "Don't you want cake and presents?"

Before she could work up an answer, the main door to our suite slammed open, the sound echoing back to us.

"Where's my baby girl?" my father called from the living room. "Grampa's got presents."

"Jesus, Dad. What are you wearing?" Ella said, her voice muffled by our bedroom door. Since when did we find my dad amusing? *How is he even here?*

"A shirt."

"That's not a shirt! It's a monstrosity." Ella's voice rose painfully.

Phoebe's bad mood evaporated and she slid off the bed. She had our bedroom door open and shot into the suite before either Dan or I could react. Swearing, I grabbed her dress and raced after the naked child. *Wasn't parenting meant to get easier?*

I stumbled into the living room to find the Rhiannon and The Brightside guys crowded around the sofas and dining table, grinning at my daughter. She'd flung herself into my father's arms like he might vanish with the next blink. My mother hugged Ella, catching my eye with amusement twinkling in hers.

"Surprise."

Ella snorted. "I'm not sure Phoebe likes surprises."

The child in question chatted excitedly to my father, entirely oblivious to the attention fixed on her. She might have been the only one not staring in horror at the fabric covering my dad. *Were those photos?*

"Given her bad mood seems to have evaporated, I'd say you're onto something, Els." My eyes narrowed on my father's shirt and I edged forward to get a better look. Ella mirrored my movements and my growing horror.

"Tell me those aren't…baby photos," Ella whispered.

"Told you they wouldn't appreciate it," Our mother said, stepping away from him. "Nia, dear, why don't you show me where to place the presents."

Chuckling, Nia detangled herself from James's arms and sprung to her feet. "Sure thing, but let's hurry. I don't want to miss this."

"Oh my god, they are." Horror dripped from Ella's voice. "Mel, he's got our baby photos on his bloody back."

"I'm not sure I want to see." I rubbed my eyes. "Dad, please go change."

"What? No. I worked hard on this shirt."

"It's embarrassing, Dad." Ella pointed at an image on his arm. "I'm in the *bath* in this one. That is so not appropriate for public wearing."

"Wait, I want to see this." Jared scrambled off the sofa and rushed across the room wearing a massive smirk. "She claims she's so perfect. I need evidence that she's human like the rest of us."

Ella rolled her eyes at her boyfriend. It had been nearly eleven months since they surprised us with that little development. I mean, it was kind of predictable and Alys and I may have had a hand in causing it… Didn't make it any less of an adjustment though. My baby sister, in a serious relationship with a reformed bad boy rock star? Yeah, I might need therapy one day.

Still, she made for the perfect full-time childminder, and considering she and Jared were still sussing each other out, I was content to let her figure out her next step in life on her own terms. It also helped having the extra familiar support on tour. Nia tried to be a constant but her job required her to be with the guys as much as possible. Couldn't exactly take behind the scenes shots if you were locked in a room with your best friend, though sometimes we shared a workspace while I fielded the latest brand disaster in the UK and she edited her photos.

Having Ella on tour made everything seem like less of a big deal. We were just normal people, spending time with our friends and family, doing our jobs.

While seeing the world.

"Tell you what, we'll compromise," Dad said, all jovial. "I'll change before the hockey game. How about that?"

"At least put a jacket on," Ella groaned.

"Not a chance." Jared held his arms out in front of her. "I'm not done cataloguing yet."

She glared at him. Someone was going to put himself in the dog house.

Dan took the dress from me and helped my father wrestle Phoebe into it. Time was quickly running out. Thanks to Lily, we had box tickets for the Toronto Titans hockey game against Philadelphia later tonight. I guess it helped that Lily and her band would be taking over the arena in two days for the first of their Toronto dates. Hockey was new for me so I fully expected to spend the entire thing sipping water and corralling Phoebe while everyone else cheered on the Titans.

Dan's arm slipped around my waist, pulling me into his chest. My hand smoothed up his plaid shirt – someone had bought far too many Canadian shirts since we crossed the border.

My breath caught in my throat when my gaze rose to his.

Then again, unlike my dad, I didn't care what he wore, as long as he kept looking at me like *that*.

Love, happiness and heat shone in his gorgeous green eyes. His fingers danced up my back until they slid into my hair, tilting my head. He didn't so much as hesitate before meshing our lips together in the sweetest kiss – and I'd know, considering I couldn't get enough of him. We'd gotten used to almost never being alone, gotten good at bottling our need for one another until we finally stopped at a hotel.

I leaned into him, absorbing the passion and returning it in turn. Who cared if our friends and my parents were watching? Touring cured you of the slightest slither of modesty.

The right moment hadn't presented itself yet, but I had every intention of locking this loveable giant down. Soon.

The door opened again and someone cleared their throat, dragging out attention back to the room. Lily's blonde head peeked into the room, of her body and whatever she hid behind her back blocked from view.

"Who's ready for some cake?" she shouted, eliciting an answering "Yes!" from her boys and Phoebe.

She let the door swing open, revealing a hotel trolley carrying a huge chocolate fudge cake. Phoebe's eyes lit up and not just because of the inferno of candles crowning the cake. I'd debated the sanity in ordering her favourite cake for all of five seconds. We'd just have to deal with the cleaning bill from the hotel.

Dan left my side, collecting a grinning Phoebe from my parents. He lifted her into her seat at the head of the dining room table as Lily wheeled the trolley towards her. Kneeling next to her, he whispered in her ear, and the little terror giggled as if she hadn't spent half an hour glaring at me over the pretty green dress she now wore. The sight of the two of them together still sent tingles down my spine. Nothing had ever felt more right.

"Mammy, stop stalling," Phoebe groaned. Her tiny fists bounced on the glass table top. "I want cake."

"Then you'd better make a wish, so we can cut it up." I settled beside her on my knees, sharing a knowing smile with Dan across her copper locks.

Lily stopped the trolley in front of us and Phoebe jolted forward trying to get at it. My heart leapt into my throat but Dan was ready for our little hellion's every move. He wrapped his arm around her waist, holding her in place and away from the flames.

The room erupted in a round of *"Happy Birthday"* and Phoebe pouted until they were done. I bit my lip, struggling to contain my amusement. She reeked of impatience. If there was ever any doubt that she was Dan's, that aspect of her nature drove it home. He was her mini-me even though he'd missed out on the first few years of her life.

"Make a wish," he whispered in her ear.

Not ready to say goodbye to the Rhiannon men?

Turn the page for a sneak preview of *Defying Ella*.

Will Ella be able to see past Jared's bad boy front or will it take a week shut in a cabin to make them see eye to eye?

Or grab it now
Books2Read.com/DefyingElla

DEFYING ELLA EXCERPT

Six hours.

I had to survive six more hours with Jared Michaels, and then freedom would be mine. I'd lasted an entire month on tour with his band, Rhiannon. A couple more hours wouldn't kill me. I hoped.

"Five minutes to soundcheck," Matt, the band's manager, shouted as he barrelled down the hallway.

For some reason, I'd expected him to be like Dan, my sister's boyfriend. Upbeat and easy to deal with. After one show with him, I quickly realised that the only thing Matt and Dan had in common was the red tone of their hair. The man acted like a drill sergeant, and I'd happily leave his girlfriend to unpack that. I had a wily toddler to find.

One look at Matt's determined face, and the roadies around me dived out of his way. Hell, I dived out of his way and I wouldn't normally give standing up to the man a second's thought. His focus fixed on me nevertheless and I resisted the urge to gulp. *Maybe I should have dived further.*

"Ella, have you seen Jared?"

No one ever asked me for the manwhore's location. There was no earthly reason I should even know it.

Except, I normally did because I was a hyperaware idiot when it came to that man.

Five months ago, when Rhiannon decided it was time to grace Wales with their permanent presence after ten years away, I made a big, huge, idiotic mistake.

I slept with Jared Michaels.

Of course, I didn't know that at the time.

His reputation and his affiliation to Rhiannon were a mystery to me. I didn't learn that he spent his days playing music until weeks later. He blinded me with the tilt of his flirtatious smile and the intrigued light in his eyes.

The static thrill that kissed my skin whenever he brushed close to me in the club and the tattoos crawling up his neck might have done some sweet-talking too...

I shouldn't have let him touch me, but then again it was only meant to be a night of fun. A night turned into a week. One amazing week. After which his unfocused flirting ways reasserted themselves pretty damn quick, and I cut my losses.

It wasn't like I wanted a serious relationship anyway.

What twenty-four-year-old trying to enjoy her life does?

Especially one who hadn't long returned from a year of travelling and needed to find her feet.

And definitely not with someone like him.

He seemed so ungrateful for the massive career-affirming opportunities chasing his band. It boggled my mind how someone could have their life's dreams come true and not revel in it. If I had the tiniest clue what I wanted to do with my life and I found myself in his position, I'd hold on tight, nails dug so far into it that no one would ever separate me from it.

Anyway, when I saw that same flirtatious expression resurface and directed at someone else, I kicked myself, but I moved on. I ditched him, deleted his number, and tried to push all thoughts of his almost never-ending store of energy out of my head. Life continued in its weird uncertain way, but the memories fought suppression. The man had probably forgotten me, yet my dreams wouldn't let it go.

And then bam!

The bastard sat in my sister's flat, playing with *my* niece and making nice-y nice-y with *my* family. What the *absolute* hell?

"Why don't you check a storage cupboard?" I sneered.

Matt nodded like it made perfect sense, which it would, because the drummer had a history of doing stupid shit. Matt glossed over the bite of irritation in my voice and brushed past me.

A twinge of guilt settled in my chest for the groupie Jared had snuck in there.

Quit it. She probably knew what she was getting into better than I had.

I continued down the concrete hallway, trying to shake off the tension riding my shoulders.

Mindlessly, I dodged roadies prepping for their final soundcheck of the tour and continued my hunt. For my sister.

I'm not sure how she expected me to babysit my niece when she kept randomly vanishing with her. I joined the tour specifically for that reason, and in the last few days, I'd spent a load of it twiddling my thumbs or sightseeing. It felt weird, being paid to be a childminder and not having a charge.

I wouldn't even touch the weirdness of working for my sister, but Mel needed me and I'd been rather absent the last year. Guilt could be a powerful motivator.

Yes, the sister who invited Jared into her flat like it was no big flipping deal. She let the manwhore touch my niece with those hands that had been god knows where. It made me want to wipe Phoebe down with alcohol wipes.

I still kicked myself for not knowing, for not connecting him to Phoebe's dad.

And then I would tell myself to chill out because how could I have known?

We hadn't exactly spent a lot of time together growing up. Sure, we went to the same school but he played no part in my sister's or Dan's lives then and with five years between us, he wouldn't have paid me any attention anyway.

I might have purposefully avoided asking the obvious questions — where are you from, where did you go to school, do you know X? Every time those words left my lips, I'd learn something off-putting and at the time, I just wanted to get off. I didn't need to know his connection to an ex or a former best friend, or worse, childhood enemy.

Rhiannon hadn't formed until years later. The first time I laid eyes on their drummer, it was through a press still after they signed with a label, and let me tell you, the images did not match reality.

What the hell happened to the scrawny, lanky kid with bedraggled hair?

I could have resisted that person with ease.

Plus I'd been blissfully unconnected for a year. I never concerned myself with the whereabouts of Wales's latest hit band, even before catching a plane off the island. Of course, just because I didn't pay attention to them, didn't mean the universe had any issue messing with me.

Was it too much to ask that I be allowed to enjoy my life without the consequences of rash actions coming back to bite me at the most inappropriate of moments?

But enough of Jared. I had a small child to locate.

"Has anyone seen my sister?" I shouted above the ruckus of the black-shirted crew rushing around me.

"Phoebe, no!" Mel's voice echoed down the hallway before any of them could answer.

A loud crash followed and everyone around me winced.

"Try the stage," a black-haired guy with a goatee called over his shoulder.

"Thanks," I muttered. Not that I needed help now.

Why was she on the stage when she had work?

Frowning, I headed in that direction.

I stepped into the auditorium and groaned. Half the drum kit lay on its side and Mel stared at it, red-faced, dragging her hands through her hair while roadies were picking up the pieces. Phoebe danced around her feet, gleefully oblivious to the destruction she'd wrought.

"Now don't you wish you left her with me?" I called from the side of the stage.

Mel spun to face me, her light brown hair whipping around her. Despite her being three years older than me, we generally looked alike. Lately, we'd diverged quite a lot. I'd lost the will to wash my hair with the back-to-back tour stops. Dry shampoo was my friend while Mel somehow maintained her denial.

I shouldn't chuckle at the pained grimace on her face, but we'd had this conversation so many times at this point, we had a script. Mel had spent the first four years of Phoebe's life a single parent before she let Dan back into her life. Taking her eyes off my hyperactive niece might have been a challenge for my dear sister.

"I'll take that as a yes."

"Auntie Ella," Phoebe screeched, throwing herself at me. I grunted, too slow to catch her before she whacked me in the stomach. "I played drums. I was great. Right, mam?"

Mel bit her lip. "Sure, just don't tell your dad."

"You really mean don't tell the band, right?"

It didn't look like Jared's kit but he'd probably still lose it. Unpredictable piece of work.

Just the thought of him being pissed off filled me with joy. I spun the little delinquent in a circle as a reward and she squealed in delight.

Mel smirked, seeing right through me. She'd clocked our bitter familiarity that first day in her flat and spent the next few months trying to get the whole thing out of me. I refused to give in. There was no need to drag a mistake into the open like that. No, it could just fade into the past. One day, I wouldn't feel disgusted whenever he opened his mouth or aroused when he stepped off stage, topless and plastered in sweat.

"When's mam and dad getting here?" I asked, placing a pouting Phoebe back on the ground.

Mel shrugged. "Any minute now. They were going to do some sightseeing before stopping by for the munchkin."

The munchkin being Phoebe. We hadn't told her that she'd be heading home with our parents while we drove down to the Alps for a much-needed girls' fortnight away from the guys. After a month on a tour bus with them, we all needed a break. So, the moment the show ended, Mel, Alys, Nia, Daphne and I would be Lutago bound. A fancy-pants lodge in the Italian Alps awaited us.

Two weeks of blissful escape. Hardly any signal, great company, and a lot of wine.

I couldn't wait.

"What the hell happened?" Jared roared from the house floor.

Mel chewed her lip, watching him approach, but I didn't bother turning. I didn't need to see the fire in his eyes to know he was about to set me on edge and maybe push me over it. It didn't take much these days. One well-placed jab and we were at each other's throats. To think I'd hated the predictability of my boring call centre job a month ago. If it meant escaping him, I'd go back to the call centre, even though I knew it would never lead me to my purpose.

Not wanting to give Jared any of my time, I crouched in front of Phoebe, pasting a huge grin on my lips.

"Shall we go count the pieces?" I held my hand out to her and allowed that mischievous feeling I always got fucking with Jared's mood to surface.

For a second she chewed her lip, but I knew she wouldn't

hold out on me. My niece loved to play. Her smile was slow to grow, but then she nodded at me, a sly look in her own eyes.

"Just a little accident," Mel said, facing down the raging bull without a moment's hesitation.

"The kit is trashed. How is that a little accident?" Jared growled, gesturing wildly.

I turned away from him and led Phoebe over to the kit. We settled on the ground, our legs crossed and our backs to the glowering asshole.

"One." I pointed out a part of the dismantled drum set.

He pounded across the stage. The vibrations thumped through my chest, but still, I refused to look at him. Instead, I focused on Phoebe, mouthing the next numbers to her as she counted. I couldn't get angry with such cuteness before me.

"It's not trashed. They'll have it back together before you know it." Patience filled Mel's voice.

I could feel the burn of her gaze on my back, on Phoebe. The awkward smile she favoured whenever Phoebe was around for arguments probably claimed her lips.

"Who did it?" Jared bit out.

He stepped up to the kit and robbed me of the ability to ignore him. For a moment, he was just a black blob in my peripheral vision. If only I were strong enough to not look.

If I'd been that strong, I would have saved myself a whole lot of pain in the last month. Wouldn't have seen him flirting with other women, leading them backstage or onto an empty bus.

But if I couldn't see him, I conjured up extreme situation after extreme situation and tortured myself. It was better to look than imagine.

I sighed as my head turned, almost against my will. My eyes immediately trailed along his body. Why did he have to start working out? It would have been so much easier to ignore the bastard if he didn't fit my type to a tee… if he hadn't started hitting the gym twice a day and still looked like the skinny rake I vaguely remembered from school.

For some reason, he'd decided to buff up between Rhiannon signing and my meeting him. Someone in their PR team had helpfully forgotten to circulate new press stills.

Or I'd blanked their existence out.

Anyway, the result was a ripped six-foot-plus guy with short, dirty blond hair, striking green eyes and a contagious grin — if he chose to break it out in your vicinity.

Yet another reason I didn't recognise him that fateful night in the bar.

Notice how I glossed over the tattoos painted across his chest, arms, back and creeping up his neck? They highlighted his hard muscles far too much for my peace of mind.

Maybe if he never took his hoodie off, I'd finally stop having to fight to resist him.

"Who did it?" he roared again, ignoring Mel completely and I ground my teeth. He stared around the stage, eying roadies with a hard expression. "Was it you?" he growled at a poor unsuspecting guitar tech, catching his t-shirt and pulling him closer.

The guy shook his head and scrambled away, taking my ability to ignore the pain in the ass with him.

"Go to your mam." I helped Phoebe stand before giving her a gentle push towards Mel.

I jumped to my feet, the low burn of annoyance itching against my skin. His eyes widened for a fraction of a second as I stomped toward him. He clamped the surprise down fast, directing that scowl at me.

"Phoebe did it. Are you going to shout at a four-year-old too?"

Jared glared down at me as I squared up with him, toe-to-toe. I glared right back at him, my temper boiling high enough to outdo him if he wanted to start throwing his toys out of the pram. He could be a reasonable, nice guy when he wanted to be — I'd seen it. My sister wouldn't let him anywhere near Phoebe if it wasn't the case. I'd even seen him play with the munchkin and talk to his friends like a normal human being.

Today wasn't going to be one of those days.

He had a manic glint in his green eyes. The last time I'd seen it, I'd caught him at a bar, late for our date, and all over another woman. I still hadn't figured out where our wires crossed, and I had no interest in trying.

"Mel, why don't you take Phoebe to the green room?"

Silence followed my request. I glanced at Mel.

"Are you sure?" she asked, eying me with concern while Phoebe hugged her leg.

That set my blood on fire. My niece barely knew the meaning of the word fear!

I turned back to Jared and crossed my arms. "I've got this asshole. I'll meet you there in a couple of minutes."

Jared's brow rose while a smirk claimed his lips. The fragments of memories unearthed by that look were not welcome. They could stay buried beneath my bed and not haunt me with the sight of him groggy in the morning, his hair sticking up at all angles. Nope. That image no longer resembled the guy standing before me.

"No, Phoebe, that's a bad word," Mel said as she herded Phoebe off the stage. "Auntie Els needs her mouth washed out with soap. You don't want that."

My lips twitched at her pointed threat. I still hadn't come up with more child-friendly but equally as insulting words to direct at Jared. I'd get right on that after I escaped this tour.

The side door closed, finally allowing me to breathe.

"Go back to your flavour of the day, Jared. Let the roadies fix this."

Confusion swept away the intensity in his gaze. "What are you talking about?"

I sighed. "Where did you leave today's girl? Matt'll tear

your head off if he finds strangers wandering around backstage."

A frown morphed his features. "What girl?"

"You're unbelievable," I hissed, my indignation stronger than my will to hold the words in. "They have feelings, Jared. You can't just use someone and toss them aside."

The heat of his body buffered me in the freezing cold arena. A couple of months ago, I would have leaned into that warmth, would have taken comfort in it. Hell, my gut reaction still urged me to lean into him, to give into the itch in my fingers to trace away his frown.

I schooled my features, hiding the interest I'd never been able to extinguish. Nothing was off-limits with him. If he figured it out, he'd find a way to use it against me. Why, I couldn't explain.

His expression cleared as his lips curled. "Don't worry, El. You'll have plenty of company at your next 'I hate Jared' meeting."

Such an innocuous thing shouldn't have flared my temper but combine the jab behind the words — I was just another girl he'd used — with the lazy, playboy smile, and I could almost breathe fire.

"Great. Thanks for building my army for me." I forced a cruel grin to my lips. "Have you ever wondered what happens when a group of women you've used and abused get together in a room?"

He shook his head, his amusement unmarred. "I don't give much thought to my conquests. You know that, El."

You were nothing but a notch on the bedpost.

I refrained from clenching my jaw, but my body burned with the force of my anger. I stepped closer to him and bared my teeth.

"Then maybe you should start sleeping with one eye open. One of these days, someone won't take too kindly to your wine and dine routine, pretty boy."

With that, I breezed past him, my shoulders pulled back, and my head held high.

"Nah, I'll just wave goodbye to my mousy haired shadow and enjoy my life," Jared shouted after me.

I didn't turn around, didn't so much as acknowledge his newest claim that I'd only joined the tour for him. He'd worn out the jab at this point. I kept moving while the roadies flowed around me, unravelling millions of wires, lining up cases and hefting heavy-looking lights into the air.

To them, it was just another day on the road. Some of them were probably sad to be finishing the tour.

For me, it should have been a happy day. Escaping Jared, a holiday in the Alps and another new experience to add to my growing list. All I felt was the sizzle of anger as I rushed back down the hallway.

And irritation with a dash of sadness.

Why do I let the asshole get to me?

I stepped into the green room, my head pounding. Deep breaths did very little to calm the anger. The rest of the band sprawled out on the sofas, their other halves tucked into their sides. Mel took one look at my face and shot to her feet, leaving Phoebe tugging at Dan's tightly trimmed ginger beard.

Seeing the pair of them together, with identical ginger mops of hair and the same mischievous grin, cooled some of the fire in my veins. *Too cute.*

Mel caught my hand before I could take more than a couple of steps. She guided me into the corner, away from the drinks table and the scattering of people.

"Are you okay?" she whispered, leaning close.

My eyes fell shut as I tried to force my breathing to even out. Jared was an asshole. I already knew that, so getting upset about it was a waste of energy. I blew out a breath, opened my eyes and smiled at Mel.

"I'll be fine." Even I could tell my smile was wonky. "Only five more hours to go."

"One day, you'll tell me what went on between you two, right?" Mel squeezed my hand, concern creasing her eyes.

I bit my lip. If I could help it, I wouldn't utter another word about Jared to anyone.

Mel's gaze shifted to Dan and Phoebe. I could see the cogs turning behind her eyes. What those cogs were, I had no clue. Dan stared back at her quizzically, equally in the dark.

"Listen," she turned to me, leaning in close again, "why don't you head to the lodge early?"

"But Phoebe —"

She shook her head. "Don't worry about Phoebe. It's your day off."

Is it?

Well, that would explain why she and Phoebe had disappeared without a word.

"There's no reason for you to stick around and breathe the same air as him." She smiled, a careful but encouraging look in her eyes. "Mam and dad will be here soon to take Phoebe. It's less than four hours to the lodge, you could be there before the guys even go on tonight."

I hummed in agreement. Very seriously tempted despite the guilt of ditching them all.

"Andy said the keys are in a lockbox. I can text you the code. The place is fully stocked so you wouldn't have to do anything but pick up another hire car." Mel smiled, silently imploring me to take the escape hatch she offered.

Who was I kidding? I didn't need that much convincing. My body already vibrated with the need to skip out of this place with my bags in hand.

"Are you sure? The others won't hate me for ditching out early?"

Mel snorted. "Don't be ridiculous. We'd all go with you if we could." She tapped my arm and gave me a little shove towards the door. "Now go. Before Jared reappears and steals that tiny happy buzz from you."

"Thank you." I pulled her into a hug and squeezed tight.

"No need. Just look after yourself, Els." Her arms tightened a little harder and then she stepped back. "I know a thing or two about running from difficult things, remember?" Her eyes screamed at me with a mixture of suspicion and understanding. "Now, go."

I didn't need to be told three times.

For the first time in weeks, as I dashed out the door, it didn't feel like I carried a three-pound weight on my shoulders.

Freedom, here I come.

If you'd like to know what happens next, *Defying Ella* is available on all platforms and can be requested by most bookstores. Check it out here: Books2read.com/DefyingElla
Or request it from your local library.

ALSO BY MORGANA BEVAN

True Platinum Series (Rock Star Romance)
(Rhiannon)

Chasing Alys – Ryan (Resistant to Love)

Charming Daphne – Matt (Force Proximity)

Winning Nia – James (Second Chance)

Enticing Mel – Dan (Secret Baby)

Needing Emily – Emily (Accidental Marriage/Runaway Bride)

Defying Ella - Jared (Close Proximity / Snowed-In)

(The Brightside)

Braving Lily - Lily (Opposites Attract)

Daring Ceri - Alex (Second Chance)

Marrying Olivia - Lewis (Accidental Marriage)

Kings of Screen Series (Hollywood Romance)

Between Takes (Enemies to Lovers)

Married Blind (Marriage of Convenience)

Acting Counsel (Close Proximity, Forbidden)

Fashionably Fake (Fake Dating)

Sign up for Morgana Bevan's mailing list: https://morganabevan.com/mailing-list/

ABOUT MORGANA

Morgana Bevan is a sucker for a rock star romance, particularly if it involves a soul-destroying breakup or strangers waking up in Vegas. She's a contemporary romance author based in Wales. When Morgana's not writing steamy rock star and movie star romances, she's working in TV production in the UK.

She enjoys travelling, attending gigs, and trying out the extreme activities she forces on her characters.

Find Morgana online at morganabevan.com.

Support Morgana on Ream and gain access to a new monthly bonus chapter and gain early access to her next release: https://reamstories.com/morganabevan

Morgana's Facebook Reader Group: https://www.facebook.com/groups/498919364708263

Printed in Great Britain
by Amazon